DUST AND ASHES

AL KALIMA

BALBOA
PRESS
A DIVISION OF HAY HOUSE

Copyright © 2016 Al Kalima.

All rights reserved. No part of this book may be used or reproduced by any means, graphic, electronic, or mechanical, including photocopying, recording, taping or by any information storage retrieval system without the written permission of the author except in the case of brief quotations embodied in critical articles and reviews.

Balboa Press books may be ordered through booksellers or by contacting:

Balboa Press
A Division of Hay House
1663 Liberty Drive
Bloomington, IN 47403
www.balboapress.com
1 (877) 407-4847

Because of the dynamic nature of the Internet, any web addresses or links contained in this book may have changed since publication and may no longer be valid. The views expressed in this work are solely those of the author and do not necessarily reflect the views of the publisher, and the publisher hereby disclaims any responsibility for them.

The author of this book does not dispense medical advice or prescribe the use of any technique as a form of treatment for physical, emotional, or medical problems without the advice of a physician, either directly or indirectly. The intent of the author is only to offer information of a general nature to help you in your quest for emotional and spiritual well-being. In the event you use any of the information in this book for yourself, which is your constitutional right, the author and the publisher assume no responsibility for your actions.

Any people depicted in stock imagery provided by Thinkstock are models, and such images are being used for illustrative purposes only. Certain stock imagery © Thinkstock.

Print information available on the last page.

ISBN: 978-1-5043-5231-4 (sc)
ISBN: 978-1-5043-5233-8 (hc)
ISBN: 978-1-5043-5232-1 (e)

Library of Congress Control Number: 2016904105

Balboa Press rev. date: 04/07/2016

He throws me into the mud
And I am reduced to dust and ashes
I cry out to You O God
But You do not answer
I stand up but You merely look at me

-Job 30:19 & 20(NIV)

DISCLAIMER

This book is a work of fiction but it is based on real events that happened in the past and continue to happen even now. The major characters in this book are fictitious except for historic figures like Presidents Nasser, Sadat, Mubarak and his wife, Suzanne. Coptic Pope Shenouda is also an actual historical figure as well as the major characters in the Denshawi Incident and a few other people. The Denshawi Incident really happened, and The Egyptian Bread Riots of 1977 took place. The rest are fiction couched in fact and are meant to illustrate the author's lesson.

Al Kalima

CONTENTS

Introduction xi

Antecedents 1
"Normal" Times 15
The Good Old Days 24
The Upheaval 36
The Turnaround 47
A New Beginning 58
Training 66
Married 73
Stresses 82
Asibi 89
On the Move 95
A Mission Field 106
Ramadan 116
Memuna 129
Qasim 137
Pregnant 162
Camp of the Mothers 173
Mothers and Babies 184
Miriam 192
Amira II 200
Winds of Change 207
Hope 217
Escape 227
The Cost of Freedom 242
End of the Road 265

Glossary of Non-English Words 283
Acknowledgements 285

INTRODUCTION

I wrote this book because I feel there is a need to address what is happening in the world now. The events described in this book continue to happen, perhaps even escalating. The aim of this book is not to arouse animosity against Moslems or to showcase how lily-pure, righteous, but oppressed, Christians are. Far from it!

What I intend to show in this story is how both sides have their heroes and their villains; but whereas the Moslems tend to be more militant in their beliefs these days, especially as much as it focuses on fighting jihads, Christians seem to have lost sight of what they really believe. Many Christians are more conversant with modern and ancient fables than with the tenets of their faith. Only a very small percentage of Christians nowadays have read the Bible, can navigate through it, or are willing to stand by their beliefs, to live by, or to die by them! Someone once put the picture this way using the events of Genesis 3: "God put enmity between the woman and the serpent. The serpent never forgets this but the woman does not seem to always realize this!"

It is not an equal battle when opposing sides do not equally realize the gravity of the issue at hand. I am not advocating that Christians go to fight jihads or anything like that. This is not a call to the return of the crusaders. No. It is a call to return to faith! What I am advocating is that Christians become more aware, better grounded in their faith, and more tuned to what they believe and what they should be doing about their beliefs so that even in adversity, they would find something to hold onto, and keep growing.

Many people in the so-called developed areas of the world believe the battle is so far removed from them. Not anymore! It is nearer now than ever. Teenagers born and bred in the West, often with Christian parents are converting to Islam and going off to the Middle East to fight in Islamic wars because they are given something to believe in and to hold onto. "Home-grown Terror" is taking root and very soon, kidnappings might be happening in our big cities. Jihad Training camps might soon be holding in our remote villages. How is a Christian to react to all of these?

I do not advocate meeting fire with fire though a firefighter explained once to me that one needs to fight some fires in this way. What I advocate is that Christians train themselves, and insist on teaching their children the fundamental doctrines and values of their faith so that not only will they be able to stand under fire, they will also have enough light in themselves to overcome the terrible darkness around them. Beyond that, they will hopefully switch on the light in other people around them.

If these pages inspire as many people as read it to dig deeper into their faith and have a more meaningful relationship with the Lord Jesus Christ, then I have not written this book in vain.

Al Kalima (The Witness)

ANTECEDENTS

Do you know how difficult it is to kill a human being, even oneself?

It is very difficult. I should know, I have tried, and seen others try it as well. I know some people may disagree with me but I am speaking of things I have seen firsthand; yes, things which I have experienced. Like so many experiences in life, killing a person goes through stages. In the first stage one thinks about it like a passing thought; and then the thought takes hold like a log smoldering after it has caught the flame of a fire.

In the second stage one actually begins to plan how to carry out what had been going through the thoughts. Some people plan in very organized manners, some others have vague and scattered plans but there is that planning phase; and it is very essential. This phase might be as short as minutes or seconds even. More often it takes hours, days, weeks, months, or even years. Of course a lot could happen within this phase including honing of plans, change of tactics, or a decision not to go through with the thought after all.

Finally there is the stage when that plan is carried out. Not many people get to this stage. More often than not, the people that do are those who did not spend a lot of time on the first two stages. More often than not, these are the ones who do not succeed. Those who spend time on the first two stages often, invariably, and irrevocably succeed. Most of the attempts that I saw failed, and often with more dire consequences than before the attempt was even considered. Many times the failure of the attempt served as a more powerful deterrent than any other thing to those who witnessed it, to those who were still at the earlier stages of thinking about it or planning on how to carry out their thoughts. At the end, we felt it was better to live from day to day in despair than to contemplate suicide or murder. Some might call this a cowardly decision but they were not in our shoes, and might not react any differently if they ever got in them.

On the very few occasions when the plans succeeded, it was often fraught with regret, especially when it was already too late and there was no recourse to any remedy.

But death is just one possible outcome to all these phases. My mother once said to me that when anyone fell down, there were three things the person could do from that point. The person could stay down and be trampled by others; stand up and keep moving with the tide; or get up fighting, more determined than before the fall. This is the lesson of the challenges of life in a nutshell, and that is partly what this story is about.

When does a story begin?

Does a story begin merely with the events which happened a few hours or days before a crisis? Mostly, the catalysts for the crisis arose from events which occurred years, decades or even centuries earlier. Should those not be the beginning of the story even as the roots of a tree are the beginnings of the plant? But even before those roots were the seed, the soil, the rock that made the soil, the climatic conditions, and the weather changes. Parts of life are just like a continuum in a line of eternity and still begs the question of what came first, the chicken or the egg. We all come on stage as Shakespeare said, play our parts and leave it for others to come and go. Past events have ways of influencing whatever current events which led up to a story, if only one had the courage and the time to connect the dots and create the linkages. And a story does not always end in how the prince and the princess got married and lived happily ever after. A wedding is often just the beginning of a marriage, of a family which is about to be formed, tried, tested, grown, face its own challenges, sometimes triumph, and sometimes fail in woeful disgrace. Where we live and breathe are often infinitesimal sections of eternity, and in the face of eternity, our times are often meaningless, and when we tell our stories, it is often one segment of it that we choose to tell. To us, it might be our triumph, but to our predecessors, it might be the destruction of all they ever fought and gave their lives for. The triumph we crow over now might be seen as an impedance of progress by those who come after us, and they have the rights to change their lives and their decisions to influence the beliefs they have at the time they would be living after we are dead and gone, sometimes sooner rather than even later.

    My name is Prisca. I am an Egyptian and this is a segment of my life. I am happily dying. The doctors say so. Of course doctors have been wrong about these things in the past but I very sincerely hope they are not in this case because you see, I really want to die. I have wanted to die for over forty years but God chose that I should remain alive still, and that, for a reason. I think my work here on earth is done and it is time for others to take over. I look forward to that blessed rest promised to the saints.

In the past, and for the bulk of my life, I have answered Briska. From birth I was Priscilla, but Mike calls me Prisca and that is what most people know me as for these past few years. I know some people refer to me as "That old woman" and that is what I must seem even though I am just fifty-five years old. At an event last week, I met a couple of other women who were about my age, give or take a few years, and they seemed about two decades younger compared to me. My skin is swarthy. My back is stooped. My neck has become so stiff that to turn around I have to move my whole trunk. And then there is my face! My face is full of scars and wrinkles. I like the wrinkles because they hide most of the scars, even though they make some of them more livid and gruesome. Mike says my most remarkable features are my eyes and my smile. Mike is usually right, especially about such things. The friends I have made over the past few years tell me that I look frightening at the first meeting but that when they take time to look into my eyes and see my smile, they feel totally at peace. Perhaps so, the eyes are said to be the windows of the soul after all and I have complete peace in my soul. It has not always been like this but this story is about how I became as I am.

People also get startled when I say I am Egyptian. Muriel exclaimed the first time I told her, "An Egyptian? I would have taken you for a Spaniard even though your accent is very difficult to place!" Muriel, I should say, has made a lifetime hobby of traveling all over the world, meeting people and making friends so she is quite an authority in such things.

However, her observation is not surprising at all. What really is the prototype of an Egyptian? That cradle of civilizations has seen so many races pass through its dry barren sands and its lush, fertile oases. She has nursed people from the very dark-skinned Nubians to the very fair-skinned Greeks. In between there have also been the Arabs, the Turks, the Romans, the Portuguese, the English, the French, and so on. My mother tried to outline our lineage to my brothers and me once. It was not just the contamination of one dominant race or two but a thorough admixture of so many races. I even had some Jewish cousins whom we used to visit on special occasions until they were suddenly transplanted to Israel and we lost all contact with them. The memories of them dimmed like a dream fades with daylight. So to be mistaken for a Spaniard was not a big deal at all. I have also been mistaken for an Indian, a Syrian, a Kenyan, and once for an American Indian!

So where should my story start? Perhaps it should begin from the Denshawi Incident even though there were years, decades or even centuries of events which led up to that particular point in time but in modern Egyptian times, the Denshawi Incident is still reported with a capital letter "I" as an epoch-making event.

The Incident really happened even though in the telling and the retelling of it, it has grown out of proportions and seems like one of those myths and legends of ancient times. It is also always retold with a lot of bias depending on who was doing the telling. In our elementary school history class, the teacher began by telling us this was what led to the fight for Egypt's independence from the colonial masters of Britain. Later in High school, we discovered that the fight for independence had been on for quite a while before then but the Denshawi Incident served to garner support and sympathy worldwide, even from the British overlords. It had inspired so much discontent and bred courage among the nationalists that it renewed their courage and gave them a further rallying point to push home their arguments and sentiments.

The bare facts of the Denshawi Incident were that some English gentlemen deployed to Egypt decided to relieve their boredom by going bird-hunting. Most of the wildlife described from ancient times was long gone from Egypt by then. At the most only very few wild animals were left except in the zoos. Nevertheless, these men went to the village of Denshawi to hunt. Seeing no wild life there, they decided to shoot at the pigeons which they saw. Now, these pigeons were more or less domesticated and often served as the only source of meat for the impoverished villagers. They were not afraid of human beings as such and could not have proven much of a challenge to the hunters. When the villagers saw their source of livelihood being decimated for sport and without as much as "By your leave", they were angry and frightened at the same time. They dared not protest to the overlords who were holding loaded guns, but they could not just stand by and do nothing while the pigeons were wiped out. What they did instead was to try to gather indoors as many of the birds as they could, out of reach of the British. It became a contest of which side would be faster in getting the birds, especially as the pigeons in question were not taking sides and did not know what was required of them.

Apparently, the frantic actions of the villagers added excitement to the hunt for the bored Britons. They took up the challenge. In the ensuing melee a village woman was shot and wounded. That was the breaking point! Suddenly, the subservient villagers could not take it anymore. Their anger overcame their fear and they attacked the hunting party which was made up five Britons and two Egyptians. Whereas the villagers had sticks, stones, domestic implements, or just their bare hands waving articles of clothing as their own weapons, the Britons had guns and live ammunition but they were overwhelmed in number. They shot into the crowd. Some people were seriously wounded but the villagers just kept coming. They were fueled by anger and fear. In desperation, the Britons set fire to a nearby wheat field which was almost ready for harvesting, hoping to divert the villagers.

If the villagers were incensed to begin with, they were now very much inflamed. Killing the pigeons had meant no meat with their food. Burning the wheat field meant no food at all! What was more? This was a farm almost ready for harvest. It was the end-stage result of weeks and months of backbreaking labor, patience, and hope. It was all going up in smoke, literally! They overpowered the hunting party, disarmed them, and beat them very severely. If not for the intervention of the village elders, the mob really meant to kill the Britons and their native attendants. But the village elders intervened and spoke some sense into their people. In fact, after the beating, some kind villagers took the wounded men in and nursed them despite their own losses.

Two of the white men managed to escape however. One of them got to an army outpost to report what had happened. The other man died of his wounds and the abominable heat of the desert. A peasant from a nearby village found him wandering in his fields and tried to help him. The man was beyond the help of an ordinary Good Samaritan. When the peasant saw that he was beyond help, he set off to find other Britons to report the death and perhaps get some reward.

The following day, the British cavalry arrived at Denshawi. En route, they met the would-be Good Samaritan coming to look for them. Through an interpreter, the peasant told them what had happened. The wounded man had stumbled up to him in his field; he had tried to help him but could not do much more than give him all the water in his skin bottle. This had not helped much and the poor man had died anyway. He led them to where he had kept the corpse, all the time reassuring them, "Your friend did not die alone in the fields like a mere animal, and without human contact. I tried my best to comfort him and make him comfortable with all I had. I tried to keep him alive but he was too far gone to return."

Later, the interpreter would keep emphasizing the fact that he did a good job and that the peasant's message did not get lost in interpretation. It will never be clear if the British Cavalry were too angry to understand the peasant's story, or that they just disbelieved him. In any case, the reward they gave him for his kind deeds was to execute him there and then. They left his corpse in the fields while they sent the corpse of the Briton back to their army base.

They then marched on to Denshawi with vengeance in their hearts. No proper inquiry was made nor any investigation carried out. They set up a kangaroo court for the incidence of the previous day. The primary concern and mandate of the court was that the insult on the Britons be avenged, and any insurgence put out. "These men were here as your guests and you did not honor them," the presiding commander said. "You received them by beating them, and chasing them around until one of them died! What kind of hospitality is that?"

"What kind of guest goes about wiping out your means of livelihood?" one of the elders asked. "What kind of guest takes pleasure in shooting at your women and children? When strangers behave in this manner, we do not call them guests because they do not seem to have kind intentions towards us in any way!"

Now I don't know if anyone said these actual words or if it was just a figment of our teacher's imagination but we all had to memorize those quotes verbatim!

Dust and Ashes

The British soldiers rounded up the villagers. They disregarded the testimonies of the villagers, and the Egyptian members of the hunting party. They selected the people whom they felt were the leaders of the insurrection and sentenced them to death or to live-imprisonment. Abdelnebi, who was the Mosque leader and the titular head of the Moslems at Denshawi, was sentenced to life imprisonment. This was so unfair because his wife had been the first shooting victim. It was his field which had been set on fire. Almost all his pigeons had been wiped out.

Mafouz was the oldest man in the village and therefore the chief of the elders. A gallows was erected in front of his house and he was hung from there as an example to the other villagers. All his pigeons had been shot. The British hunters had started with his and he had not been able to take them in. He had shouted for others to gather in their own pigeons and was seen by the kangaroo court to have in this way roused the sentiment of the other villagers resulting in the eventual "Riot". When Mafouz saw that the hunting party was taking it as a game and firing among the women and children who were trying to gather in the pigeons, he had hit one of the soldiers with his walking stick and told him to stop doing such dangerous things. For hitting a white man with a stick, and for inciting the villagers, Mafouz was strung up as an example to the people of what they should not be, and what they should not do.

Four other people were hanged with Mafouz. Perhaps, the most humiliating punishment was having all the elders of the village flogged in front of their wives, children, and all the other villagers as a lesson against insurgency. Even the ones who were hanged were first flogged. These lessons were very appropriately degrading as the Britons had calculated them to be. Native Egyptians revered, and still revere the elderly. In a culture that believed in ancestral worship, the elders were close to being gods. As everyone inevitably grew to be elderly and would soon come to the point of also being revered, old age was not just respected, it was venerated. Flogging an elder was the highest of all sacrilege. The Britons knew this, and that was the real aim of this object lesson. The Denshawi villagers, and indeed the whole of Egypt learned a lesson all right but not the one the British Cavalry wanted them to learn.

Our teachers told us that the Egyptians in the hunting party really tried to speak up about the injustice of it all but they too were flogged and put in prison for not protecting their commanding officers. Later, amidst criticisms, the British pointed out that there were also some Egyptians in this kangaroo court. If this was meant to appease, it only inflamed the people even more. "They pretended to give us a voice but instead they actually muzzled us more! They punished us, trod on us, and expected us to respectfully thank them for being so condescending and so oppressive!" Our history teacher cried passionately at this point. I actually saw tears and some of us wept right along.

Apart from the rest of Egypt, the rest of the world, the British parliament, and even the ordinary man in Britain were incensed by this incident at Denshawi. It lent credence to, and became one of the rallying points in the events which eventually led to the Egyptian independence about sixteen years later in 1922. Independence for the rest of the British colony in Africa as a whole followed eventually.

Of course people would conclude that is how it passed into history but there were other forces at play which were never considered. Up till then, Moslems and Christians had peacefully coexisted in Denshawi. There were minor skirmishes and expected competitions from time to time but that did not prevent them from coexisting as tolerant neighbors. They did business together and even intermarried despite petty squabbles. A Christian in Denshawi was likely to have Moslem cousins and vice versa. Religion was important but not anything to die for until the Incident. In the aftermath of the Incident however, a very great Moslem-Christian conflict ensued. I have heard some West Africans in Mike's circle argue that the white man came to their countries with the Bible in one hand and the slave chain in the other. He stole their land, their sweat, their crops and produce, and even their young men and women. And then with the Bible he shut their mouths so that they would not protest, promising them their rewards would be in heaven in the afterlife.

That is basically how people were taught to see the presence of the white man even in Egypt of that era. Inevitably, the early colonial masters were linked to Christianity; and Christianity was linked to the British. "Christianity is from the West, and everything from the West is Christian! To be anti-West is to be anti-Christian, and to be anti-Christian is to be anti-West!"

In actual fact, Islam, Christianity, and Judaism all originated from the same loins! It is just that whereas the Moslems trace their ancestry to Abraham through Ismail or Ishmael, the Jews and Christians trace theirs to the same origin through Isaac! Jesus Christ of the Christians, and Prophet Mohammed of the Moslems both walked under the same Eastern skies and baked in its sands. Both Christianity and Islam were cradled in Egypt. To this day, the Coptic Cathedral said to have been established by Saint Mark in the first century, is still in use for worship, and as a Tourist attraction in Alexandria. So also is the Al-Azhar Islamic University established six centuries later when Islam was still in its infancy. Islam is a relative newcomer to Egypt compared to Christianity, and Egypt was Christian long before the so-called Western World caught any whiff of it. Jesus Christ lived in Egypt as an infant! In any case, the white man might have come for the commerce. Like good businessmen, they maximally exploited the opportunities they saw. They brought in their soldiers with their superior weapons to help lord it over the natives but the missionaries spoilt the show for them. The truth is that they might have got away with so much inhumanity if not for Christianity. That is my own heartfelt opinion. The missionaries came with a quest for educating and enlightening the natives. This group of white men saw the natives as people, people with souls, people with potentials, and people in whom God had an interest. They agitated both in their native countries and "on site" with the natives to get them educated. I have listened to lively debates which said that the education of the natives was so he could be the under-clerks for the colonial masters. I have also heard one that propounded the theory that it was just so they could read the Bible and be subdued, nothing else. Incidentally, Egypt was not like these other African nations. By the advent of Britain, Egypt was if anything, more civilized than Britain. Egyptians could read, write, and were well advanced in the sciences, arts, and religion including Christianity. I mention these arguments because they continue to have strong bearings on current issues in Egypt, and on this story in particular. Islam was a very late comer to Egypt but in its usual fury, it all but overwhelmed Christianity which had been in place for centuries before it. Christianity in Egypt was, and still remains the cradle of many Christian doctrines in spite of dissenting claims.

Anyway, back to the Denshawi Incident, the unfair executions immediately bred a lot of animosities among the villagers. Abdelnebi's wife was shot. His field was burnt. His pigeons were wiped out. Above all, he was going to jail for the rest of his life. Mafouz and two of the other people who were hanged were Moslems. The perpetrators and the executors were "Christians"! Never mind that some of these people might not have seen the insides of a church for years. They probably had no meaningful relationships with Christ except for the "Christian names" they bore. Never mind also that the helpful peasant who was unfairly executed, and the rest of the people that were hanged with Mafouz were Christians. Never mind that the elders who had been flogged for not containing the insurgency better were almost all Christians. It did not help that the Egyptians in the hunting party who had also been unfairly punished for trying to speak up; and the Egyptians in the kangaroo court who had been humiliated and muzzled were also all Christians. It became an all-out Moslem-Christian war in Denshawi.

With Abdelnebi gone to prison, the Moslems in Denshawi had also lost their leadership. They did not wish to remain under the other Christian elders left in the village. The vacuum thus created was filled by angry Moslems who infiltrated from neighboring villages. They further incited and encouraged the strong anti-Christian sentiments in the community. The remaining Christians in the village were no less disheartened by the Incident. They lacked the zeal to fight back and had no desire to stay with the pall of the Incidence hanging over them. The next year promised to be difficult with their crops almost all destroyed. One day, they packed their remaining belongings and left en masse. They all went in the same direction settling down along the way as they went towards Alexandria. Some went as far as one creek of the Nile near Alexandria, settled and had families, established businesses, built residential houses, schools, and churches. Several decades down the line of history,

I was born and learned about the aspect of the Denshawi Incident in my family lore. The Moslems did not stay at Denshawi for long either. Perhaps they left one by one or perhaps they also migrated en masse like the Christians. I do not know that part of the story but today in Denshawi, I am told there is not much left either of people or of infrastructure. In the late 1990's, there was talk of establishing a Museum there. In any case, if not for the Incident, I might not have been born where I was born, or shaped by the beliefs I was brought up by. Without it, maybe this story would have taken a totally different shape.

"NORMAL" TIMES

My parents are not related, almost. In our culture, it is normal for first cousins to marry. Even half siblings are allowed to marry. Well, history has it that my paternal and maternal great-grandfathers were very good friends. They were also adventurers, who in search of their fortunes left their village of Denshawi to Cairo. They found Cairo overcrowded. Hearing of Alexandria, they went westwards. To survive, they hired themselves out as farmhands, rickshaw drivers, plate washers, security guards, and so on. Many young men found their fortunes in those days by joining the army or the Resistance for Egypt's independence from Britain. These two abhorred both war and politics and so they could not make their fortunes quickly enough.

In the course of their adventures, they reached Hosh Issa which was a small village that felt large in its own importance. Here they met two girls who were remarkable in their beauties and famed for their closeness as tight friends. They fell in love with the two girls. How each found the distinguishing uniqueness in the girl he admired has formed the basis for some other family folklore. The telling of these will be too much of a digression here. In any case, they married the girls, decided they were the fortunes they had been seeking all along, and returned to Denshawi with their brides. With the money they had saved, they bought stocks and farmlands and settled down to being local farmers.

They would have lived there happily ever after except that by the time the Incident happened, they were among the families that decided to leave Denshawi. Many of the migrants went only as far as Tanta and settled either in the city or the neighboring villages. Their two wives, longing for home, and mindful of family ties, persuaded them to go back to Hosh Issa. That is how come we regard Hosh Issa as our roots. My grandfathers were still in their pre-teens when this migration took place and so to them Hosh Issa was more of a home than the dimly-remembered Denshawi.

There had been a few intermarriages between the two families. I cannot now tell why the marriage of my parents was more outstanding than all the others. It probably was not any more so except perhaps in my own imagination and with the self-importance of childhood. In any case, as the families grew and expanded, my parents both found themselves in school at Damanhur. My mother was studying to be a nurse, and my father to be a teacher. They had known each other since childhood and were always together at family occasions and holidays. How they became romantically involved and eventually decided to get married to the delight of their parents, grandparents and their numerous other relatives is the subject of another very interesting family lore. In the course of time however, she worked as a nurse at the government hospital at Damanhur, while he went further to study Agriculture

Economics to a Masters Degree level and eventually worked as the head of planning and personnel department at the Cotton Ginnery at Damanhur.

I have a very big extended family of very mixed background. I even had Jewish and Moslem cousins. The animosity which drove my great grandparents from their home in Denshawi did not shut their bowels of mercy towards Moslems. They did not force their daughters or sons not to marry into Moslem families but anyone who chose to do so received lots of lectures in advance. I particularly remember a female cousin who wept and insisted on marrying her Moslem suitor. Her parents had many misgivings about the boy's family. At last, they chose to have her peacefully married to her paramour than have her elope and severe all contacts with them. Her husband was very kind and sweet as I remembered him. Unfortunately his parents were not as tolerant as hers. When he died in a motor accident three years later, her in-laws forced her out of his house and his meager possessions. She returned to her parents with her 18 month-old son, a three-month old pregnancy, and nothing else except for the clothes on their backs. Her parents took her back and supported her. They were relieved that they had not cut her off entirely at the outset.

Another male cousin married a woman who had converted from Islam to Christianity and was facing severe persecutions from her parents. The story was that they had disinherited her and sent her out of the house. To make taking her in decent, my cousin married her so he could legitimately protect and provide for her. At least that was what I heard but some of my female cousins said he married her because he could not get a wife by any other means. I have always had a romantic heart so I chose to believe the former story. Since they were very happy to all outward appearances, I think that was likely the true story.

Al Kalima

Not all the Moslem-Christian alliances in my family are this dramatic but the Moslems in Hosh Issa coexisted peacefully with their Christian neighbors as they had at Denshawi. When the Moslems were very good, their goodness shone even brighter than those of the Christians around. In my memory, there was no truly bad Moslem at Hosh Issa. Their cranky old men or eccentric women were not more so than their Christian counterparts. Their boys were not meaner, nor their girls saucier. Being a Moslem was not much different from being a Christian at Hosh Issa. One of the pillars of Islam required that they do good and give alms at least once a day. Some Moslems took this so seriously and would not dare get to sunset without their having done at least one good deed. I remember how my maternal Grandfather Moussa would call out to his neighbor Ahmed, "Ahmed, have you done your *Zakat* for today?"

To this Ahmed might answer, "I already did…" and recount which good deed that had lent him the relief for the day. A few other times though he would answer woefully, "Not yet but *Inshallah* I will do something before the day is over."

My grandfather might then tell him to do some sundry duty like "Please help me bring in our clothes from the line outside…" or "Help me carry this message to Mr. Dawoud…" or any such guilt-assuaging errand which Ahmed would run, full of gratitude that he had received the opportunity to do his *Zakat* for that day.

Whatever his answer, my grandfather would still remind him at the end of it all, "It is not by your works of righteousness, Ahmed. We Christians believe that it is by the finished work of Jesus Christ."

But not all the Moslems at Hosh Issa were like Ahmed. Ali the butcher was the very opposite. He never missed an opportunity to rip anyone off. If someone appealed to his sense

Dust and Ashes

of religious duties he was always known to answer, "*Zakat? Zakat!* That is why I need you to pay me so I can do *Zakat* for my wife and children."

And his wife and children were famously always in need of *Zakat*. They were the most ragged and hungriest-looking individuals in the village. One wondered what Ali did with all the money he scammed from his customers. He was so uncharitable and tightfisted. In this he was not much different from Nebi the village tailor. Nebi also happened to be the loudest bass singer in the church choir. Outside of their religions, the two were also very close friends. They were close collaborators in most scams that happened at Hosh Issa. They were both tolerated, and even cherished as a part of the total village life.

As a child I enjoyed listening to the endless, amicable religious arguments among the adults about how one could get to heaven. I usually agreed with the Moslems that the Christian philosophy of just believing and having faith in the work of Christ was just too simple. It left a lot of room for negligence and laziness on the part of the believers. "A Moslem, on the other hand has to work very hard to fulfill the five pillars of Islam. At the end of your life, if your good deeds are put on a scale and they outweigh your bad deeds, then you are allowed into paradise!"

It was quite a simplistic argument. Who could not agree with that? The five pillars of Islam were easy too. First, acknowledge that there is only one God and Mohammed is his prophet. Second, pray five times a day facing Mecca. Third, perform *Zakat* by giving alms or such good deeds. Fourth, fast during the month of *Ramadan*. Finally, make (or contribute for someone to make) the pilgrimage to Mecca at least once in your lifetime! It sounded like a lot of fun. This was all that was needed to get into heaven! In my mind, I already acknowledged that there was only one God even though I had problems with Mohammed but I dared not say this aloud. Children were to be seen and not heard. The Christian arguments about the conditions which got a Christian into heaven sounded more complicated and too simple at the same time. It went like this, "Believe in Jesus Christ and His finished work on the cross and then live every minute of your life as if Christ was living through you". It did not make much sense to me then as a child until much, much later.

I also listened to the discussions of what heaven would be like. There would be lots of perfumes and *houris* (virgin girls) for Islam. To this my grandfather always wrinkled his nose in disgust. He was a retired college principal and had quite a repertoire of facial expressions that could speak volumes. He felt that the overpowering scents of the Middle East could be quite disgusting. I remember that he was always outspoken about how the subtlety of a perfume showed high class. And as for so many *houris* for one man, he felt this would be a personal hell. "One wife is already more than I can handle. I have seen what having multiple women can do to a man's life. I do not desire that at all. I certainly do not wish it even on the worst of my enemies! One man's paradise is indeed another man's hell" he would conclude.

I was so puzzled by this as a child since I knew how much in love he and my grandmother were, even in their old age! Would it not be wonderful to have more of Grandma, younger and even more beautiful? That was how the mind of a child worked.

The subject of Mohammed was a very delicate one and they always carefully skirted it. Moslems minded a lot if one said the name without also pronouncing a special blessing on it. Christians did not buy into this. They would rather avoid saying the name altogether. The Moslems around me as I was growing

Dust and Ashes

up generally felt that Christians did not take their Christianity seriously enough. As Moslems, they also revered the name of Jesus as a great prophet and wondered why we should use his name so often and so unnecessarily. "Imagine, you would even use His name in profane language!" they would say with a mixture of awe and disgust.

On the other hand, in school at Damanhur my Moslem schoolmates could bandy about the name of Jesus. They would talk about what he had done or not done. They would even use His name as a cuss word with impunity. I remember how they made fun of the film *"Jesus Christ the Superstar"*. We were in high school then, and it was the year that witnessed a lot of upheavals in my life. "The film portrays how Christians really see Jesus" some Moslem boys taunted us in school.

From magazines, we read about how the film got a lot of positive reviews and endorsements, even by Christians. Locally however, it was deemed culturally inappropriate. I distinctly remember one of my father's friends in church saying he would not allow his children watch the film. I never got to watch it myself but at school we heard a great deal about it from the Moslems! The taunts hurt but we felt Jesus was God and should defend himself. We tried to tell them that the film was a fiction but we did not have much ground on which to argue. Most of us had been forbidden to watch the film by our parents or other authority figures. We told them that if they wanted the nonfictional truth, they should check their Bibles. Some did, and were silent afterwards.

Most Moslems had at least the New Testament Bible, curtsey of Gideon Ministry. There was also a local Imam who peddled anti-Christian propaganda. He asked the Moslem faithful to collect Bibles and mark certain passages with which to refute Christian arguments. He asked them to study certain passages

Al Kalima

which showed how controversial the Bible was. He claimed that the "Original Bible" had been tampered with by the British, and that certain segments in both the old and the new testaments foretold the coming of Mohammed after Jesus. The Moslems therefore had Bibles that they could use as reference.

The majority of the Moslems in my school were respectful but the handful of troublemakers was really very loud. At one point, two of these taunted Bitrus, a Christian boy in my class. "Why don't you Christians just admit that Mary Magdalene was really the mistress of your Jesus Christ?" he asked.

Bitrus retorted, "That is certainly not so! Even if it were, that is still far better than your prophet who was a pedophile!"

I think the troublemaker did not understand what Bitrus had said at the time. He must have gone home and asked the meaning of the word because the next day at school, there was a riot. Some riffraff arrived at our school gate armed with stones, clubs, metal rods and all manner of crude weapons. They demanded that Bitrus be brought out and stoned to death for desecrating the name of the prophet. We were all very frightened. In retrospect, it was lucky it had happened this way. Nothing was to prevent their waylaying Bitrus on the way to or from school and doing just as they had threatened. As it was, the principal and some teachers met with the mob at the school gate. They promised to look into the matter. After they left, Bitrus' parents were summoned to the school and asked to take him away immediately. Afterwards, an emergency school assembly was called where we were told that Bitrus had been expelled. The principal warned all of us about making derogatory comments about one another's faiths and practices. The other boy who had started it was not even suspended but at least everyone seemed mollified. My parents were acquainted with Bitrus' parents. We understood that after this incident, he had been sent away to school in England. The rest of the family moved away to Aswan thereafter.

From this occasion I learned more than one lesson which I needed later on in life. On the whole, the Moslem-Christian dynamics at the earlier stages of my life was quite stable, very manageable and even agreeable.

THE GOOD OLD DAYS

I was born in the Golden Days of Nasser's reign in Egypt. My great grandparents and my grandparents had been relatively well-to-do and very hardworking but they said that in those days, no matter how hard one worked, one could never rise in society. It was assumed that the colonizing British made it so. Being used to the feudal system where a small ruling class accounted to the king while keeping all the other citizens under serfdom, they encouraged this system in their colonies. The result was that the rich got richer, and the poor, poorer. My parents' families were land and business owners but they had to work very hard to meet even the basic necessities of life. Not all of their children were sent to school. Only the ones who showed strong interest or very good aptitudes went on to any formal higher education. Their parents could not afford the school fees for everybody. Reading and writing Basic English and Arabic were compulsory and could be acquired at home, in church, or in the mosque. People were literate but people were also very poor.

Dust and Ashes

Nasser's reign changed all these. Suddenly, everyone who wanted to go to school could do so. There were opportunities for the training of professionals in all fields. Anyone who worked hard and saved hard could also own land and move up from lower, to middle, and to upper class. Jobs were created. Indigenous industries flourished. Egypt shook off the shackles of the colonial masters. She also shook off those of the indigenous monarchy. It was the rise of the common man and my extended family prospered in it all. In fact, Nasser was so much revered that many children were named after him including my parents' firstborn child.

My childhood was a very happy one. I had an elder brother Gamal, a younger brother Yohana, and a baby sister Amira who was twelve years younger than me. My parents called her their Sunset Baby, the child of their old age. We all loved and spoilt her shamelessly. My mother worked at the government hospital at Damanhur and my father at the cotton ginnery. We lived at a block of flats owned by the ginnery. There were five other families in that block. All the fathers worked at the ginnery. The flat was set in a field where we all played together as children. I do not now recall any animosities between our parents even though we had varied backgrounds. I know for sure that there was a mixture of Christians and Moslems in the block. I also knew that the Christians and the Moslems were not all the same type. They did not go to the same places of worship. With the power of hindsight now, I guess the Christians were Coptic and evangelical. The Moslems were Sunni and Shiite. During Nasser's regime, these differences were not at all significant. One was first an Egyptian, and then all those other things besides. I remember the debate among the adults around me over the 1967 war against Israel. Even in such matters, what mattered most was that we were Egyptians first, regardless of our sentiments towards the Israeli question.

Religion played an important part in my childhood but it never overshadowed other things. My grandparents on both sides had become evangelical Christians sometime in their lives long before I was born. This earned them some degree of ostracism at Hosh Issa where the majority of Christians were Coptic. My parents had continued in their footsteps. I grew up to family prayers and devotions. I had to attend Sunday school and Christian youth camps. I also had the privilege of participating in Coptic worship especially during extended family events like weddings, funerals, and special holidays, or anniversaries. The Coptic form of worship was so regal, dignified, and full of symbolisms compared to Evangelical worship. I felt more at home with evangelical worship however. It was somewhat freer, and I derived more meaning from it. However, I am the first to admit that upbringing must account for a lot of my biases.

All said, between the six families at our block of flats at Damanhur, there were about twenty children ranging in age from months-old babies to young adults in their early twenties. We all went to the same schools depending on age. In the mornings we all trooped off, boys together, and girls together. In the afternoons, we came back the same way. We had a loose general alliance formed on the basis of our coming from the same block of flats. We would defend one another in fights, share our lunches, or cheer one another on during school competitions. Smaller alliances formed on the proximity of our ages. My best friends were Hoda and Salma. Salma's family lived in the flat across from ours. Hoda's family lived directly above ours. Coincidentally, three of us were in the same class at school. I remember once that a boy at school took Salma's lunch and threatened to beat her up. Smaller than her age and shy by nature, she huddled in a corner weeping until Hoda and I came upon her. Where Salma was shy, Hoda was fiery. She marched up to the bully and demanded Salma's lunch back. The boy laughed at her. He threw the empty lunch bag at her face and ran off taunting Hoda to try and catch him. We went crying to Gamal and his friends. When they heard what had happened, they had us point the boy out at the playground. They then consoled us and made us share our own lunches with Salma. The following day, they waylaid the boy on the way to school and beat him up so badly that he did not come to school for the rest of the week. When he returned, he was a very subdued person. The school could not have done anything about it because they never heard of it. Even if they had, the event happened outside the school, outside their jurisdiction.

Of course such things also worked both ways. We heard of members of our own group being threatened with beatings outside school. Alliances also broke down and reformed but one's best bet was never to be alone or without friends. These were just childhood skirmishes and there was never any incidence of true lawlessness. We all seemed to have an intrinsic sense of fair play and mutual respect. In other words, I had a very normal childhood. I guess these events were also my basis for developing adult loyalties, friendships, and values.

When my younger brother, Yohana, became old enough to go to school, my mother charged me with keeping an eye on him. I tried to obey her, but Yohana preferred to tag along with Gamal and his friends instead. By the time Gamal graduated and went on to secondary school, Yohana was old enough to form his own alliances and would not be caught dead walking to school with girls. As we got nearer to school, other groups from other blocks and houses joined up. By the time we reached the school we would be quite a reasonably large crowd.

School was fun. Our teachers really were interested in teaching and the students were very eager to learn. The major examination then was the *Thanaweya Amma*. It signaled the end of high school and more or less the formal beginning of adulthood. The results determined whether one was university material or should be apprenticed for a skilled job at a vocational or technical college. It was not just enough to pass it, but to score high enough marks in order to get placement into one's choice of course or university. I never got to worry about this exam for myself but we were all involved when it was Gamal's turn. I knew it would be my turn soon enough. That three-year gap between Gamal and me was sometimes too short and went too fast. For the moment I had to worry about the *Adaadiya Amma*, the quasi-entrance examination into high school proper.

The last three years of basic education helped our teachers decide if we could join the next three years of secondary education that would involve intense preparation for *Thanaweya Amma*. My friends also worried about whether they would even be allowed to further their education given that we were merely girls. I knew that in my own case, going to university was not an option. It was a given! Not only were girls in my extended family encouraged to go to school by all means, Nasser had virtually eliminated the gender bias in education. Any interested girl could go to school, often with the family not needing to sell off their assets or rob a bank. My parents were not only well-to-do, they were fanatical about "Proper Education". They also thanked God for giving them children with "Brains to learn".

My childhood days were carefree and full of love and discipline. I knew that I mattered a lot to those who loved me. Some events still stand out clearly in my mind especially all the wisdom I absorbed from my grandfather and his friends just by being allowed to linger in the background as they talked. I was loved by my grandparents, my numerous aunts, uncles, and cousins. I was loved especially by my parents. There was a *Sham Ennisim* when I was about five years old or so. Yohana was just a year old at the time and was just beginning to toddle around on unsteady feet. That day I learned that my mother was a fighter and could give her life for her children.

Sham Ennisim is a national holiday celebrated the week after Easter. It was probably a pagan festival that predated both Christianity and Islam. It was supposed to be the beginning of the first day of spring. People went out to open places to "Smell the fresh breeze". *Sham Ennisim* was usually a family event with get-togethers, picnics in parks, boat trips on the Nile, and so on. As with almost all holidays, we got away from Damanhur to Hosh Issa to celebrate it with the wider family and catch up with one another. We all went for a picnic at a field near the Nile creek. Towards the end of the day when we were packing up to go, suddenly out of nowhere a swarm of angry bees came straight at us. We screamed and ran in different directions. "Quick," yelled my mother, "Get under my skirt!"

It was the only protection she had. Gamal, Yohana and I did as she said. She covered us with her skirt while she waved her scarf above her head and screamed at the bees. She was stung more than once and had swellings for those stings by the next day but her children were perfectly safe and untouched under her skirt! I was still very young at the time but that incident made a very deep and lasting impression on me.

Another memory that also stayed with me was the day I came back from school with a zero on my Math test paper. I must have been about nine or ten years old at the time and we were doing long divisions in class. My parents were both in the living room when I got back. I thrust the paper out to my father and simultaneously announced, "I'm never going to understand long division!"

"Oh yes, you will" said my father. "You are a very smart girl. Now let us do it together. It starts with mastering your multiplication table."

I was not listening to him anymore. I had stomped off to my room. Memorizing the times table was compulsory in school. The previous year I had mastered two, three, four, and six times' tables. Five, ten, and eleven times' tables were easy because they had patterns to them. I saw the trick to the nine time's table but I just found myself stumped by seven and eight times' tables. I gave up on ever understanding the multiplication table until that Friday. I just was not interested any more. There were other more interesting things demanding my attention, like reading.

My father said I should take my time and study the entire times table from two times to twelve times during the night and recite it to him the following morning. He added that I was not allowed to go out to play the next day until I could say the whole table to him. Dismissing him in my mind, I had my supper and went to bed but not to sleep. I had a juicy story book I was in the middle of. I loved to read and was advanced in that area beyond my classmates. I hoped to become a teacher or a journalist when I grew up. What did mastering the times table have to do with this ambition?

But my father was determined. The next day after breakfast he asked me to recite the times table to him. I quickly parroted the ones I had mastered. "Yes?" he waited expectantly.

"That is all" I replied. "I have done most of it."

"'Most of it' is not good enough" he stated firmly. "You can do better than that. You are not permitted to go to play outside today until you have mastered it all."

Dust and Ashes

I shrugged nonchalantly and was about to go back to my room to finish my storybook but my father meant business. He was home from work that day and was just lolling at the dining table. "Bring your pencil and rough notebook, and come and sit here. You will work at it until you get it. First, write out the ones you don't know, and then try to fill in the blanks from memory then from your textbook. When you're ready to say the whole thing to me, I will be here, waiting."

I dragged my feet trying to find the pencil and notebook until he sent Gamal to fetch me. I sat at the chair opposite him gazing at the blank paper with tearful eyes while he read his newspaper. I thought of the book under the pillow in my room which I could then be finishing. I had just got to the interesting part, filled with suspense; and I hated my father with my whole heart. He must have read that newspaper over and over for a hundred times but I was not thinking of him. My mother came and went. I could hear the noise of other children playing in the field. Around midday, my mother and the boys came in, ate their lunch around us, and then went out to visit a friend at the other end of town. My father and I sat on at that dining table. At his behest, neither of us had been served any lunch. At last, seeing that he was not going to relent, I started doing what he asked.

It must have taken me less than an hour from the time I finally began to work but at last I looked up and told him I was now ready to recite the entire table to him. He put down his paper and looked straight at me. With tear-choked voice and a bowed head, I went through the times table, from two times to twelve times without a single mistake. At the end, I looked up at him and discovered that he too, had tears in his eyes. He opened his arms wide and I ran into them. We sobbed together and he said, "I am very proud of you. I know that whatever you put your mind to do, you can always accomplish it. You are my girl!"

With that endorsement, we went out and got ice cream and lollipops for ourselves and for the rest of the family. That was a very rare treat. From that day, whenever I was stumped by any problem, I would remind myself that my father believed very much in what I could do if I put my mind to it. I would then go about methodically finding a solution to that particular difficulty. I did not know it then but that lesson upheld me in years to come.

The year I turned twelve, there were some major changes in my personal life and in the life of the nation. With two brothers, I never really felt the lack of a sister because I always had enough cousins and friends to fulfill the need for female companionship. However, like all girls, I loved babies. My friends and I were forever volunteering to help out wherever there were newborn babies in our apartment complex. Sometimes the babies would actually be the siblings of my friends. I would go home at the end of the day filled with envy because they got to keep spending time with the baby while I had to go back to roost in my own home.

For whatever reason, my parents had stopped childbearing after Yohana. I remember once begging my mother to have a baby for me just like Ester's mother had for her. My mother replied, "Don't worry, you will soon be old enough and have your own babies for yourself."

I did not fully understand this. I felt that having my own baby was still too far in the future. After begging for some time, I resigned myself to the fact that she was never going to have any other children. And then the year I turned twelve she started getting fatter. Her tummy grew big and round. One day

Yohana asked her, "Why is your tummy so big, Marmee? Did you eat too much?"

She simply answered "Yes" but my father used that opportunity to tell us that come July that year, we were going to have a little brother or sister.

"She's pregnant!" I shouted as the light of understanding dawned on me. "Marmee is pregnant!"

I could not contain myself. I drew up a calendar to keep count until July. I had a barrage of questions to ask her and I must have driven the poor woman crazy. I had to tell all my friends. There could not have been a better time than July. We would be on long vacation. There would be no school. My friends would be the ones visiting my house and having to leave at night. Gamal and Yohana were understandably not as excited as I was. At fifteen, Gamal kept his thoughts to himself. Yohana, at eight years old, was not jealous or anything like that. He hoped fervently it would be a baby boy for him to treat as Gamal treated him. I hoped it would be a girl to balance us out but it did not really matter to me even if it turned out to be a boy. What I wanted was my very own baby.

Amira arrived right on schedule. My mother's elder sister came to stay with us for about two weeks. When she left, I got to be my mother's major helper. That baby belonged to me in every way, especially when my mother resumed working again, albeit on part-time basis. Gamal and Yohana loved her too, and we all spoilt her. We were on the lookout for her smiles. Every achievement she made from holding up her head by herself to sitting without support to cutting her first tooth all called for celebrations. We were a close family before Amira came along but she served to bond us even more tightly.

When Amira was two months old, another major change happened that affected the whole nation. President Nasser died of a massive heart attack! To the nation, his death was so sudden and so unexpected even though there were rumors that there had been little signs of his failing health known only to his close associates. We were all plunged into deep and genuine mourning. He was loved that much. Maybe we had begun to think of him as immortal, especially those who remembered his offer of resignation soon after the failed Israeli war of 1967. Some people remembered previous failed attempts at assassinating him. He had brought Egypt further than any other leader in recent memory ever had. I remember people standing in the middle of the streets, looking dazed and numbed like a street dog caught in car headlights at night. Everywhere, people talked about "What is to become of us now?" as if we had suddenly been orphaned, and without hope. We did not understand it all as children but we could feel the atmosphere of sudden calamity. Like the rest of the nation, we felt suddenly bereft and exposed.

When we visited Hosh Issa that weekend, the talk among the adults was also mostly about "What is to become of us now?" and "So who is going to take over now?"

Everyone agreed that whoever was elected to take over would never be as good as Nasser. His intentions were very pure. His shoes were too big for any one man to fill. "My fear", said my astute maternal grandfather, Moussa, "is that they will choose Anwar Sadat to succeed him. I never have trusted that man with his half-open eyes like a snake meditating on his prey."

I remember that phrase in particular because subsequently every picture of Sadat I saw reminded me of that word picture which my grandfather had so skillfully painted. All the other events of his reign also always brought it back to my mind. That is how biases begin, I guess, but are these biases always wrong?

Dust and Ashes

Just as my grandfather had feared, Anwar Sadat was chosen to fill Nasser's shoes. "Temporarily" we were told, "until elections can be held."

Those elections held but by some sleight of hand and some well-orchestrated maneuvers, Sadat's opponents either mysteriously disappeared or died. His stay became more permanent. Perhaps he was just unlucky where Nasser was lucky but he overtly undid much of the good that Nasser had done, seemingly with the best of intentions. He shifted national and international allegiances. He minimized the power of growing indigenous industries thereby cutting jobs and increasing unemployment. Most of all, he lifted the clamp which Nasser had put on religious militancy among other things. Suddenly, being patriotic became secondary to things like religious and racial affiliations. People began to defend and speak up for their religions more than ever before. Racism became a real issue in Egypt. I for one had not felt the differences until then. People became suspicious of their neighbors even in quiet Hosh Issa, not to talk of cities like Damanhur, Alexandria, and Cairo.

The standard of living fell. The gap between the rich and the poor widened again. Even my parents, who up till then had been secure in their jobs, became jittery. We all became restive without knowing why; but life still went on anyway.

THE UPHEAVAL

To hear my grandfather tell it, Sadat was responsible for all the problems in Egypt. With the mind of a child, I do not think we appreciated much of these problems. We went to school right on schedule as before. We ate as we usually did when we were hungry. Our parents went to work and came back. Nothing much had changed as far as we were concerned. But then there were subtle changes that even we, in our innocence, noticed. Unemployment was steadily increasing. People were laid off at the factories, and offices. Small private enterprises that depended on the patronage of these people also ground to a halt. All these redundant people came to depend more and more on those of their relatives who were still employed. Many of my cousins and uncles who had been working in various towns and cities returned to the village. They could not go back because they had no jobs or accommodations to go back to. Two of my cousins came to live with us while their parents tried to find other jobs. It felt good to have them move in with us even though the house was now rather crowded.

Dust and Ashes

Crime rates soared as unemployment rose. There were more reports of robberies. Robbers broke into people's houses or held them up on the roads. These things used to happen before but very, very rarely. Everyone became more vigilant. Doors that used to be kept unlocked were now secured by more than one type of locks. They had to be checked and rechecked before going to sleep or going on an outing. Road trips became full of apprehension. People planned their trips to be along busy roads and to get to their destinations before dark. The robbers grew bolder until no time, and no road was totally safe. Even joyous celebrations that used to occur with abandon became marred by increased vigilance. Strangers were no longer so openly welcomed and entertained. Even supplies at feasts became more meager and less varied.

Perhaps the most bothersome of these subtle changes was the increase in awareness of our religious differences. Whereas we had always known we were different and believed differently, we were now more aware of what these differences meant. Whereas we had loved and played with one another with abandon, our interactions now shrank to being painfully polite to one another, sometimes exaggeratedly and embarrassingly so. We could no longer eat together nor closely interact with and play with one another. This was very difficult for those of us at our block of apartments who had grown up together and were used to sharing so much. Suddenly for the first time, we became introduced to the word, "*Kafir*". Anyone who was not a Moslem was *Kafir*.

Our Moslem neighbors became more devoted to their religion. Every Friday afternoon they would troop to the mosque and when they returned they would be so subdued and solemn until the next day. By Sunday they would have loosened up enough and almost be back to normal. By Wednesday we would all be playing together, as near normally as the times allowed until they went back to mosque again the following Friday. Once, unbidden, Hoda began to share with Salma and me what they were being taught in mosque. They were taught that there was a need for the purification of their religion. Those that truly believed were not to be tight friends with unbelievers. We had never heard such nonsense before but it meant a lot to our Moslem neighbors. Gradually, new alliances formed along religious lines. We started looking at one another more suspiciously.

In my family, 1971 was also a year in which we were living out our own peculiar tensions. Gamal was to sit for the *Thanaweya Amma*. I was to sit the *Adaadiya Amma*. Gamal's exam was far more important than mine. The teachers were already working very hard to prepare us but my parents did not leave anything to chance. They took time to still coach us at home. Gamal wanted to be a doctor. He had hoped to go to University of Cairo or the American University but my uncles advised strongly against this. "There is a subtle pressure to admit more Moslems and less Christians" they said. "You stand a better chance at Tanta or even Alexandria."

They knew what they were saying. One of them was a university lecturer at Alexandria. The other worked for the education ministry and knew about intakes and admissions. Gamal therefore dutifully chose Tanta as his first choice, South Valley as his second, but he still defiantly put University of Cairo as his third choice.

As for me, my parents had the confidence that I would do well at the *Adaadiya Amma*. I was not subjected to as much scrutiny and extra coaching. So far there was no known discrimination in who went on to the next three years and

Dust and Ashes

qualified for higher education even though my grandfather prophesied there would soon be. My mind was firmly made up. I was not going any further than Damanhur in order to pursue higher education. When in three years' time it was my turn to choose universities, I was going to apply for Education or Teacher Training at Damanhur, Media at Damanhur, and maybe Education or Teacher Training at Tanta to complete the choices. I was not that ambitious but everyone was entitled to his or her own dreams.

Preparing for, and taking the exams were tension-filled moments. Waiting for the results was, if anything, more so. Gamal got up and went out each morning. He came back late in the afternoon and roamed restlessly around the house. My parents were worried when he went out. They were irritated when he was at home. Even Yohana and Amira felt the tension. I was not unduly worried. I was one for reading a book with full concentration, but when there was not much to do at home I took three-year old Amira, settled her on my hips and went out to the fields to play. To my delight, she had chosen me as her favorite just as Yohana had chosen Gamal. She followed me about everywhere. I read to her from picture storybooks. When I read for myself, she was content to just stay beside me, leafing through her own picture book. My name was the first word she learned to say, even before she learned to say "Marmee!" She would follow me around calling, "Pi-a! Pi-a! Pi-a". Whenever I was not around, I heard of how she searched for me behind drapes and closed doors calling. That little girl was indeed my pride and joy.

At last the results came out. I had done very well as expected, but Gamal had done spectacularly well. "In fact," said Uncle Zach, "You are in the top 3 percent of the whole country. If you wanted, you could have gone to University of Cairo!"

"Could I? Could I?" asked Gamal excitedly.

But Uncle Zach still advised caution. My grandfather seconded it. "My bones tell me that there are bad things brewing in Cairo. Exercise caution. Even if you want to go to live at Cairo, give it some time. There will be time for that yet. Let us see first what that snake has brewing for this country."

Obeying one's elders was too inbred in us. With more than one person telling him, Gamal did not think of doing otherwise despite his own dreams and desires. He agreed to go to Tanta but I overheard him telling one of his friends, "Tanta is closer to Cairo than it is to Hosh Issa and Damanhur. Who is to closely monitor what I do at school?"

The spring of that year also, I had the experience which changed my whole outlook to life. Different churches organized various youth programs at about this time of the year. My parents always encouraged us to go. This particular year, the theme for one youth conference was "Know Ye Your God." The program was organized by the evangelical church that we attended but some Coptic seminary students had also been invited as speakers. Somehow in our hearts, we had come to think of members of the Coptic Church as not being as serious Christians as we the evangelicals, but we went anyway.

We listened as various speakers talked on different aspects of the theme from the Old Testament, the New Testament, the writings of the church fathers, contemporary periods, and so on. The highlights of such programs were usually the music, games, and interactions among the participants. It went on for a whole week from one Sunday to the following Saturday, ending with a thanksgiving service the next Sunday.

It was on the Tuesday I had the encounter that changed my life. I had honestly come for that program with every intention of enjoying myself with the entertaining music and games as

I had in previous years. With each new topic however, I was asking myself over and over, "Do I really know my God?"

I knew a lot about God, having been raised by my parents in the way they had. I knew what my parents, my grandparents, and numerous relatives believed about God. I certainly believed there was God, and I believed in Him but did I know Him as *my* God? My mind must have been primed by such questions, or as it was explained to me in the days that followed, "The Holy Spirit must have been convicting" me.

In any case, on that Tuesday, this young Coptic seminary student came up to speak on his topic. He did not use notes or even quote a lot of Bible passages. He simply shared with us the testimony of his own life. Out of a life of piety, one day his eyes were opened to the fact that he did not know God. He ended with, "I was the worst sinner there ever was, even though nobody else would believe it. I was worse than the demons. At least knowing God made the demons tremble. I was not worthy in any way but I pleaded for forgiveness and God heard me. I opened my heart and pleaded with God to please make our relationship very personal. My life has never been the same ever since. I daily live in the assurance of what God has done for me."

It was not the most dramatic of testimonies. I had heard more moving ones but suddenly his was also the story of my life. I found myself weeping uncontrollably. I must have disturbed those around me or perhaps they too were equally touched by the testimony. When the call was made to the altar that day for those who wanted to know God and be known by Him on a deeper level, all of us on that row of seats, the row in front of us, the row behind us, and several others beside us got up and went forward to be prayed for.

The activities for that week went on. Unlike other years when I could not wait for the long breaks to begin socializing, or for the end of the day so I could go home, I enrolled in the short and intensive discipleship program. For the next few days, those of us who made decisions to follow God more closely on any of the days of that week-long program were taught the meaning of the decisions we had made. The counselors instructed us in changes to expect in our lives, and what God expected of us now that we had come to this level of relationship with Him. I was like insatiable soil, soaking up every drop of water that fell on it. Suddenly, the Bible had new meaning to me. Words I had read before became more alive. Stories I had heard or read before took on color and real meaning. I could not stop talking about my experience whether at the program or out of it. There was a small new testament Bible that Gideon International had come to distribute to us in school. I had never really had much use for it but now we became inseparable. It was small enough to fit into my pocket and every day I was making new discoveries in it as I read.

My parents smiled indulgently. My brothers did not pay much attention to me. Amira looked at me as adoringly as always. I told Salma and Hoda. Hoda blinked and looked away. Salma told me the young Copt must have been very cute and that I must have fallen in love. We were at that age when we fell in and out of love every day. The young Copt really was cute but I had hardly noticed this. To me, this was additional evidence that I had indeed fallen in love but not with the young Copt. I was in love with God!

At the conclusion of the program by that Sunday, a baptismal class was announced. I promptly enrolled. It was a further voyage of discovery. In fact, for the whole of the long vacation that followed, I enrolled in everything spiritual, not just in our own church, but also in the nearby Coptic Church. My taste in books changed. I no longer had time for adventure novels or even the romance novels which we were just discovering. I was reading the Bible and everything that pertained to spiritual questions. I had not even known our church had a library but I now found out. From there I discovered all manner of absorbing materials, from the apologetics of the church fathers to the writings of modern American Evangelists. They were all very enlightening even when I had differences of opinion with the author, or totally disagreed with them. I was on a voyage of spiritual discovery.

One day, my mother remarked that she felt these things were beyond my age. "You should go out and do what normal girls of your age do. You can be young only once. Go out and play. Enjoy the parks and the sunlight before school resumes again."

Surprisingly, it was my father who came to my defense at this time. "Let her do what she feels compelled to do right now" he said. "It might be a passing phase or God might be preparing her for something we don't yet know about. She is obviously enjoying herself so let her be."

How prophetic those words turned out to be! However, we never know what we are being prepared for until we start living it out.

September rolled by. The new school year began. All of my friends and I had done well in our *Adaadiya Amma*. This meant we were qualified to go to secondary school and prepare for *Thanaweya Amma* over the next three years. Over the long vacation we had grown as tall as, or even taller than our mothers. We had filled out in places where we were flat before and had become more conscious of ourselves. Alliances had again re-formed and changed. We still all walked to school together but Hoda now chatted with some Moslem girls from the block next to ours. My cousin, Miriam, now joined our group. Her elder sister, Regia, was two years older than us. In the course of their parents' difficulties, she had lost one year of schooling, and did not do so well in *Adaadiya Amma* the following year. Offered the choice of repeating the class and the exam, or going to technical school, she had chosen the latter to the disgust of my father but everyone felt it was her choice to make. The technical school and the mainstream school were in the same compound except that a large playground separated them. Sometimes a student from the mainstream found it difficult to cope with the pace set by the teachers and was sent across the field to join the technical stream. More often, it was the students from across the field that excelled, by dint of determination and extra coaching, and came to join the mainstream. Regia was neither willing, nor apparently able, to be in this latter group. She did whatever she was told to do very unwillingly and just well enough to avoid trouble. She sulked most of the time and did not join in our games or conversations. She always chose to walk by herself even though her classmates were often part of our groups.

Walking to school together was not just for the sake of the companionship that it offered. It was also for security reasons. One of the crimes which were on the rise in Egypt then was kidnapping, especially of young girls. The story we heard was usually of a girl on her way to school, work, an errand, or some such normal activity, and was never seen again. Everybody reasoned that when people moved in groups, they were less likely to be kidnapped. The larger the group, we were told, the less the chances of this happening. We all knew this. Regia knew this but she chose to walk alone. Even though she walked alone, she was never really far from the main group. Sometimes we stalled, waiting for her to catch up but she had a way of

Dust and Ashes

hanging back if she noticed this. After some time we would just give up and keep going. It was true these kidnappings happened but it had not happened to anyone that we knew yet. In any case, life was not worth living if one was constantly worrying. We were cautious but we were young! We were carefree! We were invincible!

The general unrest in the country filtered into our schools. The dichotomy between Christians and Moslems increased. We understood that in mosques they always spent considerable time and effort being instructed on the flaws in Christianity. They were told how it was a mortal offence to associate with or, heaven forbid, convert to Christianity. A Moslem man might marry a Christian girl but it was anathema for a Moslem girl to marry a Christian man unless he was willing to first of all convert to Islam and consent to raising his children as Moslems. I never heard such sermons against Islam in the churches I went to. I am not saying they were not preached, but that year I was so embroiled with discovering why God made me who I was and had chosen to give me His special attention by my experience that holiday. Someone had told me that we were "Saved to serve". I was fully occupied with the questions of how and where to serve God. What I am saying in essence is that it is quite possible that such anti-Islamic messages were being preached from Christian pulpits, but that fortunately for me, I missed them entirely.

The religious dichotomy and unrest were not helped by President Sadat himself. That year, he went to war against Israel to try to regain the Sinai Peninsula. All the remaining Jews we knew around Damanhur and Alexandria fled the country due to severe persecution. The Moslem Fundamentalists were delighted with Sadat's actions. Christians were expected to take sides but right from time the relationship of Israel and Egypt had always vacillated from that of bosom brothers to that of sworn enemies. Even so, the then Coptic Pope, Shenouda III, came out openly to say that Sadat was not wrong in going to war against Israel, only his timing was. My grandfather said, "Whatever happened to 'We are Egyptians first'? That snake is on a course to disintegrate this country! There are so many more important things to do than to go to war at this time just to seek popularity. He's currying favor with the Moslems and trying to see what the rest of us will say and do. He should try to redo and continue what Nasser started. We need jobs, we need schools, and homes. What we do not need is war! Nasser realized war with Israel is not what we need now!"

Later that year, Sadat officially declared Islam the State religion of Egypt, and *Sharia* the laws to live by. The Islamic fundamentalists hailed him as a hero but he did not garner as much support as he had hoped from the rest of the country including the conservative Moslems. This faction was certainly more in number. Demonstrations were held but they were very easily squelched by government troops. President Sadat just rounded up prominent people and put them in jail. The country languished but life went on as normally as it could.

THE TURNAROUND

Once, when I was about thirteen years old, our teacher gave us an assignment to write an essay titled "A Day I will Never Forget."

We were given two weeks for this monumental essay and were allowed to discuss it among ourselves and with our families. My friends had so many suggestions. Should we write about the festivities we had attended, games we had won, or other things we had done together? My family had so many other suggestions. My grandfather suggested I write about the day Nasser declared war on Israel or the day of the almost-successful assassination attempt on his life. Although I was big enough when these things happened, I was still very much a child and such events had more meaning to the adults than it did to me. The assignment was before Nasser died, apparently healthy and full of life one day, and announced dead to the entire nation by the next day. That did have a profound effect on all of us. I remembered being afraid that it could happen

Al Kalima

to my father, grandfather, or any of my beloved uncles. I had nightmares about it for some weeks.

The usefulness of the exercise was that it got all the students and members of our families thinking and talking. Long after we had completed and handed in the assignment, our families kept discussing what was significant and insignificant in their own lives. In the end, I think I wrote about how my mother went into labor one evening, was driven to the hospital, and came home two days later with a baby girl! To me, it was probably the most momentous event in my life up till then. I had really longed for a baby sister without fully being aware of how much.

Despite the significance of Amira's birth in my life, the day we were kidnapped overshadowed it. It indefinitely defined the whole of my life, even up to that point. That day was Monday, December 10, 1972. The day I will never forget.

The day started like any other day. Usually in the complex where we lived, the first sounds of morning would be mothers moving about very softly, taking time perhaps to be alone first and then to organize the rest of the day for their families. About an hour later would come the Moslem call to prayer and then the noise increased as men and boys congregated at the small mosque at the corner of the street to pray. Afterwards, the noise rose to almost a crescendo as lunches were packed, people got dressed and rushed about to get out to work or school. Mondays were always a bit noisier, a bit more stressful, and a bit more demanding following on weekends. Fridays on the other hand were more of the opposite, in anticipation of the weekend but the routine never varied except for holidays.

This particular Monday was not any different; neither did my family do anything differently. Even with Gamal gone to University at Tanta, our family size had become increased with the coming of Regia and Miriam. Despite the passage of decades, it is the little details which still stand out in my mind. My mother was to go to work later that evening but she had woken up first as usual but was moving rather slowly. She begged us all to be quiet because she had a headache. She had been getting those headaches quite frequently and they usually put her in a very bad mood which only made her yell at us more irritably at every slight provocation. We all tried to tiptoe around her, except for Yohana.

Yohana was looking for his blue socks and he went about it as noisily as possible. He was flinging clothes about and demanding loudly if anyone had seen them or was hiding them. My father said Yohana had been very lonely, feeling lost and displaced since Gamal left. He told us the boy was just expressing himself in crankiness in a houseful of girls only. Besides, those blue socks were a gift from Gamal. Used to missing second socks, my mother had bought him lots of white socks so that even if he wore mismatched ones, the difference would not be too obvious. Yohana preferred those blue socks, perhaps for the novelty of it amidst all the other white ones. At last when he had finally been persuaded to use an alternative for the day, he found the blue socks! They had been inside his canvas shoes all along. He had left them the previous day so he would not have to look for them!

In the midst of all the drama and noise, my father sat calmly at his customary place at the head of the dining table leafing through the day's newspapers. He usually went out to get newspapers from a vendor down the street immediately after our morning devotions. He did not sit there like a Buddha but more like a solidly built ship moved only very slightly by the buffeting of the winds and the waves. Once in a while he would chastise or tease someone, contribute to an ongoing discussion, or smile secretly at what he perceived as a joke. He would sometimes lower the newspaper and glower at us over the rim if there was a squabble, or if he felt the noise was getting too much. That single look usually would discipline us effectively. Other than that, we accepted his presence as a normal fixture for getting ready for school. In fact, the only morning he was not there, it was an ominous sign. It turned out he had to rush off to the bedside of a dying uncle. My father loved what it meant to have a family, and I believe he enjoyed every moment of those early morning chaos. The other fathers in our circle, I knew, preferred to read their newspapers at the office, in the relative comfort of their bedrooms, or elsewhere in the house but not my father. That fateful Monday morning it was not different in any way either.

At last when we were about to burst out of the door and go to school, Amira came toddling out of the bedroom she still shared with my parents. She was to have moved into my room but with the coming of Regia and Miriam, my father said she had to wait until one of us went off to University. Amira was still toasty warm and flushed from sleep. Every face in the kitchen softened, even Regia's usually sullen one. Amira beamed at all of us happily but it was to me that she came. She hugged me with her chubby arms chanting "Pi-a! Pi-a! Pi-a!"

I gathered her up in my arms for what I did not know was for the last time. To this day, four decades later, when I close my eyes, I still get whiffs of her. I can still feel her chubby arms round my neck. Mike teases me about choosing *Johnson* Baby products as my cosmetics. They still remind me of Amira and that is the most pleasant memory I cherish of that fateful morning.

The other thing I remember about that morning was the conversation we were having as we walked to school. After my spiritual encounter, I had started attending a Youth Bible Study at our church on Saturday evenings. It was also a preparatory class for baptism. That last Saturday, we had continued on the Theme "In God's Service". The leader that Saturday had spoken on "How far are you willing to go for Christ?" I was sharing with Salma and Miriam about how we should be willing to die for Christ. We were dissecting how Peter had declared his willingness to do that very thing one day, and less than twenty-four hours or so later was denying every knowledge and association with Christ, not just vehemently but even with oaths! With typical youthful abandon, we were talking of the "Maybes."

"Maybe he was caught up in the heat of the moment…"

"Maybe he wanted to divert attention…"

"Maybe he meant something else, but just had a slip of the tongue!"

"Maybe he wanted to do a covert operation…"

"Maybe…"

We were laughing as we made more and more absurd suggestions. Our enjoyment was infectious. People coming from other complexes joined in. Hoda and the other Moslem girls walked in another group, a little removed from us but they seemed to also be listening even though they did not join in. They were probably mindful of the school's prohibition on making fun of other people's religions. It was a very normal day in every way when suddenly, everything was shattered.

A truck screeched to a halt across the path in front of us, blocking our way. Four men jumped out of it, wielding long guns. We screamed and made to run in different directions but they had chosen their position well. There were no open fields to run into, no doors faced the street where we were. As we turned backwards the way we had come, we saw that there was another truck also blocking that way with another set of men and their guns. We kept screaming in panic until one of the men shot his gun upward and ordered us to be silent "or else…"

The silence was immediate. We stared at them with very wide, frightened eyes. "Into the trucks" ordered the man who had fired.

We tried to resist, but what could gently-raised school girls do against strong, muscled, and armed men? They shoved and dragged us into the two trucks and made us sit on the floor of their beds. They threw our school bags and lunches in after us for those of us who were not clutching tightly to theirs in terror, as if they provided any useful shield. It was over in only a few minutes. No other person had passed by. No other vehicle had rounded the corner. No curious windows had opened to find out the cause of all the screaming and the loud gunshot. I suspect even the curious would hide more deeply at the report of the gun. That was what I would have done if it were me. We were less than a hundred yards away from the school gate. Although students and pupils would be coming from other directions, we were not yet close enough for any of them to see us. As the trucks sped off, I saw Regia coming round the corner from the corner of my eye. I opened my mouth to scream a warning but one of the men hit me with the butt of his rifle. I wondered if Regia had seen what happened. Her tardiness and unsocial behavior had proven ironically protective on this occasion contrary to what we had been taught, believed, and practiced up till then. Could she get help for us?

I was not the only person who got hit with the butt of a gun. Anyone who tried to speak, or that squirmed significantly was hit by the butt. It was not just a gentle tap either. Those men hit to hurt. They showed us they meant business. The trucks drove very fast. In our confusion, we did not think of taking note of

Dust and Ashes

the directions we were going. I just noticed, very gratefully, that Salma and Miriam were in the same truck as me. So were Hoda, Jehan, and a few other Moslem girls. Our kidnapping was very unusual. It was neither late evening nor early morning; it was in broad daylight. We were not moving alone, we were moving in a large group. Not only Christians but also Moslem girls were kidnapped, and almost at the school gate! It was not in the open field. Granted, it was in an alley but it was not an unusually lonely or long alley. This was either a very well-planned operation or it was just a quirk of fate.

The thoughts that kept running through my mind were: "This is a nightmare from which I shall soon wake up", and "Did Regia see us? O Lord let it be that Regia saw us."

We could not talk to one another so we were all occupied with our own thoughts. I prayed, how I prayed very fervently. Since my encounter with God, He had been answering all my prayers pronto! It was as if I had made His list of favorite mortals. I had every confidence He was going to answer this one too and we would be rescued by the end of that day.

We must have gone on for about an hour or two when we stopped at a place that was probably outside the city limits. The population density was not much, as evidenced by the number of trees and buildings we could see from the bed of the open truck. Our captors did not talk to us. They dispelled every thought that we had of this being the end of our journey. With practiced efficiency, they covered the open truck with tarpaulin so that we would not be visible from the sky or to any casual observer on the road. The Egyptian heat was just beginning to rise with the late morning sunlight and we were stifled and sweltering. There were holes in the tarpaulin but they were so inadequate in the small enclosure of the truck bed, holding nine girls. I had counted by now, having nothing better to do.

Al Kalima

The only good thing was that after the tarpaulin was put up, the men with the rifles did not stay with us anymore but we were still too terrified to talk with one another. When it had been open, at least we could see one another's faces and tears, and tried to talk with our eyes. Afterwards, we became dimly outlined shadows to one another. We did not know how close our captors were, what we might or might not do. We bore the heat as much as we could. Maybe we slept. Maybe we continued to fantasize in hope. In all likelihood we probably just passed out from the heat. I do not know how long, how fast, nor in which direction we went. The truck stopped about two times that I was aware of. At those times I heard indistinct conversations but the tarpaulin was not removed. We sweltered in the heat. My eyes burnt and felt sore. My tongue felt very heavy. There was a lump in my throat which I could not swallow. I wondered how the others felt.

When at last the tarpaulin was removed, it was late in the evening. The sun had almost set. By this time we would have long been home from school. Our most immediate response was sighs of relief at the feel of the cool evening breeze. We had heard stories, the morale of which had been that if one was kidnapped, one must avoid the food and drink offered by the kidnappers because these were usually drugged. We had listened to our parents and we still found ourselves in the predicament we were in. If our parents were still there, we would still have been guided by their instructions out of a lifetime habit of doing so. But our parents were not there and our primal instincts for survival were far louder than any embedded voices of conscience. When we managed to stagger or fall out of the trucks, the very first thing we saw was a metal bucket and a sawn-off metal drum filled with water beside a village-style well. There were about a dozen chipped metal cups beside the bucket. A slight woman robed in black was standing beside the well. She asked if we would like some water. We did not need a second invitation. No one remembered all the advice we had been given. We were so faint with thirst and dehydration that we fell to drinking immediately. It was only after my third cup that I thought of how sanitary the water, the bucket, the drum, and the chipped metal cups could be but I kept drinking anyway. It was probably after my sixth cup that I remembered the warning about drugged food and drinks and then I stopped drinking. That first drink of water was so cool and so welcome to my parched throat.

The well was at the center of a hamlet, surrounded by native limestone and wattle buildings with river reed on the roofs to keep it cool during the day. There were two accesses by dirt roads to where we were then standing. From how the trucks were positioned, we had come through one of the accesses and the trucks would be exiting through the other. There was no glimpse of any major road, and no sound of passing traffic. In fact, for a city dweller like me, the place was eerily quiet.

It was dusk when we were disgorged from the trucks. When we paused in our drinking, we were immediately herded into one of the houses whose main door opened unto the village square. The woman who had offered us water seemed well-acquainted with this procedure of dealing with kidnapped school girls. Through the door was the main visitor's area, and then through that, another door opened into a courtyard, surrounded by several doors. This was still not our destination. She herded us to another door at the end of the compound and we came upon yet another courtyard, completely surrounded by a high wall. On either side of this courtyard were two low-roofed buildings. Each building had two doors and a row of small windows. "You will sleep here" she said. "You can choose any place you like."

Her voice was not unkindly. Her eyes were sad and compassionate, and at the same time looked resigned and tired. However, she was the enemy that we could see. We viewed her with universal hatred. With one accord, we all turned into the building on the right. It was like a long empty hall, devoid of any furnishing except some mats on the floor. We stood in the middle of the room, huddled together, and wept silently. We forgot all our alliances and differences. Right then, we were just a group of frightened and confused girls together, wrenched from their homes and their normal lives, and put into the kind of predicament one only heard of in stories but thought could never happen in real life.

Nobody came to chide or to comfort us. O for the normalcy of a scolding mother, a punishing teacher, or even a yelling camp counselor! Anything that was familiar! We had left our school bags and lunches in the truck when we tumbled out so we did not have even the familiar comfort of those burdens. We only had one another so we clung together and wept, asking over and over, "What are we going to do? What is going to happen to us?"

We knew our parents must be looking for us by then but what was to guide them in the right directions? Did Regia see us nabbed? Could she describe the trucks? A quick count showed there were nineteen of us altogether, some Christians and some Moslems. There were two sets of sisters, Ester and her eight-year old sister, Sara; and Khadija and her seven-year old sister, Rawya. With my cousin, Miriam, and me from the same household this meant that sixteen households were affected, of which three households had lost two girls each. I knew everyone by face if not by name. Kidnappings had become rife with the

Sadat regime but I had never heard of almost twenty people kidnapped at the same time. Surely, the government would react with a massive manhunt. Surely, all our parents would do something and we would soon be rescued…

We hoped. We theorized. We wept and consoled one another until we slept off from sorrow and exhaustion. Our uneaten lunches were in our bags which we never saw again. Although nobody offered us food, hunger was not our major concern. We did not go to the laid-out mats. We slept where we were huddled instead. Throughout the night nobody came to disturb us. That was our first night in captivity; Monday, December 10, 1972.

A NEW BEGINNING

I woke up in a panic at the customary time I normally would on a school day. My first thought was "O Lord, I'm going to be late. What did I forget to do? Was there a due homework?"

My next thought was "Where am I? Why is my left arm so numb?"

And then reality came flooding in. We were kidnapped and our parents had no idea of where we were. I had prayed that we would be rescued before the end of the day but God had not answered that prayer with a "Yes". Nothing spectacular had happened and we were still where we were. It was not an unpleasant nightmare either. I wanted to feel bitter and disappointed at God but I was more frightened than angry. Everywhere was unnaturally quiet. I realized I had been holding my breath. All I could hear was the thumping of my heart, and other heartbeats for that matter. In the distance we heard a voice calling faithful Moslems to Morning Prayer. This meant we were very far from any township. Even big villages like Hosh Issa had at least a megaphone to wake the faithful to the hour of prayer. I shivered. Our parents would

Dust and Ashes

have no way of knowing where we were, and that we were so far from home.

That was when I realized that my co-captives must all have woken up to this new reality. This was the usual time for us to wake up to start getting ready for school. Apparently we were all holding our breaths collectively and wondering. Suddenly, we let out a collective sigh and the whisperings began. "Where are we?" "What are they going to do with us?" "What should we do?" "Do you think the police are looking for us by now?" "Do you know of anyone who got missing and was eventually found?"

Suddenly, out of the whisperings came a very loud wail. Sara was telling her big sister, "Ester, I want to go home. I want to see Marmee! I want to go home!"

Almost at the same time Rawya wailed, "My tummy hurts Khadija. I want to go home."

Reasonably efficient and caring big sisters that Ester and Khadija were under normal circumstances, this was too much for them. They started sobbing as they tried to console their little sisters. We all began to sob and cry noisily. One had to let off steam somehow. That was when there was stirring at the end of the room. The slight woman who had tended us the day before emerged from the gloom. "Stop! Stop this, all of you" she said in a voice which was strong and authoritative.

We obeyed her at once. The sobs were immediately cut off. Full terror returned. Not even a whimper was to be heard. "Spare your tears for what is yet to come. Conserve your strengths. You haven't even met Ummi. Does anyone feel like going to urinate?" We stared at her mutely in the half gloom of the dawning day. She waited a bit for any answer which was not forthcoming. She looked briefly into each of our terrified faces, and then continued. "Anyway, whether you want to or not, you better come and see where such things are done. You might not get another chance to be shown to it."

With that she exited through the only door into the walled compound we had passed the previous evening. We meekly followed her. We went further into the complex. In a corner she showed us the facilities. It was a low thatched building with two holes in the ground, pit latrines. Even at Hosh Issa, the toilet and bathroom facilities were no longer so basic. "Return to the dormitory when you are done" she said. "The little ones are probably very hungry. You better let them eat something before Ummi comes."

That was the second time she had mentioned "Ummi" as if it was someone or something to be feared. *Ummi* meant "Mother". Yes, there could be terrible connotations associated with that word especially when one needed to be disciplined but it generally meant love, comfort, and security. Why was this Ummi to be feared rather than loved and respected? But we did not pay her much attention then. There was time enough and we were soon to find out.

The slight woman left us then and went away. We discovered that we really did need to pee. It was the most natural thing one did immediately after waking up and we had not gone since the previous morning, despite the large quantities of water we had consumed the previous evening. We took turns doing this, two at a time, while those waiting squirmed and jogged at a spot. The next natural thing back home would have been to wash our mouths but we saw nothing for this purpose. In the adventure books I had read, now that we were left together and unguarded was a good opportunity to explore our surroundings and look for an escape route. In real life however, none of us thought of exploring at all. We were too scared to make any moves at all. We were even too scared to get out of sight of one another. We waited

Dust and Ashes

for the last person to finish her business and then we trooped back to the dormitory like automated robots and sat huddled in the middle of the room wondering what would happen next.

We did not have long to wait. The slight woman returned with a large tray of *koshari*. *Koshari* is a staple Egyptian meal, made up of rice, lentils, corn meal, and whatever else the cook's imagination might drum up to add. That imagination, besides the affluence of the people going to eat the meal or the influence of the cook would determine what meat, vegetables, other spices, or whatever else might be added. The *koshari* we got that first morning looked cold but whatever spices were in it wafted to our nostrils. It reminded us that we had not eaten anything for about twenty-four hours. We looked at one another warningly. When she had put the tray on one of the mats on the floor and gone out again, we put the warning into verbal terms. "Remember, don't eat anything they offer you. It may contain poisons or sedatives."

"I am hungry Khadija" Rawya wailed. "My tummy is hurting."

That was a plausible explanation for the tummy ache. By then we were all beginning to feel it too but who was to say it was not also due to fear? Nobody went near the food. We must have stared at it and at one another for close to an hour when the door suddenly burst open and one belligerent, mean-looking, fat woman burst through it. Nobody needed to tell us that this was our inaugural meeting with the famed Ummi.

Her first words to us were, "And who says you are here to waste perfectly good food? Do you know how difficult it is to get food? You spoiled brats! This is not your rich homes where food is easy to get and to waste. Finish this food right now otherwise I will whip you until your bottoms are too sore to sit on for a whole year."

Al Kalima

Perhaps it was her appearance, her voice, or the fact that she had a long whip to back up her threats, but we immediately went to the food and began eating as fast as we could. We paid no mind to the taste, the warmth, or coldness of the meal. We swallowed the *koshari* down as one would swallow pills. In almost no time at all, the tray was empty. This was not really saying anything because the entire meal was just enough to give us a few mouthfuls each. We ate with our fingers. No form of cutlery had been provided. We could feel Ummi standing over us. She watched our every mouthful. We were very careful not to let even a crumb fall to the ground. Satisfied that we were done, she yelled "Asibi, get them water to wash their hands. They can go to drink at the well later on."

The slight woman who had tended us came in with a bowl of water. We now knew her name to be Asibi. We all washed our hands one after the other. Of course, the last people to wash their hands did so with very grimy water but no one dared complain.

When we were done, Ummi pointed to a corner of the dormitory and ordered "Now, sit over there and look at me." We did so. We stared at her with wide frightened eyes. "We owe you no explanations as to why you are here. While you are in this compound or any other compound where I am in charge, you must do as I tell you. The first thing you must do is forget your parents. You will never, ever see them again. I run a very efficient camp and I will tolerate no disobedience. This whip here is my friend." She lifted the whip and cracked it loudly in the air. "It is made of treated cowhide and I know how to use it very well. Anytime you fail to do what I say, I will let you have a taste of it on your bottoms. I don't believe in beating someone who deserves a beating with only one stroke or two. If you ever need to be punished, you shall be punished very thoroughly.

Dust and Ashes

Do you understand?" she yelled at us. We only stared dumbly back at her. She roared, "Do you understand me?" Petrified, we bobbed our heads in assent but she was not satisfied. She roared louder, "Is everything that I have said clear to you? When I talk to you, I want to be answered in words. Don't just nod and gesticulate like dumb camels. Did you understand what I just said?"

"Yes, Ma" we chorused, loud and clear.

"Very good" She continued. "The first thing we shall do is to separate those who are already Moslems from those of you who shall soon become Moslems. "All Moslems please move over to this side" she gestured towards her right with the whip.

There was a shuffling of bodies. We soon discovered there were seven Moslems and twelve Christians. "Good," Ummi said. "Now, those of you who are *Kafir* will start your education today. The rest of you, follow me." The seven Moslem girls got up and followed her out. It was a week before we saw them again.

As soon as Ummi left, Asibi came in again. "That was Ummi" she said. "Just do as she says and everything will be easier for you. If you disobey her, you will get her whip. She means it."

We now saw Asibi in a new light. She was the lesser Enemy. "Come" she said. "You better drink some water before the training begins."

I expected her to take us to the outer well where we had been when we arrived the previous day. That way, I hoped, maybe we could get a glimpse of the outer world and begin to plot a route of escape. She took us instead to yet another section of the compound and had us drink water from a similar well. All the wells were guarded by a low wall of stones which narrowed at the top, usually put there so that animals would not fall inadvertently into them. A metal bucket on a nylon rope stood nearby for drawing up water. There were also several metal cups close by for individual drinks. Ummi had not been joking when she called this a camp. In this part of the compound, there was a rudimentary outdoor kitchen such as my great grandmother had at Hosh Issa. There were huge cauldrons, sacks of food, basins, and utensils which showed that the meals prepared there were for large numbers of people. We saw about three women tending to the cooking. Asibi chatted easily with them. One of them asked, "Are these the new ones?"

Asibi said yes, and then added "These ones are for training."

When we had drunk about two cups of water each, Asibi led us to a nearby hut with dwarf walls and open sides. There were mats on the floor facing a blackboard at one end of it. The other end was obviously used as the kitchen storage area because there were sacks of meal, raw vegetables, tins of oil, and so on. We were hardly seated when Ummi arrived with her long whip.

"You are all unbelievers" she thundered at us. "You are not fit for this world but you are lucky to have been brought here. The prophet has taught that girls taken in war can be converted to Islam and redeemed by marrying good Moslem men. You must learn that there is no other God but Allah, and Mohammed is his prophet. That is your first lesson. Now repeat it after me."

We all stared at her, dumbfounded. "Say it after me" she thundered. "There is no other God but Allah, and Mohammed is his prophet." When we still continued to gaze at her mutely she snapped the whip in the air startling us with the whistle and cackle of it. Meekly we all mumbled something incomprehensible.

"Insolent fools!" she roared. "I will show you how to mumble!" She ordered us to all lie down in a row on the mats and started whipping us at our backs, including little Sara. It was obvious that she gained a lot of enjoyment from doing this. Her hand went up and down powerfully and rhythmically until she was out of breath. We all lay there on the floor wriggling and weeping. All of us had more or less been coddled all our lives. We had all been whipped in punishment at some time in our lives but not with this kind of savagery. I looked over at Sara. She was whimpering like the rest of us but Ester had thrown herself across her little sister and taken the brunt of the punishment for both of them.

Evidently tired but satisfied with the morning's job, Ummi left us. We must have lain there for quite some time, tired, in pain but above all confused as to what was expected of us next. Was the ordeal over or was this just a break? After some time Asibi came to the door. She looked sadder than ever. "Come," she said. "She will not return again today. If you want to make it shorter and easier for yourselves, just do whatever she says."

We dragged ourselves up from the floor. Moving stiffly with pain, we followed her back to our dormitory. This was our initiation into the life of slavery.

Again we stayed huddled together in the middle of the room to give one another whatever comfort we could. We did not even have enough energy to discuss what we had just been through. We wept ourselves to sleep wondering where God could be. When I thought of what we had been through, it was obvious to me that our kidnapping and so-called training was a religious ordeal. Why did they separate us from the Moslem girls? Why was it so important that we recite the Moslem catechism? Obviously this was what they meant by our "Training". What would a child of God do in this kind of situation? I had prayed. There had to be something more than, or other than, praying.

TRAINING

And so the pattern of our days was set. We woke up before dawn, before the first calls to Morning Prayer. As Asibi, who shared the dormitory with us, left for her daily chores, we were free to go to use the bathroom. Asibi then came back with our daily dose of *koshari* which we were obliged to eat, no matter how reluctantly. We then went to do what passed for washing our hands and mouths and thereafter it would be time for the training.

Apart from this all-important sentence, there was nothing else that was required of us. After the first day, before the cane descended, practically everyone in our group of twelve girls was belting out that they believed there was no other God but Allah and that Mohammed was his prophet. Practically everyone that is, except for a few people and Sara. Sara was crying too hard to be able to say anything. By accident or by choice Ummi overlooked this for the next two days but by the third day she decided to address this inconsistency.

Dust and Ashes

Incidentally, the first sign of rebellion was from my usually quiet, submissive, and easily dominated cousin.

On the fourth day of our training, as Ummi was about to raise her whip, Ester threw herself across her little sister sobbing, "She will say it! She will say it!"

Almost at the same time, Miriam threw herself across Ester screaming, "It's not true! That is not true."

This drew the attention away from Sara all right. Ummi now faced Miriam with the full force of her anger. "What did you say?"

"There is only one God," Miriam said, "and Jesus Christ is His son whom He sent to save the world."

Infuriated, Ummi raised her whip and beat Miriam over and over again. "Unsay that" she screamed. "Unsay that immediately."

As her arm rose and fell, so did her voice in a kind of an unnatural scream. I had wondered what to do for three days. What kind of a Christian was I who would deny my faith at the least sign of torment? I thought of all those secret believers in the Bible. I had recently come across the story of Obadiah in the Bible who outwardly served King Ahab during the intense persecutions of the prophets of God by the king and his wicked wife, Jezebel. Using his position as a statesman, he had hidden and fed some true prophets, to his own peril. There was also the story of Naaman the Syrian leper who after his healing and conversion by Prophet Elisha sought to show his allegiance to the only true God by standing on imported Israeli soil while bowing down to the Syrian idol, Rimmon, with his king. Were they not honored by God even though they were outwardly doing lip service to other gods while believing in the one true God in their hearts?

On the other hand were people who had stood up for their faith, ready to die for it like Daniel and his three friends, or Queen Esther. I also thought of those martyrs of whom I had recently been reading in *Foxe's Book of Martyrs*. Even in our own contemporary times, there were numerous stories of secret believers, not just in the Arab world but in the then-oppressive communist countries. We were hearing about them and praying for them through the ministry of Richard Wurmbrand. These were Christians who staunchly refused to deny their faith and were tortured, imprisoned, and even killed. Did God honor these ones differently? What would it matter to just confess this silly phrase even though I had a totally different belief in my heart? Should I defy Ummi's indoctrination, be tortured, and killed? Had I not been praying for God to be honored in my life?

These were my thoughts. They had occupied most of my waking hours both day and night. I had not discussed them with anyone, certainly not with Miriam. However, we were among the few who refused to chorus the liturgy to Ummi. Seeing how Miriam was bravely taking the brunt now, I found courage to launch myself across her back screaming, "Kill me too! Kill me too!"

This seemed to give courage to the remaining girls. We all piled on top of one another screaming. Our voices became louder than Ummi's. Ummi became briefly disconcerted. Apparently she had not yet experienced this type of resistance. Her upraised arm seemed to freeze in the air. After what seemed an interminable minute, she brought it down and savagely bit out, "All right, I will kill you! I swear that I will! I will kill all of you!"

As her arm was about to descend again, a voice full of authority said, "What is going on here?"

Dust and Ashes

Through tears I saw another woman outside the dwarf wall studying the scene. The voice belonged to her. She was taller, certainly slimmer, and also looked older than Ummi. "Were you not told to be sure not to mark the girls? And you are planning to kill them?" She asked.

Visibly shaken, Ummi now said in a whiny, deferring voice, totally unlike what we had known of her so far, "They refuse to recant and convert. I was trying to make them do so."

"Of what persuasion are they? Remember that the people of the Book are acceptable too. Are they Christians, Jews, mere idolaters, or atheists?"

"I don't know Mother" replied Ummi. She used a term which did not necessarily mean that the other woman was her mother but someone she respected and deferred to.

"Then I suggest you find that out before you kill them. Convert them only if they are neither Christians nor Jews" she said and left, just like that. It was a small victory. We might not have achieved much but we had set the precedence for those who were to come after us. That day, we learned, and our tormentor learned, that no Christian girl needed to convert to Islam if they did not want to. What then did they want of us?

Training was over for that day. We went back to the dormitory to nurse one another the best we could until the next day. Asibi usually brought a small plate of food for Sara in the evenings. Apparently, once daily feeding with *koshari* was our allowance. By the fifth day, in lieu of Ummi's training, we were put to work at the kitchen. We were to clean, sweep, wash, and so on. We were not directly involved in cutting up the ingredients or preparing the actual meals. From the quantity of food cooked, there must have been at least a hundred people being fed. From the conversation around, this was also not the only kitchen. Ummi made a brief appearance that day. She looked at all of us with so much distaste and asked, "Who among you is a Christian?"

We all raised our hands. She grunted in disgust, glared at us, and with another "Humph" she left.

When we went back to the dormitory afterwards, we were more animated than the previous days. Perhaps our victory of the day before, the little exercise we got that day, and our having been allowed outside, engaged in some meaningful activity did us some good. We discussed what our captors had in store for us. We wondered at the steps our parents were taking to find us. Would they ever succeed? We speculated on what must be happening to our Moslem co-captives. "Maybe they will return them to their homes. Do you think they will be kind enough to tell our parents how to find us?"

Opinions were varied. Some people thought they would work hand in hand with our captors. "Don't you know that betraying those who are not fellow Moslems is a shortcut to them for getting to heaven?"

Some people felt some of the Moslem girls were too kindhearted for that. "They will certainly tell our parents what happened, but will they be able to find their way back to this place?"

We talked of what our captors would do with us. "Maybe they're holding us for ransom. They're always looking for more money to buy guns and things."

"Maybe they'll sell us as slaves, you know, like in the olden days. We will go to work at American plantations."

"Maybe they just want to convert us to Islam and then send us back to our homes to convert other people."

There were even wilder speculations. Someone suggested it was probably related to the Bitrus incident at our school which had happened about nine months earlier. "That is why they're taking it out on us. Why did they separate the Moslem girls?"

We had no comfort to give to one another. The most heartrending was seeing little Sara suffer. Like Amira, she was the "Sunset Child" of her parents. At home she was totally spoilt and petted by everyone. She was so unused to this kind of life, more so than the rest of us. I tried to tell her stories to while away the time. The stories which came most easily into my head were the Bible stories I had been reading recently. We realized that everything had been taken away from us. Somehow, the only thing that remained was my pocket new testament because it had been in my pocket and not in my school bag. I told her stories by memory from the Old Testament, and I would also read aloud from the New Testament. Having nothing else to do, everyone listened to my stories too. Even Asibi listened when she was not running one mysterious errand or another. Having a rapt audience I also shared my newfound faith. By the fifth day, we began a ritual of holding hands to pray. We asked God for a miraculous deliverance from our captors.

On the evening of the sixth day, Ummi appeared and announced we were going to take the bath. Used to bathing twice a day at home; and not having had a bath since we were kidnapped, we were overjoyed. God had not answered our prayer for deliverance yet but surely this was one small light at the end of the tunnel. We were so excited that we did not remark she had said we were going to have "The Bath", not "A Bath". Asibi was less animated than we were at the news. She did not appear at all happy but we were too excited to take any note of her countenance. By now we were beginning to see her as less of an enemy and more of a friend, especially with her ministrations to Sara and wanting to be with us. She was even asking us questions and making little contributions during our storytelling. We attributed her reticence on this occasion to some sort of jealousy. Maybe we were about to be released and she did not wish to see us go.

The Bath turned out to be a ceremonial one. It held very early the next morning, supervised by Ummi. That was the seventh day of our captivity. We all gathered outside the low building housing the pit latrines. She ordered us to undress. By some instinct, I had hidden the pocket Bible under a mat in the dormitory. We bathed with soap and cold water in buckets over which Ummi had made some incantations. Thereafter each of us received a long black robe similar to what Asibi habitually wore. This type of robe characterized married Moslem women all over Egypt. After the bath, we were taken to the kitchen for our daily *koshari* rather than its being brought to us at the dormitory. We were then asked to wait there until someone came to get us.

We looked at one another with uncertainty. The day was not going as we had anticipated. We thought we would be given back our clothes and school bags and then taken to meet our parents. We squatted on the floor or sat on the mats apprehensively, telling stories to while away time. We were not as carefree as the day before.

Sometime long after noon, Ummi came and bid us follow her. She led us to another part of the compound, through a door in the wall to an adjoining compound, and then into another dormitory, not dissimilar to the one we were coming from. Here, to our great surprise, we saw the seven Moslem girls from whom we had been separated a week earlier. What a reunion it was!

MARRIED

I think up till that moment we had harbored hope, tinged with jealousy of course, that the Moslem girls had somehow been released. If they had, there would certainly be hope for the rest of us, whether they told about us or not. It came as a great shock and a crushing disappointment to realize they were still captive, albeit at another part of the camp. After this came the dismay that they were not in any better state than we were. True, they did not bear the wheals of Ummi's whip but their faces were a study in misery. Ummi barked at us, "No talking to one another!" as she went away.

We gazed at them dumbly when we would have liked to ask them so many questions, at least I did. They on their part sat huddled separately in their misery. They gaped at the floor mutely, refusing to meet our eyes. Even Khadija and Rawya sat near each other but they were not touching each other. Ummi did not stay away for long. She came back and said, "You, *Kafir*, follow me!"

Al Kalima

We followed her in a single file except for Sara who walked beside her sister, hanging unto her hand. We passed through several courtyards and buildings but never left the walled-in compound. As we got farther we began to hear voices, as of people in a celebration. The voices were deep male voices; men who were past their puberty. They were talking and laughing and the sound grew louder and clearer as we approached. Eventually we burst into yet another courtyard and came upon the owners of the voices. There must have been up to fifty of them. There were stones raised in the courtyard in the shape of a prayer enclosure. When they saw us, the men grew a bit quieter. Ummi went to one of the men who seemed to be in charge. I did not hear them clearly but Ummi mentioned something like "...twelve of them now" so I knew they were talking about us.

The man raised his hand and all the others grew even quieter. He gestured for Ummi to take us into the prayer ring and sit us down in about four rows facing the leader's niche. He then proceeded to call out some names. Each time he called, a man stepped into the circle amid the cheers of the others, and came to sit beside one of us. Ester and Sara were seated right in front of me; and Miriam to my left. The last man to be called came to sit beside Sara and I saw her shrinking towards Ester as if wanting to melt into her big sister. Ester on her part reached out her arm to hold her even more protectively.

The man in charge now stepped into the leader's niche and began to speak. It took a few sentences for me to realize that what he was chanting was the Moslem *Nikka*, the contract of marriage. I knew this because I had attended enough Moslem wedding ceremonies at Hosh Issa. It dawned on me that this man was marrying us, even Sara, to the men seated beside us. I gripped myself in horror. I looked over at Miriam and saw that she had realized this too. I tried to reach out to her but there was

Dust and Ashes

a man between the two of us. My heart felt paralyzed but my feet jumped up of their own accord. The man beside me held me down firmly. Perhaps it was this commotion or the other girls also now realizing what was happening because mass hysteria broke out. All the girls started wailing and crying. The leader just went on unfazed. He did not even bat an eyelid or miss a beat. Either he was so inhumane or he was used to, and was expecting this kind of commotion anyway. He continued and concluded the *Nikka*. He then said, "You can now take your wives to your tents."

At this point all the men cheered, including the ones outside of the prayer ring.

The man beside me grabbed me in a firm hold. I was struggling with all my might but I had time to glance over to see Ester trying to reach out to Sara. Sara herself seemed to have fainted. This was quite a mercy, all things considered. Amidst the crying and the wailing, the men carried off their brides like so much slaughter at a game party.

I fought and scratched and bit in all the ways of self-defense that I had learned growing up but it was to no avail. This man was not only more than two times my size but seemed to have been through this sort of thing before. He knew how to get what he wanted. In fact, the only sentence I remember him making was, "I am so lucky in this one. I got a fighter and not some cold dead fish!"

My fighting only excited him as far as I could see. I tired after some time. It was not difficult for him to divest me of my clothing. After the ceremonial bath, all our clothes including our underwear had been taken away. All I had between me and his savagery was that simple black robe. He wrapped it around my upper body, effectively immobilizing me and pinning my hands under me. He then held me down with the weight of his upper body. With his elbow he turned my biting mouth to one side and held my head there, to the side. He jammed one of his knees between my thighs. In mere minutes, all my romantic notions were shattered. My dreams, my mother's dreams, my father's boasts, my grandparents' expectations were all gone in one poof. It was painful. It was very, very painful. It was not at all like what we read in the romantic novels nor like the stories we had been hearing. This was not at all how I had imagined, hoped, nor expected that my first sexual experience would be.

When he finished, the man lay panting. I curled myself up in a ball at a corner of the room weeping. There was blood all over my thigh and legs. I ached in every joint but the emotional wounds were far deeper than the physical pain. From my heart I wailed, "God, God, where are You, God?"

The man was not finished with me. Three more times that night he raped me. By the fourth time there was no fight left in me. I just lay there while he had his way. When he finished he slapped me several times across the face shouting, "Dead fish! Dead fish!"

I just lay there sobbing. I did not care anymore. I wished I were dead. I closed my eyes tight but the tears kept coming. I did not sob anymore. If only the breath would also leave my body and I indeed became like a dead fish. I held my breath and wished to die there and then but after some time it would burst out of its own accord in renewed sobbing. I must have passed out or slept off. I did not know when the man left. The next time I became aware, Ummi was harshly ordering me to get up and go to bath. She pulled me by the robe and forced me to my feet. I was not the only one having the ceremonial bath. All the other girls were there but O what a difference from the bath we had the previous day. Then, we had been full of joyous anticipation that perhaps we were going home. Now, we could not meet

Dust and Ashes

one another's eyes after the horrors we had just been through. It explained what had happened to our Moslem mates. We scrubbed and scrubbed but the wounds were more than water and soap could get rid of. Stiff in every joint, it was difficult to even bend down to take up the water with a cup and pour it over my body but I was motivated, not that it made any difference.

That was when I tried to kill myself for the first time. Feeling deserted by God, I hit my head over and over on the wall of the bathing enclosure but it made no difference. I punched myself over and over in the tummy until I collapsed to the ground. None of the other girls paid me any attention and I did not pay them any. For all I knew they were also all doing the same thing. I must have lain there for some time but I did not die. I did not even have the blessed relief of becoming unconscious.

About thirty minutes later, one of the women came to take us to the section of the compound where our Moslem counterparts were still huddled on the floor in separate heaps. What a far cry from those first days when we had huddled together for comfort, seeking security in the closeness of one another. Now we all wrapped ourselves separately in our soiled black robes and did not want to be touched by another human being. After our ordeal, another human touch felt noxious and repulsive rather than comforting. Someone brought a plate of *koshari* but none of us paid it any attention. Ummi did not try to come to force us to eat. We did not see her at all until she came again that evening. This time, she selected thirteen of us. The following night it was fourteen. The night after that it was eight; and so on. Once, it was even only three and at another time they needed twenty-two but there were just nineteen of us. No matter the number selected, I was always among. It was a different man each night. In the next ten days, I was married ten times, to ten different men. Some were brutal and slapped me around in addition to raping me. Some were less fierce and went only one or two rounds. One man even apologized afterwards but in my heart I said, "For what?"

I never again fought as I did that first night. I merely twisted and turned with discomfort but I learned that lying still and having it over and done with as quickly as possible was a better strategy. Always, there was the ceremonial bath, so as to present us as pure brides. This was followed by the sham wedding so that what happened next could not be daubed fornication. Afterwards, on the next day, they served us *koshari* with meat or fish. We never could fathom the significance of this but we never had appetite for it anyway.

None of the men ever asked my name, nor did they mention theirs. Most of the time, the wedding happened at dusk or after dark immediately after the fifth prayer of the day. There was no provision for bride and groom to see each other's faces. I admit this had its advantages in a way. Always, the men would leave before the call for Morning Prayers but before they did, Ummi would come to collect us. In her presence, the man would say "I divorce you. I divorce you. I divorce you."

This three-fold declaration made by a man in the presence of a witness was sufficient to dissolve a marriage. I found this out on the second day when I had remained conscious. Once, I had a man who was still asleep when Ummi came. She scolded him roundly for being lazy. The man got up, made his pronouncement and then left to join the others for Morning Prayers. The girl usually, was supposed to say nothing. In my own case, I did not even look up. He could have been talking to Ummi for all I cared.

Among the girls, we had stopped talking to one another. We had nothing to say. We were so sad and bruised in body and spirit. We were ashamed of ourselves and of what our bodies were being made to endure. From the second day, I had stopped scrubbing myself so vigorously, knowing that my body would yet be violated again and again. I simply bathed with the water and soap and put on my robe again until the next ordeal.

Apparently the Moslem girls had been going through this for a week before us. When I had time to think about it, I wondered if and how they were doing with Rawya and Sara. They were just seven and eight years old, where the rest of us were sixteen, give or take a few weeks or months. I did not know how they were coping but I did notice that Sara had become quieter. She was no longer calling for her mother nor did she want to be held by Ester as at the beginning of our ordeal. She must have learned that Ester could not protect her from the harsh realities of the life we found ourselves in. Rawya was probably in the same predicament. Now they stayed by their sisters but not too close to them. They too, now abhorred human contact. One would have thought that when selections were made, and there were enough girls to go round, the little girls would always be left out but that was not the case. Apparently some men specifically requested for them. After all, according to Moslem traditions, Aisha was only six years old when the prophet married her. She was a debated eight or nine years old when the marriage was consummated. She was not the only wife of the prophet that was that young either. In fact, I was later told that the older wives often deferred their rights of copulation with the prophet to the child-wives.

And then one day, there was nothing. The compound seemed quieter than usual after Morning Prayers. There had always been the rumble of distant conversations but it was particularly lacking that morning. Ummi had witnessed our divorces as usual, collected us, and made us have our ritual baths. When it was the usual time for us to be served *koshari*, Asibi appeared instead. "Come on" she said, "We're going back."

We had no idea of what she meant when she said we were going back. Back to where? Back to our homes from where we had been forcefully taken? Did we have the strength to bear the shame? But we did not question her. Our spirits had become so crushed in our misery that we had become used to simply obeying orders. We simply got up and followed her like zombies. She led us by the way we had come mere ten days, or a lifetime, before. We again came to the door in the wall, passed out of that compound, and into the compound we had occupied initially. It was not exactly a homecoming but it signified the end of nights of sham marriages and tormenting sex. That was what we thought. In actual fact, it was only a respite.

I do not know how she did it but Asibi managed to get us buckets of hot water and soap to bath with. She even brought some rags and showed us how to massage ourselves. She got us a double serving of *koshari* and begged us to eat. "Cry too, if you want" she said. "Sometimes, crying helps to bathe the soul."

We cried and wept in our separate corners as much for our misery as for this unexpected kindness. This was a patch of kindness for the first time, in an otherwise bleak world of terrible wickedness, in what appeared to be a long waking nightmare. When we had bathed and wept and eaten, Asibi told me, "I have a special present for you."

From the folds of her black robe, she brought out the pocket New Testament which I had hidden under the mat before our first ceremonial bath. She proffered it to me. "I hid this for you so that Ummi would not get it. One day you will read it to us again" she said.

I snatched the book from her extended fingers and flung it in anger at the opposite wall of the dormitory. "No! No!" I screamed. "I don't want this anymore. Where has God been while we have been suffering all these? Did He not see us? Was He not mindful even of Sara and Rawya? No! I don't want anything to do with this God or His Word anymore." I started sobbing afresh. Truly, at that moment, I felt totally betrayed by God. I understood what Jesus meant at the cross by feeling forsaken by God.

Calmly, Asibi walked over to the fallen Bible and picked it up. "I think you're making a mistake" she said. "I know your God was here. He was here for me at least. I felt it. I will keep this for you now. One day you will need it again and I will have it ready. For now, why don't you all sleep and rest. The soldiers will be gone for some time. Who knows what your God will do before another set comes?"

We were too drained physically and emotionally but we began to understand what this was all about. We were kidnapped for satisfying the sexual urges of the militant Islamic soldiers. However, being good Moslems, everything had to be "properly" done including the conversion of the girls and the sham marriage ceremonies. In emergencies like shortage of women, legalities could always be dispensed with, re-interpreted, or bent. It was just like using sand for ablutions when water was not available. Ordinarily, I knew that following a divorce, Moslem women were supposed to wait for an obligatory three months before marrying another man. This was to ensure she was not pregnant with the child of the last husband. In my own case at least, I had been married to ten different men in ten consecutive days. There was no obligatory wait. The divorce witnessed by Ummi was deemed sufficient, and the purifying bath the next day enough fulfillment of this exigency.

One wise man once said that understanding a phenomenon makes it easier to tolerate. Maybe this would be so under different circumstances. We understood better what was happening to us all right but the very next day, Khadija tried to kill herself and her little sister.

STRESSES

My brief outburst about the proffered pocket New Testament, misdirected though it was, served as a kind of catalyst that woke most of us up from our stupor. We started sobbing as if our hearts would break. Suddenly in our collective hysteria, we found a common bond. We fell into one another's arms. There were no more distinctions between Moslems and Christians as there was when we had first arrived. We were now bound by this common misery of forced marriages and unwanted sex. I found myself holding not unto Miriam but unto Hoda. We wept until we all fell asleep. At the call to Morning Prayers the next day, we did not wait for Asibi. We went to the communal bathroom and had a truly cleansing bath, not with water which had been sanctified by Ummi's incantations, but with the desires of our souls. Returning to the dormitory, we met Asibi. She directed that we were to come and work at the kitchen. This seemed reasonable. The time we had worked there in the past had proven therapeutic in some measure. Besides, with the soldiers gone and no need for further training, someone must have reasoned that we might as well be occupied and useful. We were to wash and clean. Apparently also, with less people to cook for, there were only Asibi and one other woman whose name we learned was Fawzia, working in the kitchen. It was there in the kitchen area that we began to share our different experiences.

I thought I had been maltreated. The stories told by some of the other girls were horrific. Miriam told of how the first man had tied her legs to posts and used his fingers to forcefully tear her apart. Another girl told of how a man used his gun to penetrate her vagina to see how far it could go. One girl said she was so tight that the first man used a dagger to enlarge her vagina and she bled for days afterwards. The pain was still there but the bleeding had made her unfit for further marriages.

These were besides the tales of sodomy, having more than one man per night, or having other people watch when all this was going on. I began to feel grateful that at least my own degradations happened in the dark, with one man per night. There were no pleasant tales at all apart from the man who had apologized to me afterwards. And we were still the same girls, who until a few short days before were full of the usual adolescent romantic dreams and tales from romantic novels. We were still having our fantasies, fleeting crushes, and shunning boys of our age while at the same time being infatuated with unattainable television and movie icons.

Most of us were willing to talk but there were a few who said nothing at all. What they had suffered still hung over them like a heavy pall. The two babies among us were in this group. Sara and Rawya said absolutely nothing. In fact, both of them never talked again. We could only imagine the horrors they had been through. The first days after we were kidnapped, Sara always wanted to be in Ester's laps. She would wind her arms around

Al Kalima

Ester's neck and nuzzle under her chin. Yes, their mother was not there but her big sister was enough as a surrogate mother. Of course after our first night of abuse, we all abhorred any human touch. Sara did not come to Ester, and Ester did not reach out for her. After the catharsis, Sara allowed Ester to carry her and put her on her lap but she held herself there rigidly. She would not cuddle or nuzzle anymore as she used to do. In the morning, she allowed Ester to bath her but when we finished preparing our *koshari*, she would not eat. Ester tried feeding her but she held the food in her mouth and would not swallow. When eventually we suggested Ester gave her water, she spat out the food that was in her mouth but managed to take and swallow a few sips of water.

Rawya also did not speak of her ordeal. Her big sister, Khadija, did not either. They stayed close to each other but neither talked to, nor touched each other. They did not also interact with any other person for that matter. When we went to have our bath, two of them remained in the dormitory but when we went to the kitchen area, they roused themselves and tagged along. When we were cleaning and washing up, both of them did not participate. When the *koshari* was ready, it was served with a large communal tray. We allowed it cool a bit and then gathered to eat together. Rawya and Khadija did not still come closer. Asibi put some into a smaller plate and went to coax Rawya to have some. She stared at Asibi vacantly but would not so much as open her mouth. "I will just leave it here for you" Asibi said kindly. "I hope you will soon feel hungry enough to eat it."

"What we need" said Fawzia maliciously, "is for Ummi to come and whip some sense into the two of you. Why should you waste good food? Do you know how difficult it is to get it?"

While we were trying to clean up after the meal, there was a sudden, loud, and unnatural scream. We all turned towards the sound. It was either Khadija or Rawya! Khadija seemed to have suddenly awoken from her stupor. She grabbed the kitchen knife which was close by and plunged it into her sister's tummy. Before anybody could react, she pulled it out and plunged it into her own chest.

Fawzia and Asibi galvanized into action. They both fell upon Khadija to wrest the knife from her hand. It was quite a struggle. The rest of us stood there. We were amazed and stupefied. We were totally petrified by this new turn of events. And then Rawya whimpered. We all suddenly came alive. I got to her first. There was not as much blood as I had expected. Her robe was ripped where the knife had gone in. She held her hand over the wound and I saw a smooth pearly-grey mass protruding between her fingers. I was fairly sure it was her intestines. She was crying and moaning in pain. The others stood behind me. Nobody quite knew what to do. The black robe was already ruined. I tore it up some more and then tore out a sizeable strip to form a bandage that could wrap around her midriff to cover the wound.

"Don't do that" Fawzia shouted. "You are ruining the robe. How are we going to account for it?"

"Account for what?" I thought. I did not even bother to answer her aloud. This little girl was in mortal danger and this woman was talking about one stupid piece of uncomely garment. "She needs to go to hospital" I said instead, "She needs a doctor immediately."

"And how am I going to explain the fact that I was in charge when this kind of thing happened?" she fired back. "You were not supposed to touch the knives!" She was more concerned for herself and her vindication than for the wounded child.

By now, my rough bandage was becoming soaked with some fluid. I did not know what else to do. With fear stoking my temper, I jumped up to faceoff with Fawzia. We were soon yelling at each other while the other girls watched us. Suddenly, Asibi's voice cut through our verbal match. "Can anyone do anything for the sister?" she asked.

We turned to where Khadija had been wrestled to the ground. Here was blood, and plenty of it! Miriam went to her. There was a bucket of water nearby with which we had been cleaning up. I took Rawya's already ruined robe and tore it into more pieces. We began to sponge away the blood. Khadija did not seem to have sustained much injury. She had aimed to plunge the knife into her heart but somehow her ribs had prevented her from doing much damage. As soon as we sponged off most of the blood, we saw the wound was not that large. The flow of blood was no longer much either. By the time we finished with Khadija and looked around, Fawzia was nowhere in sight. Rawya still lay there moaning in pain. "What are we going to do?" I demanded of Asibi. "She needs help, and she needs it now!"

"I don't know" Asibi answered. "I think Fawzia has gone for help."

There was nothing to do but wait. We made the two of them as comfortable as possible in the kitchen area. None of us wanted to go back to the dormitory. We waited to see when Fawzia would return with the help. As night came, people drifted off to sleep in the kitchen storage area where we had been having our training. I stayed beside Rawya who remained painfully conscious. She kept groaning in pain. I believe she slept from time to time but even in her sleep she would cry out in pain and terror. Instinctively I started singing to her. I sang short ditties and choruses that we used to sing in church. This seemed to help; at least she would become calm for some time. The night deepened. We did not see Fawzia or anyone else for that matter. In desperation I began to pray aloud for Rawya. I forgot all my anger against God. "Please Lord, I said, comfort this little girl and get her the help she needs. Help her as no one can help her, Lord."

Rawya never opened her eyes. The cadence of her breathing did not change but she squeezed my hand from time to time as if to tell me I was on the right track and that she was appreciative. It was a very long night. We had no organized plan of how to take watches but somehow someone was always awake with me. Sometime during the night the poor little girl started running a high fever. Back home, my mother always had a pill for high fevers and then she would sit beside the person and sponge with tepid water. I had no pill to give her but the water in the bucket was not so cold. I used the remnant of the strips from the black robe to sponge her. Asibi, Miriam, or Hoda was always there to change the water. The rough bandage wound round her middle was now totally soaked but I was too scared to open it and take a look.

Khadija lay nearby. She was curled up in a fetal position with her back to us. She was not uttering even a sound. We did not know if she was awake or asleep, in pain, or at ease. We knew she was alive because she was breathing. Fawzia still did not appear. At last the long night ended. We heard the call to Morning Prayers. Soon afterwards, the tall woman who had rebuked Ummi with authority at that long ago training period appeared with another woman. The second woman was short and dumpy. She moved with crisp, practiced efficiency.

"Okay" she said, "We shall take over from here." We drew back and watched them. She looked Khadija over, opened her wound, and dressed it again with a long white hospital bandage.

Al Kalima

Without looking at us, she went over to Rawya. She certainly felt the fever because the little girl's body was really burning up. Her breathing had also become shallow. In fact, she was now breathing in irregular gasps. The woman did not make any move to unwind my crude bandage nor to examine the wound in our presence. She just picked up the slight form. Leading the way with her burden, they both left the same way they had come. We never saw nor heard about Rawya again. Did they treat her? Did they kill her? Did they send her back to her parents? I never found out. I just chose to believe that God had answered my prayer for her that night. Even if she died, I hoped she was better off than those terrible days at the camp and whatever those men might have done to her.

ASIBI

After Rawya was taken away, we all returned to the dormitory, Khadija in tow. Nobody had the strength to do much. Even the ever-cheerful Asibi had nothing to say. Exhausted by the long night, we all slept unnaturally. Throughout the next day, nobody had the appetite to eat anything and nobody offered us anything anyway. By evening, Asibi went out and came back with a small plate of *koshari* for Sara. It looked like the same portion she had tried to coax Rawya to eat the previous day. She told Ester, "It will be good for the little one to eat something."

Again Ester tried to feed her little sister but Sara just held it in her mouth and would not swallow. She still accepted small sips of water though. By that night, she became feverish. Ester woke me up. There was no water near the dorm. As we moved about, Asibi came closer to enquire into what was going on. When we explained that Sara was feverish and we needed water to sponge her, she said, "We cannot get out in the night."

"Why?" I asked. "Surely, there will be some water at the kitchen area. We just need to get there."

"There are patrollers in the night" she explained. "They shoot whatever they see moving on sight. We cannot risk it." "But we were outside last night at the kitchen area. How come no one shot at us?" "If we had tried to leave that area to any other part of the compound in the night, someone definitely would have done so."

We did not know how lucky we had been if such would be called luck under captivity. We exposed Sara as much as we could and tried to fan her with her robe. It was another long night. As soon as Morning Prayers were called, we all went to the kitchen area again. The water from the well at this time was very cold. Asibi heated some water and we used it to bath Sara there and then. She still would not eat anything but continued to take water, a few sips at a time. When she started shivering, we dressed her in her robes again and Ester sat close to the fire holding her close and weeping helplessly. Sara no longer held herself rigidly. She actually leaned into Ester and stayed there looking so weak and miserable. We all shed tears on her behalf.

"When Fawzia comes," Asibi said, "maybe she can get some help or at least some medication for her."

We hung onto this hope, but Fawzia did not appear. The person who came instead was a totally different woman whom we had never seen before. She came to supervise the making of the *koshari* for that day. All the vegetables she brought were already prepared and sliced. Apparently, no knives were to be allowed near us ever again. Asibi asked her for help concerning Sara. The woman said she did not know what she could do but that she would mention it to someone else.

With Asibi, she prepared the meal and served it with the communal tray as usual. As she left, she said something we did not hear but it had Asibi upset. "What is it?" We asked Asibi, "What is it?"

"I think they're going to move us tonight" she answered.

"What do you mean move us tonight?"

"We're leaving this compound, probably this town, tonight. Who knows where we will be going to next? It might not be as good as this place."

The news did not have any big significance to us. It was true we had developed a fairly familiar routine since we were kidnapped but this was not where we wanted to be at all. We were not as affected by the proposed move as Asibi but her discomfort moved me to ask Asibi about her own story.

Asibi was not as old as we thought she was. In her estimate, she was about twenty-two years old. She was a mere six years older than we were but she had been in captivity for about ten years. Again this was also an estimate. "At first I tried to keep count but the days come and go. The years come and go, and I lose count sometimes" she said.

She said she was originally from somewhere in northern Nigeria, a place called Talata Mafara. This explained her puzzling looks. Because of her darker skin, we had all assumed she was Nubian but somehow her features did not look quite typical. Although we did not really see her hair because of the ever-present robe, the wisps which we caught sight of from time to time did not really look like ours nor like a Nubian's. However, over the centuries, there have been a lot of intermarriages and admixture of the races that one could never really tell from looks alone.

Asibi and her two cousins had been on their way to the market when they were kidnapped and put into a truck. "We were in the truck for about six days and seven nights. It was moving continuously except for only brief periods at a time. The stops were perhaps so they could change drivers or take on fuel. Three of us wept until we were dried up. We were choked by dirt and dust, oppressed by the heat by day, and the cold by night. About two days into our journey, one of my cousins died. They stopped long enough to bury her in the sands before we continued. The two of us left mourned her as best as we could. Her death taught us what our own fate would soon be. However, after her death they took better care of us. At least they gave us more water and allowed some more air into our prison. We survived.

"There were only a few of us in those days, and many needy soldiers. In one night, one could be married and divorced three times. Everything had to be done according to the *Hadith*, you understand?

"I was about twelve years old then, but had always looked smaller than my mates. That is why I know what Sara and Rawya might be going through. Notwithstanding, I had those marriages and they told me to be happy. That was how it was with the wives of the prophet."

There was no bitterness in her voice as she recounted her story. There was only a tired resignation which was somehow even sadder than bitterness would have been.

"The only times one was exempted from the marriages were if one was on one's period, one was noticeably pregnant, or one was still bleeding after delivery. Even then, some men specially requested such people but the line has to be drawn somewhere."

Asibi had tales of horror to recount. She had been pregnant twice. The first time was when she was fourteen years old. "The labor was long and difficult" she said. "I nearly died but at the end it was the baby that died. It was a baby boy and Ummi was so angry with me. I had deprived The Cause of a soldier even though he would have been named a bastard and never been allowed to lead in prayers!"

Her second delivery was two years after that. Asibi was then more grownup. Labor was easier and this time it was a baby girl. The baby came out alive and thrived. "I was so happy with that baby. Never mind how I got pregnant for her and that I would never know who her father was. She was the only thing that was truly mine. She was the only person who felt that my existence was worthwhile. I poured my heart and my life into that baby. She made my life worth living then. I thought Ummi would be angry because it was a girl but she was not. Later I learned that baby girls are actually kept and groomed. She would have been taken away at four years old and as soon as she turned six, would become another slave like I am. I did not want that for my baby girl. I loved her and she was the joy of my days.

"And then, when she was almost six months old, she became very sick. She started vomiting, and then also started purging. Her temperature became very high. I cried out for help but she could not be taken to hospital. The other girls in the camp of mothers tried the best they could but two days later my baby was dead. I wanted to die too, not for the first time but death has always eluded me. They allowed me to dig a grave for her. By the next day I was back in the circuit of wives. I never got pregnant again. I ceased to really care about anything at all. Mine was a totally hopeless life with nothing to look forward to until you people came along."

Asibi's story explained a lot about her apparent compassion towards us. She had been like us once. She had experienced the horror, the torment, and now the despair. By the time we arrived, she had become more or less a worker among them. She was responsible for taking care of new arrivals like us. Did she ever try to escape?

"Oh yes, several times and not just me. Everyone tries to do so from time to time. I have also seen what happened to those who tried to escape. Some were shot, some were recaptured. My cousin tried to escape but she was re-kidnapped by another group and later bought back. She was punished very severely for the trouble she had caused, and the money she had cost.

"In any case, what direction would I know to go? To get here took so many days and nights of a ride in a covered truck. Since then we have moved around a lot too. Even at the best of times, my sense of direction is very terrible. I also have an idea of what happens to people who get lost in the desert."

It was only about three years before we came that she learned she was now geographically in Egypt. How would she ever find the way home and would her people still recognize her? "All these years, they must have given me up for dead!" she said sadly.

Asibi's story made our own case appear truly hopeless. We had tried keeping a chart of the number of days our parents must have been looking for us but we lost count during the trauma of the sexual assaults. One or two weeks were bad enough, but months... years... a decade...

ON THE MOVE

At dusk, the woman who had made our food came to collect us. She steered us through the compound. We thought we were being herded back into the other compound but she led us through yet another hole in the wall until we came outside the compound. It was not the way we had come by the first day we were kidnapped. However, standing by the side of the wall were two trucks similar to the ones that had waylaid us on that fateful day, maybe even the same ones. There were already two women inside the cab of each truck, next to the drivers. The woman who brought us asked nine people to get into the first truck. Jehan was the first in line. When she hesitated, Ummi appeared from the other side of the truck and brandished her whip. Meekly, Jehan got into the truck. Ester, struggling to hold unto Sara got on next. In compassion, knowing she would probably need help with the sick girl, I got in behind her. At the end, I saw that Asibi also made it into the same truck.

When there were enough people in that truck, the others were ordered to get into the second one. We sat on the floor of the truck and then it began to move, the other one following behind. We would have welcomed the covering tarpaulin against the bitter cold of the night but we did not get any such luxury. We huddled close together and wrapped ourselves in our inadequate robes for warmth. Sara was wedged between Ester and me. I could feel her very hot little body. "Maybe we should expose her." I suggested.

We moved aside a bit to increase the circulation of air around her. Shortly afterwards, maybe less than five minutes later, she started shivering and had goose bumps. We regrouped around her and hugged her close. Her eyes remained closed for the entire drive. She had not spoken now for three days, or even more, as far as we could tell. She would not even nod or shake her head if we asked her questions. The most she had been doing was to open and close her mouth when we tried to feed her. Asibi had brought water in a small plastic bottle. We tried to make Sara drink this. After one or two sips, she held it in her mouth and would not swallow. Ester clung to her, intermittently weeping and praying out loud. She pleaded with God for mercy and rescue.

The trucks moved at a fair speed. From feeling, we knew that sometimes we were on smooth, tarred roads. At some other times we bumped along as on a poorly-maintained or uncharted track. We rode through the night. By morning we were ordered to get out. Unlike Ester, Asibi and I, some people had managed to fall asleep. When we staggered out, we looked collectively like half-drowned rats.

"Get into line" barked a voice.

We saw that we were surrounded by about half a dozen gun-toting men wearing red and white checkered *kaffiyeh* which half-masked their faces. We staggered into a rough line. Sara could not stand by herself. Ummi tried to separate her from

Ester and make her stand on her own but she kept collapsing to the ground. At last, Ummi saw that it was hopeless. She allowed Ester to carry her piggyback, using the edge of Sara's robe to secure the younger girl at her midriff and then we set off.

Two of the gunmen went ahead; next came the motley crowd of the kidnapped girls in a single file; and then Asibi and the other women. Other gunmen brought up the rear. There was no telling how far or for how long we went. There were no rest stops. Ester, walking directly in front of me, stumbled. When I offered to relieve her of Sara for some time, the alacrity with which she surrendered her precious burden told me she was probably very exhausted. I eased Sara off her back and transferred her to mine. This caused the line to stop for some time. Maybe there was some modicum of humanity left in these people after all, or perhaps they saw they had no better choice in the matter. When the line paused one of the men behind shouted belligerently, "What is going on up there?"

Someone explained the situation to him, and that was the end of the matter. Everybody waited while we did the transfer. It did not take more than a few minutes and then we continued. So natural was it to carry babies in this manner that it was nothing at all. The weight of Sara on my back at first was so comforting. It brought back memories of Amira to me and how intensely I missed her. My heart ached and my eyes filled with tears. But there was no time to be sentimental. "Hurry! Hurry!" shouted a gunman from the front. Apparently we needed to be at a particular place at a particular time and we were not making good time.

Once, at school, a teacher had mentioned to us that one way to make a mundane task seem to go faster was to chant a ditty with it. He said it had worked for the African slaves on the American plantations, and for so many other people through the ages. In my heart, I had been singing a short chorus that we learned in church not long before we were kidnapped. I must have started humming it aloud because suddenly I found out that down the line behind me some other voice was also now humming it softly. It spread. Very soon practically everyone, even Ester trudging ahead of me was also humming it. We marched according to that tune. It was just humming with no audible words. Perhaps because it was being so effective, our captors did not try to stop us. Who knows, they might even have joined, albeit inaudibly. Maybe they would not have allowed it at all if they had known that the words that went with the tune was, "If Jesus gave so much for me, for me, what can I not give for him? O Halleluiah!"

The sun came up in its fury. The midday heat built up and still we did not stop. Our pace slowed. People began to stumble more obviously and more frequently despite the ditty. I felt Sara begin to grow heavier on my back. Her breathing had become more irregular and her burning little body seemed to have become hotter than ever. After some time however, her body began to feel cooler until it was quite cold. Thereafter, she seemed to grow heavier than ever. I knew that babies generally felt heavier when they slept. I was reaching a point when I was about to ask Ester to take another turn carrying her when suddenly we saw a line of huts in the distance. Our captors asked us to quicken our steps .We knew we were approaching our destination.

In Egypt, almost everyone lives close to the Nile just as it had always been from the ancient times. The Nile was the lifeline of Egypt. Sure, there were some oases but these were occupied by ancient Christian monasteries or were otherwise the domains of the Bedouins who freely roamed the land and whom everyone, even their kin who settled in towns and cities,

Dust and Ashes

slightly despised as unlearned. Every other settlement was either on the Nile, its delta as it fanned to empty into the sea, or by the coastline of the Red Sea or the Mediterranean. Every city, every town, every village had to be close to this body of water for sustenance. In fact, in some places, how close one lived to the Nile was dictated by how affluent the person was.

The village which opened to us now therefore was close to the Nile. By the bright light of the late afternoon, we could see that it was really another collection of walled-in compounds except that one side of it opened towards the Nile. From my knowledge of Geography and the position of the sun, I knew we had been heading north since we alit from the trucks. There were no signposts to tell me where in Egypt we were, but I was pretty sure we were still in Egypt. Perhaps where we were coming from was outside Egypt but from all indications we were now in Egypt.

Some people seemed to have been looking out for our approach. We climbed up a dune and as soon as we were descending, some black-robed women came towards us. They escorted us into a compound and we all sank unto the floor. They brought us chipped metal cups filled with water. Just like that first day, we did not question where it had come from or what else it might contain. We all started gulping it down greedily. As the popular television advertisement went, we had to obey our thirst.

I had put Sara down from my back as soon as we stopped moving. I laid her down on the packed-mud floor just inside the courtyard, and arranged her robe around her, making sure her little body was shaded by the shadow of the wall. After my second cup of water, I tried to give her some but she was not taking it. At first I thought she was just weak and tired as in the last few days but how she lay there so inert was too unnatural. I shook her frantically, calling her name. That drew everyone's attention. In a flash, Ester was there beside us. She too had been quenching her thirst. She called and shook Sara but to no avail. We all became very quiet and took a closer look. Sara was not breathing at all. None of us had ever seen death at close quarters. We did not even know how to check for the signs of life but one thing we knew for sure was what it meant when someone was no longer breathing. I placed my hand in the center of her small chest. It was not moving. The heartbeat was not there as it should have been. Sara must have died on my back some time during that long, hard trek. When her body had begun to feel cool against by back, all life must have gone from her by then. Now she lay there stiff and cold. Ester let out a long piercing wail. "Help me!" she screamed, "Somebody help me! O God! O God!" And then we all joined in.

Ummi and two other women ran in to see what was going on. When they saw the little body lying there and the rest of us shrieking and wailing as if there was no tomorrow, the story must have told itself. One of the women came and tried to shake her, as if we had not just been doing that. She went away again when the little body did not respond. The others did not even try to touch her. A Moslem became defiled by touching a corpse and must have to go through purification rites afterwards.

They left us alone. We wept until we were hoarse. Ester kept moaning "No, no, no!" Right beside her I echoed with "Why? Why? Why?" Some of the girls must have fallen asleep. I could not sleep despite the fact that I had not really slept for almost three days. Ester sat on the floor holding the rapidly-stiffening corpse which had been her sister close on her lap. I did not know what to do. I felt somehow responsible. What could I have done that I did not do? What did I do that I should not have done?

Dust and Ashes

It was very unreasonable to blame myself, but who else could I blame?

We sat by Sara until the following morning. Asibi had successfully pried the corpse lose from Ester's grasp and laid it there in a corner of the yard. According to Moslem rites she should have been buried before sundown but I guess the whole camp was either too shocked or too exhausted to care. Nobody brought us anything to eat or drink. We were also too sad and exhausted to care.

But a corpse was a corpse, no matter how beloved the person had been. By midday the next day, in the hot desert climate she was becoming bloated and beginning to give off unpleasant odors. Small secretions were escaping from her mouth and nostrils. Flies were buzzing unpleasantly around her. We had to bury her. Fawzia and Asibi came with a stack of plastic plates. They showed us a place on the other side of the dune, outside the village where we could dig a grave for her.

"Dig" is not quite the word for what we did. I guess the experience with Khadija made them wary of giving us any sharp or heavy instruments. With the plastic plates, we kept scooping sand out of a rough hole until it was wide and deep enough to take Sara's body. It took us the rest of the afternoon and a considerable part of the evening. When it was done, we wrapped Sara, head to toe, in the black robe which had been issued to her. It was her only possession. Every other thing had been taken away from us. I wanted to wash her body at least, but there was nothing to bring the water in. Carefully, we laid her small body in the hole face-up, but with the robe covering her face. As we began to fill back the hole, Ester who had been in a stupor all along and had not participated in the digging suddenly flung herself over the little corpse. "Bury me too!" she cried. "Please bury me with her!"

Her sudden action caused a sudden small explosion from the corpse followed by a seeping stain of some unpleasant-smelling fluid. Whether this was from one of the orifices or that she had become so bloated and then burst, we would never know. Miriam and Jehan held the hysterical big sister back while the rest of us finished filling the hole. From her robe, Asibi suddenly produced my pocket New Testament Bible. "Say something" she urged, "say a prayer at least."

I had convinced myself there was no need to ever talk to God again. I had nothing to say. However, looking at the ragged circle of filthy faces turned expectantly towards me, it occurred to me that this was not about me. It was about Sara. It was about Ester. It was about all these girls who were suddenly and cruelly snatched from living coddled and protected normal lives in one moment, and then in the next moment living through more horrors than they had ever witnessed or imagined possible. It was about the common bond of suffering which now united us, past the petty bickering which we had between us in the past. And so by the light of the setting sun, I took the Bible from Asibi and began to read from the Sermon on the Mount. I had underlined excerpts from it before and read these out now. I read the Beatitudes, God's expectations of us, what we could expect from Him; the Lord's Prayer …

And then a strange thing happened. As I read, I had the assurance that God had not deserted me after all. I stopped struggling to understand. I let go and began to weep. Everyone began to weep with me. It was a turning point. We held one another. We prayed for one another. By the time we were finally calm enough, we noticed how filthy we were – from the digging and from the fluids which had emanated from Sara. The river was nearby. A portion of it was secluded by the walls of the compound. We went to bathe in the river and to wash our robes. Those robes were the entirety of our worldly possessions for then. From this point on, we became more than co-captives. We became more than friends and colleagues in the same predicament. We now became sisters. I did not have enough boldness then. I am sure if I had called for confessions of faith and baptisms I would have had many takers. In any case, I think the bath we had that evening was indeed a form of baptism for all of us.

Nevertheless, that night, Ester tried to kill herself, or rather to get herself killed.

We had been warned by at least two sources that anything that moved after curfew was liable to be shot. We had wept ourselves dry. With the physical drain of the past few hours or even days for some of us, after we had bathed in the river, we fell into a deep sleep. At least, I did. Ester lay between Miriam and me on the mat, supposedly asleep. The next thing I remember was a lot of shouting and screaming. I could not make out any voice separate from another for some time. And then I realized that most of the screaming was coming from the girls in the dormitory, apart from one particular voice.

When I was more fully awake, I realized it was Ester's voice. She was outside the safe periphery screaming, "Kill me! Kill me! Why don't you shoot me? Shoot me! Shoot me!"

The other girls from inside the dormitory were screaming different things. Most of them were calling Ester at the top of their lungs. Some were screaming "Come back! Come back!" Some were screaming "Don't do it! Don't do it!" Some were screaming other questions or just asking "What is it? What is it?" with bewilderment.

People were screaming different things but no one was screaming an encouragement. As Ester was screaming she was moving further and further away. Suddenly, a gunshot rang out. Whoever fired that shot was either a very good shot, a very lousy

Al Kalima

one, or perhaps the finger of God just deflected that bullet. The noise of the gunfire served to immediately silence the whole group. From inside the dormitory, we could see Ester fall to the ground. For a frozen moment none of us moved and then quick as a dart, Khadija was outside, beside Ester and dragging her back into the dormitory. Jehan and Hoda saw what she was doing and joined her. Between the three of them they managed to pull her in. She was very limp and looked dazed. She was breathing and her eyes were open even though they were wild and staring. She seemed to be foaming at the mouth. Quickly, Miriam and I removed her robe. The bullet had passed through her robe and grazed her upper thigh. It did not even penetrate the flesh as such. It was bleeding but not that much. Asibi still had the leftover of the strips of Rawya's robe. With this we bandaged the wound. Asibi forced her to drink some water from her ever-present water bottle.

Afterwards she fell into a deep sleep which lasted until late the following day. She was apparently exhausted from sorrow and her ordeal. Khadija never left her side. She tended Ester like a mother hen. After three days of not being fed, we were given what looked like a double portion of *koshari*. Khadija even reserved some for Ester. When Ester woke up, Khadija fed her as if she was feeding Rawya. From this moment on, both girls became very tight friends. They were perhaps bound by their similar losses. In the olden days of school rivalry, they had both been leaders of opposing parties.

Asibi began to mean more to me. She told me, "I came to put my faith in Jesus Christ some days after you came. One night, as I listened to you read to the children from the Bible I knew there was a message in it for me. I simply accepted and believed. That was why I saved the little book for you."

If only she understood that she was the one who had restored my faith in God and in living! I tried to tell her this often but she insisted she was my disciple, and not the other way round. Asibi could neither read nor write in English. She knew some Arabic and could chant whole sections of the Quran. "There were some indigenous Christian missionary ladies who were teaching us how to knit and sew in my village" she said. That was the entirety of her formal education before she was kidnapped.

She saved everything that looked like a string. She hoarded scraps of cotton, bits of clothes, and even the rough nylon strips from food sacks. "We practiced knitting with broomsticks and so if I get any two rigid lengths of anything, I can knit with them."

Even though we were not allowed near any metals, there were always twigs and reed stems and Asibi taught us how to knit. This exercise helped us not only to maintain some creativity, but to also while away time. Most importantly though, knowing how to knit helped us to preserve some degree of dignity and privacy. Asibi showed us how to attach some of our creations inside the seams of our robes to create secret pouches. It was in such a pouch that she had hidden and carried the pocket Bible. It was inside such a pouch that she always carried her small plastic bottle of water. "Your robe will always belong to you or be on you" she tutored us. "Sometimes, you may not return to the room from which you have been taken, and Ummi might order your room to be searched and cleaned while you are away from it. You will lose whatever you had been trying to hide there" she told us from her own experience.

This advice made so much sense and we would see such things as she described happen over and over again during our captivity.

A MISSION FIELD

"Out of every evil some good always usually develops." This was my grandfather's philosophy.

New alliances formed, stronger ties were forged. We all developed a new appreciation of human lives. Miriam had always wanted to be a nurse, and I had lived all of my meager lifetime with a nurse as a mother. Miriam and I became the unofficially recognized health officers with whatever little we had to work with. This was not where we wanted to be but we were making the very best of the situation as much as we could.

With the power of hindsight, we would never know what good Sara's death achieved for us. However I have a theory that it must have prevented something terrible. Years later, Mike theorized that whatever happened to Rawya must have alarmed the organization in some way and we might have been moved as a precaution. Who knows? On my part, I believe we had been moved to this camp for a repeat performance of what happened at the other camp but because of her death and how closely involved we were with her corpse, we were probably all deemed defiled. For the roughly two weeks or so that we spent in this second place, even though we heard the voices of the soldiers at prayer and at training, we were left strictly alone. There were no marriages, no indoctrination, and no forced labor as such.

The only mandatory labor we had was that we had to dig by the riverside every day for clean drinking water. There were no wells in this compound. Digging beside the Nile was a primitive way of getting clean drinking water. One dug a hole by the riverside and then covered it with broad leaves, or plastic plates in our own case. This was so that animals would not come to drink from it nor desert windstorms arise to cover it up with sand or blow other debris into it. Throughout the night, water gradually seeped into the hole, filtered by the sand. By morning, relatively clean and potable water is the result. The hole had to be dug, or at least refreshed every day. According to my cousin who had told me this, sand has to be sterilized by the sun every day. In any case, the filtering sand also came into the hole, causing it to become too shallow and consequently useless.

During this respite we knitted and told one another stories. By an unspoken agreement, one person would not knit but read aloud from the pocket Bible to the others who were knitting. Everything we read from the Bible was interesting in this kind of bored setting. We did not read just about the life and the miracles of Jesus but even the relatively dry and uninteresting epistles of Paul and the other apostles. Asibi asked if we could teach her to speak English. All this while, we had spoken to one another in the colloquial form of Arabic commonly used in Egypt. Delving into this scheme of teaching English to Asibi became a hilarious project. We made fun of her foibles which she took in very good faith. Using tracings in the sand, we even tried to teach her how to write in English as well, going from left to right rather than from right to left.

Apart from the daily *koshari* served to us by Asibi, we saw virtually nothing of the other occupants of the compound but we knew they were there. Some of the girls started their periods and those of us who did not worried that we might be pregnant. We discussed the consequences. "If it were a few days ago" said Hoda, "I would have made definite plans to kill myself rather than have a child of rape. Now, however, I am not sure that will please God."

The rest of us agreed. And then Miriam confessed, "I actually tried to kill myself a few days ago but it did not work."

"How?" I asked. We were all curious.

"It was the same day that Khadija tried" Miriam answered. "I saw a bottle of what looked like bleach in the kitchen area when we were working there. When no one was looking, I opened it and swallowed more than half of the content, and then I panicked. I stuck my fingers down my throat trying to vomit but it didn't work. I was thinking of telling someone about it when Khadija made her move and everybody concentrated on that. Later, I saw Fawzia taking a drink from that same bottle. I knew it wasn't bleach after all. It had just contained bleach some time ago but not right then. I was so relieved. God taught me that lesson in a gentle manner, I think."

We discussed such practical matters openly now. Psychologists will perhaps say it was good for all of us, especially Khadija and Ester who surely were more emotionally deeply wounded than the rest of us. I believe these open discussions helped us in no small measure.

Inevitably, we also discussed escape. It looked hopeless but we promised ourselves we would keep a look out for a way of escape. We made tentative suggestions like swimming down the Nile but apart from the fear of crocodiles, we had no idea of where we were; or of who the enemies or our friends were. We

Dust and Ashes

called to mind Asibi's tales of those who had made unsuccessful attempts at escaping and ended up with worse fates than if they had stayed. "Nevertheless, let us not lose hope" we would always conclude. "Let us keep a lookout for any opportunity at all."

We also talked of what would happen if we ever got separated. We recognized that so far we had been lucky that we were together. "If we ever get separated and any of us manages to escape" we promised one another, "We must speak out and tell the world what we saw and what is going on in our country!"

Lofty ideas! After about two weeks of respite in this place, one moonless night we were moved yet again. This time there was a short trek first, and then a truck ride. We went to an encampment similar to, but larger than the first place we had been. The next day, five girls aged about twelve to fourteen were thrust into our group. They wore different school uniforms, and were apparently freshly-kidnapped. We tried to make friends with them but three of them wept incessantly. One was completely mute, staring at the wall with vacant eyes, while the other one was very belligerently castigating us as if we were responsible for what she was going through. We tried to understand. Had we not felt the same way towards Asibi when we first came? Because they would not communicate with us, we had no chance to tell them the fate which awaited them.

The very next morning, Ummi came in raging. Apparently, putting them with us when they had not been trained was someone's huge mistake. She ordered them put into a different dormitory at once! Five days later, the marriages started again. It was about two weeks before we saw the girls again by which time they were so dumbfounded, humiliated, and at the brink of suicide. This time when we spoke with them and bathed their wounds, they were more welcoming. They realized that we were victims as much as they were. They shared with us the story of how they had been kidnapped. Two of them were on their way to school at Alexandria when they were kidnapped. The other three were returning from school at Asyut when theirs happened. They had obeyed all the rules of never moving alone but in groups. Still they had been kidnapped. The three said they were in a group of about nine. They felt some members of their group had escaped. The two said they were in a group of about seven and were sure all of them had been taken. "The person who tried to escape was shot. The rest of us meekly shut up and did as we were told."

Did the girl that was shot die? What happened to the rest of their groups?

They did not know. They believed the girl might have died or was unconscious at the least. There was so much blood and she had lain there on the ground immobile. As for the other girls they had been kidnapped with, perhaps they went to other camps since there were two trucks each when they were kidnapped, and only one when they disembarked. Again those of us who had been together thanked God for this. We again discussed what we would do if we ever got separated.

The coming of the new girls also brought us other things. It brought us writing papers and news! Apparently, their schoolbags and personal effects were destroyed as soon as they came into camp but Asibi had rifled their belongings before then and brought us another New Testament Bible, some clean sheets of paper, stubs of pencils, and some sheets of a history textbook.

They told us of what was happening to the rest of the country. They talked of how loyalty to Sadat was divided. Things were getting harder and harder for the common man in Egypt. There was increased migration of the wealthy to other parts of the world, and so on. They told us of the increasing cost of basic

Dust and Ashes

things like food, amenities, and education. There was increased urban migration and slums in cities. They talked of how Islamic militancy was on the increase. Three of the girls were Moslems and two, Christians but after their ordeal, they renounced their Moslem faith there and then. The Christians also renounced their faith in God. "I cried and pleaded with God" said Hanan "but He did not answer. Where was He in my time of need? He didn't help me. I don't believe in Him anymore."

In addition to every other thing, Hanan's twin sister, Nadia, was among the girls whose fate they did not know about. We shared our own ordeal with them, even the aspect of wanting to kill ourselves. Memuna was the one who had not spoken a single word since we met her. After her first set of marriages, she was even more reticent. She just huddled in her corner weeping silently. She only ate when threatened by or with Ummi. Two days after the cleansing bath of the last marriage, she tried to set herself on fire. Ester and Khadija caught her as her robe was beginning to burn. They threw her on the ground and started beating out the flames with their own robes. Jehan poured a bucket of dirty water we had been washing up with on her and the rest of us started throwing handfuls of sand.

The fire was quenched but she had a lot of burns on her face, chest, legs, and her abdomen. Although she was moaning in so much pain, Ummi still came and beat her with her cowhide whip. "Now you will look so unsightly and we can only use you as a spare wife" she bit out.

Aha! Was that the trick? The more unsightly one looked, the less the marriages! As intriguing as this was, none of us was ready to suffer through the pains Memuna went through for the next few weeks. The woman who had tended Rawya came daily to slather her with some salve and to give her what I presumed was painkillers but at night especially, she continued to moan and keen in pain. She was feverish sometimes too. All that Miriam and I had to work on her with were tepid water and the rags of Rawya's robe. For a long time, she was not given any replacement robe and the scars of the burn were very scary and unsightly indeed. None of us had any spare robe or garment of any sort to give her even as a loan. At night we huddled around her to keep her warm. Of course at first she abhorred the touch of another human being but the very basic need for warmth especially in the chilly desert nights far outstripped her revulsion, and the need for modesty.

Nevertheless she was very appreciative. Once she hung onto Miriam's neck saying over and over, "Thank you, Angel of God, thank you." Those were the first words we ever heard her speak.

By now, we made it a habit to wake up before the first calls to Morning Prayers. We held a devotion of sorts. We prayed, read a short passage from the Bible, and then encouraged one another. We never failed to pray that God would somehow provide a way of escape for us. The newcomers started joining us. One day I quipped that my congregation was growing. "I should be thinking of baptizing you!"

"Why don't you?" asked Asibi. "That was what the Ethiopian eunuch asked Philip, was it not?"

For someone who was just becoming serious with the Bible for the first time, Asibi's mind was like an insatiable sponge. She caught on to things and held them. She had a simple, and yet very profound faith. She believed all things were possible if the Bible said so.

"Okay" I countered, "Don't forget the first part of that was 'here is water!' where is the water here?"

"We could draw water from the well and improvise" she suggested. "I'm sure God will understand. The prophet told his

Dust and Ashes

followers after all that if water was not available, they should use sand for ablution."

This was what destroyed the argument for her. No one wanted to be baptized if it involved any improvisation. "It will be so much like Islam" Khadija said. "You keep improvising things for your own convenience like getting married and divorced seven times in a week. I want no part of that."

But I think God saw the desires of our hearts. The next time we moved, we were again close to the Nile. We were allowed to go to bathe in it. The very first day we got there, Asibi reminded me about the baptisms. Everyone wanted to be baptized. When I pointed out that I needed to be baptized as well, we resolved the problem in this way: Miriam and I would baptize Asibi. Asibi and Miriam would then baptize me. After that, Asibi and I would baptize Miriam on the first day. By the second day, being duly baptized, the three of us would baptize everyone else who wanted to be baptized.

It was hilarious. It was solemn. Above all, it was very symbolic! We asked everyone to make a statement of faith before being dipped into the water. Everyone, including our five newcomers had something touching to say. Memuna for instance said, "I had to be totally lost to find God. Now that I have found Him, I never feel lost again. I belong to Him and He is forever near me."

Bama who had been so hostile and belligerent at the beginning said, "I renounce my Moslem faith and the faith of my fathers because in this Jesus, the Messiah, I find perfect peace!"

Jehan said, "I seem to have been running all my life. Now that I have run into You Lord, I know I have reached home."

Marta said, "Men might defile my body but I know my soul, and yes, even my body belongs to You Lord, for always."

There were so many other profound one line confessions of faith. Our captors might think they were killing us but we were finding faith in Jesus Christ as a result of our oppressions. I felt so ashamed of myself for the time I had denounced Him. That night, I had a dream. I had always known God could speak to people in different ways. I, after the encounter with Him that changed my life, had always shared how he spoke to me to the amusement of many people especially my uncles and cousins. I would come back from a church meeting or a Christian Youth Fellowship meeting blathering about how God said this or that to me. One of my uncles teased me once, "How would you describe the voice of God? Was it a deep bass or a soft soprano?"

I could not answer the question except to emphasize again that I was sure it was the voice of God which I had heard. Another cousin bore me out on that occasion. He told the uncle, "It is a spiritual thing, Uncle. When God speaks to your spirit, you cannot categorize it as bass or soprano because you hear it with your spiritual ears!"

Oh yes, God had spoken to me in the past but He had never spoken to me in a vision or a dream. This night though, He did. I was in that nebulous area of sleep when one is half-asleep, yet somewhat still conscious and alert. I was so sure it was Him. He said, "I am happy with what you did today, Briska. You have shown that you meant what you said when you said I should take you and use you in whatever way I please. You have proven yourself in the Mission field which I have given you. There is still more work ahead of you, and more of my sheep to be rescued from the enemy camp."

I woke up comforted and with a sense of purpose. This was not simply a case of making the best use of every situation. It was a sense of mission and a purpose for being where I was at this particular time. I shared the vision with only one person,

Asibi. I did not expect her to be skeptical but I expected her to be full of questions. She merely nodded instead and said, "He visited me too. I asked Him what we should do and He said that things would be revealed to us one step at a time."

That was Asibi! I had not even thought to ask questions but I was truly comforted and reassured. I was not in this alone. I was not in this to no purpose. This kidnapping was not captivity. It was God's mission field. With this change in my thinking, came a change in my attitude. Whereas it had been Asibi goading and driving me, I now saw that I was where God wanted me to be and there was a purpose in it. Someone once said that there was a method to every madness. I saw that there was a pattern to good for everything that God allowed to happen to a believer. I could give sermons on this. It felt very good to be back on very good terms with God, and this happened just in time too.

RAMADAN

The baptisms seemed to mark a new era in our captivity. After this time, things began to fall into a new perspective for all of us. No, we did not begin to enjoy the serial marriages and the rapes. We did not begin to welcome captivity; but we became less bitter about things. In fact, we began to pity our captors. We did not bottle up our experiences. We rather shared them more openly but now without bitterness. We learned from one another that the best approach was just to get in there, remove our robes and spread our legs passively, singing songs, reciting Bible passages or picturing some other nice place in our heads until it was over. Any show of resistance or modesty tended to inflame the lusts of the men and to prolong their enjoyment as well as the girls' discomfort.

The girls on their periods were "exempt from duty". My own periods had always been erratic right from when I started menstruating. Consequently I found myself on duty more often than most. Hoda and Berhan did not see their periods for a long time. They thought that for sure they were pregnant

Dust and Ashes

but their tummies were not growing. I remembered a lesson a teacher slipped in once that under pressure, some women cease menstruating altogether. Indeed, after the baptism, their periods resumed but remained irregular like mine except that irregularity for Hoda and me meant about once in six to eight weeks whereas for Berhan, she was menstruating every two or three weeks. She did not mind at all. This bought her relief from sexual duties.

Khadija and Ester became pregnant at almost the same time. We knew this because apart from missing their periods, they started vomiting in the mornings and could not stand the smell nor taste of *koshari*. Asibi was the one who made the diagnosis. She comforted them and said maybe they would have baby girls to replace the little sisters they had lost.

It sounded like cruel comfort at first but after a while, we all began to look forward to having the babies with us. Again Asibi told us mothers and babies are usually quartered separately from marriageable girls. Suddenly, when they were about three months along, after a particularly grueling period of sexual duties, they both started bleeding. At first it was slight spotting, then heavier spotting and then very severe bleeding with abdominal cramps. We did not know what to do. I remembered my mother talked of people who bled to death while having miscarriages. We appealed for help from Ummi and the kitchen women but help was not forthcoming. Frightened, we gathered round them and prayed, rubbing their tummies. Suddenly with an anguished cry, first Khadija and then Ester expelled mangled pieces of tissue at about the same time! We did not look to see if there were babies in them. We went and dug holes in the ground and buried them. After that, the pain ceased immediately. The bleeding reduced considerably but stopped completely after a week more.

Ummi ordered them to have purifying baths. Two weeks after the event, they were back in the circulation of marriageable girls. We mourned the loss of those babies but at the same time we were relieved, not just for the girls whose lives were spared but on further thoughts, for the babies as well. How would they have fared in the kind of lives we were living? Was it not better that they were lost this way? Asibi had also explained to us that as soon as the babies were weaned, they would also have been taken away from the mothers anyway. Such were the dilemmas we faced in those uncertain days. We never knew when to hope or when to despair.

When Asibi was telling me her story, I had asked her how she managed to keep a tab on the passage of time. She had replied, "By the Ramadan. Ramadan is a big event and every Ramadan something happens to make me remember that year in particular. Last Ramadan, I wished for a special sign to make me want to keep on being alive. Two months later your group came!"

What an answer to prayer! It was not a privilege we cherished but let us face it that the mysterious ways in which God works is not always pleasant for all the parties involved.

Asibi did not elaborate on timekeeping and Ramadan but we got to understand that Ramadan, in our present status as captives, was something to either look forward to or to dread. Being born and raised in Egypt in close proximity with Moslem neighbors, I knew what Ramadan was all about. It was one of the pillars of Islam. A good Moslem must fast during the daytime in the month of Ramadan in order to commemorate the fasting that revealed the Quran to Prophet Mohammed. It could be likened to the Jewish month of Yom Kippur or even the Christian Lent except that these Ramadan fasts are mostly without penitence. It was rather a testing of wills. Some did

Dust and Ashes

indeed fast for a revelation of God but these were O so few. On a special night called "The Power Night", they actually wait for a revelation of God, or as one of my cousins put it, for the revelation of the strength needed for the next mischief.

My erstwhile grandfather at Hosh Issa once said tongue-in-the-cheek that Ramadan is when there is a contest of how angry a hungry man could get. Wisely, officially, working days are shortened during the month of Ramadan in Egypt. Some private companies even moved to do their businesses at night rather than during the daytime. Like every other thing in Islam, every Moslem I knew improvised a lot at these periods so that during Ramadan, a lot of people gained weight rather than lost it. The catch was that they fasted during the day all right but as soon as the prayer to break the fast was called, they would be like a lot of little children with bottled-up energy let out for recess. They began to feast and carouse and live it up very maximally until the first Morning Prayers was called. At that time, those who could, would pray and then go to bed. They would remain there, intermittently rising to pray until Evening Prayers to break the fast was called. Even the poorer Moslems stocked up on extra nutritious food at this time. Eggs became scarce as it was seen as a wholly nutritious diet. Already-made food sold out very quickly in the evenings. Entrepreneurial Christians and people of other religions capitalized on this. In fact, I had a Christian aunt who did brisk business in cooked and packaged meals during Ramadan. She would refuse any out-of-town engagements at the peak of this her business period.

The fasting told most on those who were addicted to nicotine. One of our neighbors had the habit of drumming his fingers on the edge of a table during Ramadan. Gamal and his friends nicknamed him "The Ramadan Drummer". The drumming got worse as the day progressed but once the

Evening Prayer was called, quick as a flash, he would whip out his cigarette and lighter and then chain-smoke from that point until Morning Prayers was called, as far as I could tell. We used to like watching him in those last few minutes before the Evening Prayer was called. How he whipped out the lighter and the cigarette was very fascinating and seemed like magic to us. My father always said we had to admire his commitment, especially given that he did not really know what he was fasting for. My father believed that when one fasted, it should be for a reason, a burden, for which one needed to pray and pray through. But then, my father was an Evangelical Christian. Those ones had their own peculiarities too. He used to say to my Coptic church relatives that they did not need to fast during lent because Christ did not ask even his intimate apostles to continue this as a tradition. "Did you not read where the Bible says that if you confess your sins, He is faithful and just to forgive and to cleanse you of all unrighteousness? The Bible did not say fast over your sins. It will not carry any extra merits."

He believed in fasting but for specific burdens. I was sure that he fasted after we were kidnapped, and was perhaps still fasting. This was the kind of thing which made him fast and pray.

But not to deviate too much, our first Ramadan was truly an epoch-making event. It served to buttress what Asibi had said of its being a time marker. By that time we had been in captivity for several months, almost a year by my reckoning. Lots of water had passed under the proverbial bridge. We had lost two members of our original party. We had welcomed five new members. By then we had become fairly acquainted with the routine. For about ten to fourteen days every six to eight weeks, we were moved to soldiers or soldiers were brought to us. We were then forced into marriages with a different man per

Dust and Ashes

day for whatever number of days it took. Thereafter, they moved on and we were left to our own devices until the next stint.

For Ramadan it was different. We were moved to a large camp. From there we could see numerous minarets which told me we were very close to Cairo. This camp was like a coalition of so many camps. There were probably more than two hundred girls. The serving women were also more in number. The soldiers were even much more. Here, we were not just getting married on a daily basis but usually two or three times in a night. Once, I was married up to four times in a single night. Ummi or someone like her was always around to witness the divorces and there were plenty of Imams who conducted marriages all night long from after the call of Evening Prayers to just before Morning Prayers. It was very horrendous, but so used to it did we become that we did not even have the time to discuss our experiences in the mornings.

Because of the large number of people, we were not left alone to sleep away our days after the morning purification baths. We were put to work in the kitchen at once. We were not allowed to taste what we had cooked until the Evening Prayer was called. At that time we would quickly gulp our food and be ready for the first marriage of the night. Gone were those fellowship periods. Gone were those periods of quiet camaraderie and spelling one another. We did not so much as have time for ourselves. In fact, I found myself sleeping through most marriages.

But it did not last forever. Ramadan ended after one month. Everyone was exhausted. Once the *Eid* to end the fast had been celebrated, the soldiers disbanded and went to their various posts, I presume. We had time to catch our breath, take stock, and meet with the girls from other camps. As far as the girls from our own camp were concerned, we had not fared too badly.

We found time to laugh about sleeping through marriages. Said Jehan, "I was having myself a good sound sleep and dreaming I was at a *Sham Ennisim* picnic while this man was pounding away and suddenly Ummi bellowed at me. 'Get up. Do you think this is a luxury hotel?' I nearly began to answer her that it was not a hotel, just a riverside picnic when I suddenly realized where I was."

We all roared with laughter.

The other girls were looking at us askance as if they could not really place us as sane or insane. We, on our own part, were also curious about them. Gradually, we could see there were really two groups of girls. There were those who seemed thoroughly miserable in their captivity, and a very few who seemed to be living a privileged life even while in captivity. By listening, we gradually began to understand. Ameena and Beeba were like the most prominent members of this favored group. They did not deign to talk to us. In fact, we caught what was tantamount to just a fleeting glimpse of them one morning after the *Eid*. Two hours later, they were gone. We remembered them because they would not eat with us. They seemed to look down their noses at the *koshari* served in communal trays. They would not even come near the food. Their robes were made of new and shiny black satin or silk rather than the coarse cotton which the rest of us wore. They kept toying with their lacy black veils. We had no veils at all except for the rough cowls attached to our robes. The other difference was that even though they did not speak to any of us at all, when they spoke to each another, they did not speak in the common Egyptian Arabic, nor any form of Arabic at all. They spoke to each other in what I thought to be Farsi from a few familiar words. After they left, another girl who knew them better told us their names, and that they were Iranian.

Dust and Ashes

Aha! I thought to myself as if that explained everything. One of those childhood memories which remained ingrained in me was of a conversation between my opinionated grandfather and my very gentle grandmother. On the surface, those two were always arguing. They appeared mismatched but there was no one who could rein in my fiery grandfather as well as his small, serene wife, and that, usually with a few soft words. I don't remember the beginning of the conversation nor what led up to it but my grandfather declared, "Iranians! You can never trust an Iranian! They are slipperier than eels."

My grandmother had said, "And this from a man who says it is foolishness to generalize. You are being prejudiced. Perhaps you should also agree with the commonly stated fact that anyone who has origins in Denshawi is either a fool or a coward."

This hit too close to home and I think my grandfather may have winced but I remember him saying, "That is totally different. All the Iranians I have ever known, personally or in business, have toxic sides to them."

"How about Monsoon?" asked Grandmother.

"Monsoon is different. There is an exception to every rule but if you break it down, you could say he has his toxic side too. Besides, maybe we have not seen him pressed to his breaking point yet."

Monsoon was one of Grandfathers closest friends. A Christian from Iran, he made several journeys between Iran, Pakistan, and Egypt every year. He visited, raised, and encouraged liaison between secret pockets of believers on all sides of the borders and in so many other countries in between. I understood that he specialized in travelling with camels. I never understood if Monsoon was his real name or a nickname. His presence was certainly always like the rain storms of India that we read of in books. He was forceful, relieving, and sometimes devastating if need be. He could never be ignored. Long after he had come and gone, people would still be talking about his visit at Hosh Issa. He was always both anticipated and dreaded at the same time but my grandfather loved him. When I was still a young child, he made one of those his trips to Iran and never returned. Nobody heard of him or from him ever again. He had no close family. Ours was it for him. Grandfather mourned him for a long time but always said that even if he was dead, he had accomplished more for Christ in his lifetime than any other person he knew.

From the conversation between my grandparents however, my young impressionable mind took away two things. Iranians were not trustworthy; and there is always an exception to every rule. Apart from my dim childhood memories of Monsoon and the stories related about him, I do not believe I knew any other Iranians that closely until I encountered Ameena and Beeba. Today of course, not only do I know lots of Iranians, I have become quite intimate with a few. Fariah is one of my closest friends. If I could make any generalizations about Iranians, it will be about a peculiar grace and regality with which they carried their frames; and the fact that they tend to have deep compassion and to sacrifice themselves for other people and for what they believed in. These attitudes must have been borne in a people used to staring undisguised human suffering in the face and doing something about it. They are unlike most of the rest of the world who either looked the other way or stood by, helplessly wringing their hands. The Iranians I got to know later in life were always very proactive in good causes. They are a wonderful breed of people. But at the time I met Ameena and Beeba, I did not know all these other ones.

Dust and Ashes

The truth though is that I never really met Ameena and Beeba. Before any of us could ask why they were not eating, one of the matrons like Ummi, signaled them from afar. They got up, snatched up their veils and left. It was the reactions which came after they left that aroused my curiosity. There were hisses, clicks of the tongue, growls, sniggers, and sneers. The faces of the other girls were a study in human emotions ranging from anger and jealousy to sheer admiration. Only one face registered anything like pity or understanding, and that was Asibi's. My face and those of some others must have either remained blank or registered bewilderment. What was happening here? I looked at Asibi and she, answering my unspoken question said, "I will tell you later."

"Tell her now" said Bashra, a girl from another camp whom we had met for the first time at the beginning of the Ramadan. She was very pretty, tall, and slender with fiery eyes in a nicely oval face. Apparently, she had been very good friends with Asibi once. "What is there to hide? They are high class prostitutes!"

How could anybody use that kind of nomenclature for any of one of us, seeing what we went through most nights, albeit in captivity? If Ameena and Beeba were harlots, then were we not all the same? Which qualified kettle was calling a pot "Black"? Apparently it was not that simple. Girls like Ameena and Beeba were specially selected for "special duties". Apparently they did not get to be married several times in a week like the rest of us. They were specially selected to service the sponsors of the Jihad with whom they could spend days or even weeks at a time. They were groomed and given special treatment. While they were at their "appointments" they could have whatever they wanted, and were even sometimes specially paid in some way. "Can't you see they even dress differently from the rest of us and they smell better and higher than the rest of us?" Bashra asked.

Her voice dripped sarcasm but one could detect a lot of envy beneath it all. Ester said "But they are still very much as captive as we are or can they ask and be allowed to go home whenever they wanted?"

The other girls who knew more about this joined in the conversation. It turned out there were about twenty of these "special girls". Coincidentally they were all Iranian or seemed Iranian. They too were also kidnapped like we were, on their way to school, an errand, or even directly from their homes or schools. Hoda remarked, with a lot of pity in her voice and eyes, "They are even further from their homes than we are. Heaven knows what else they do to them for the many days they are away from other people."

Asibi later explained to us that Bashra had once been chosen as one of the special ones but later dropped. She had tasted of what she thought was the good life and then been returned to the ordinary life. No wonder her cultivated pain and bitterness.

Pain and Bitterness! Those were the two main "strong" characteristics of the girls whom we encountered from the other camps. Two of the commoner characteristics though, were despair and resignation. There was a lot of fear but incidentally almost no anger. These girls had been reduced to total hopelessness. When people are hopeless, every fight and anger tends to die in them. Some of them would not even so much as lift their heads and look other people in the eyes. They moved about, ate, slept, bathed, and did whatever else they were told to do like mindless robots. Constantly underfed as we were, sometimes fights broke out over food, or sleeping spaces. Even these were half-hearted and lacked any real fire. People only fought for what they really cared about. We had nothing to care about anymore. "The only time people show some energy or humanity is when they have babies but whenever anyone is

Dust and Ashes

due to deliver they will move her to another camp. When the children are weaned the mothers immediately return to the pool of wives" Asibi had told us.

For about two weeks after the *Eid*, after the men had moved on or gone to do whatever it was they usually did, we virtually lolled about recovering from the ordeal of the Ramadan. We recouped what we had before in praying together, reading the Bible, and knitting. We tried to involve the girls from the other camps but although a lot of them were interested, we were met by outright opposition and hostility in some quarters. One girl reported to Ummi that we were hiding a Bible in camp. When Asibi heard she was coming for a search, she ripped the inside of our two Bibles out, divided them into sections and had each of us that she trusted hide them in our robes. She then filled the jackets of the Bibles with the pieces of paper which we had gathered. When Ummi came for the search, Asibi actually led her to where these were hidden under a mat. Without even so much as opening them to see, Ummi cast the "Bibles" into the fire and swore she would whip anyone who promoted such unbelieving propaganda in any of the camps again. Ester, Miriam, and I were identified as the ringleaders. She beat us on our bare backs twelve lashes each with her cowhide whip.

We went underground after that. Up till then, we had gone through the New Testament at least three times together and could quote sections of it by heart, albeit not always verbatim. Now we went through it again more thoroughly and a bit feverishly, striving to remember as much as possible in case our Bibles ever got totally taken away. We did not know it then but we were doing what persecuted Christians of old did long before us. And also like them, the more they persecuted us, the stronger we grew. Those of us in that original group of twenty-two plus Asibi formed a core of discipleship. We met in secret and more earnestly discussed what we would do if we were separated. "Thank God we have sections of the Bible at least in some parts. Never let it go and if we meet from time to time we can exchange what we have."

"Don't ever get discouraged trying to tell others of this hope in Christ. The voices of the ones who want to hear and need to hear are usually drowned out by the few who do not want to hear."

"Whenever you have any opportunity for baptisms, go ahead. I think God recognized the one we did."

And then every time, constantly, we reminded one another, "If you see any opportunity for escape, take it and inform the rest of the world of what we're going through."

"Even if we die in captivity, remember we shall meet again in heaven."

Again, without knowing it, we were holding what big churches would call ordination and leadership training meetings. A few days later, our fears were justified. Camp broke up and we were scattered. Of the original group of twenty-two, only Jehan, Memuna, Hoda, Lubna, Asibi, and I remained together. The others went to other groups, some we saw again at the next Ramadan when the groups again broke up and reformed. As God would have it, three years later, we were all reunited but how this happened will come later in another part of this saga.

MEMUNA

From our previous life education on the consequences of sex, one would have thought that with all the sex which was going on, there would be lots of babies, but it was not so. There were the occasional prolonged periods that we assumed might be pregnancies but there were only a few proven pregnancies by our reckoning. Even these ended in miscarriages sooner or later. Once, when it was brought up in our discussions, I felt that perhaps it was because we were all too malnourished to sustain pregnancies anyway. Jehan said, "How can a pregnancy survive when the body is pounded like that continuously?"

I did not have a lot of experience in these matters but what she said made a lot of sense. The only person who ever had a sustained pregnancy among us till then was Memuna. She was a standby wife. Ummi hardly ever brought her out to be married because of the scars she got after her burns. She only got married when there was a dire shortage of wives. Whereas the rest of us had got used to just lying spread-eagled on the mat with our thoughts somewhere else while the men did their business, Memuna never got past squiggling, squirming, and twisting in revulsion. The morning afterwards, she would linger over her cleansing baths. She would be depressed and in tears, refusing to eat for a few days until we got through to her again. This happened over and over even though she was forced to get married only for one day every two months or so.

About three months after Ramadan, she missed her period. She had not been keeping count anyway and did not take any particular notice of it. It was when she started refusing her *koshari,* would be repulsed by the very smell of it and on two occasions vomited at the very sight of the food that we became worried. Apart from the occasional sniffles and cough, none of us had ever really been sick. As at the last occasion with Ester and Khadija, it was again Asibi who connected the dots. "You must be pregnant" she told Memuna bluntly. From calculation and other things, we placed her at about two months pregnant then.

Predictably, there were tears. Never quite robust from the beginning, she lost even more weight. No matter how much we tried, we could not get her to eat. Asibi got some sugar from Fawzia and made Memuna take sips of sugared water. Unlike Ester and Khadija that began to accept and look forward to the baby after sometime, Memuna remained adamantly opposed to her pregnancy. She was not talkative from the beginning, and she now retreated even more into herself. Often, she would allow herself to be held and comforted by one of us while she wept but mostly she abhorred all human touch. Even before her growing tummy became noticeable, Ummi stopped marrying her to anyone. By the time she started showing, Ummi would often look at her and snicker with satisfaction. This gesture was enough to make Memuna start weeping again. I often heard her mumbling "Why me? Why me?" She prayed for a miscarriage but the pregnancy progressed. We could even see the baby moving through the very thin skin of her tummy. The woman who had taken Rawya away came twice and gave her injections. She left what we presumed were iron and vitamin tablets for Memuna who threw them all away once the woman left.

One day, when she was about six or seven months pregnant by our reckoning, we overheard Ummi telling Fawzia that Memuna would have to soon be taken away. Asibi had explained this was customary. Apparently Memuna would be taken to this separate camp for nursing mothers and their babies. Once the babies there were up to about four years old they were weaned, "harvested", and taken away by force for training while their mothers were returned to the circulation of wives.

The same night that we overheard the conversation, Memuna became feverish. By the next day she was unconscious and delirious. We tried to get one of the women to come and see her but they all seemed to be very busy elsewhere. Only Asibi was around. "I think they went to arrange for transportation or a way of moving her to the camp of mothers" she explained.

We sponged Memuna with tepid water, exposed, and fanned her. There was nothing else we could do. By evening she started groaning intermittently, accompanied by some restless thrashing about. "I think she's in labor" Asibi opined. "I think the baby is coming."

In between the groans, she would be quiet and seemingly asleep. As the night progressed, the groans and thrashing became more and more frequent. There was no one to call. We could not even leave our dormitory or we would be shot. Apart from Asibi, none of us knew what childbirth was like, nor ever witnessed one. Our sex education ended with how babies were made. It did not extend to how they were born. In our respective homes, we only saw them after they came back from the hospital with our mothers, aunts, or whoever delivered them. Even then, we did not get to cherish them until much later when they had become cute.

As dawn broke, two things happened simultaneously. Memuna's water broke, and she started convulsing. Her robe was soaked by the smelly fluid so we used it to soak up the remaining fluid on the floor and to clean her up. We had nothing else to cover her with. The only possessions each of us had were that robe apiece, and a few strips of rags allocated to us for our monthly menstrual periods. We had saved a few pieces of rags after nursing Rawya but these were inadequate pieces and really terribly ragged by this time. Naked, Memuna started shivering with cold so I sat by her head trying to cradle her and cover her with an edge of my own robe at the same time. Lubna sat towards her feet and tried to do the same pitifully inadequate covering.

Memuna convulsed two more times. In between convulsions she was groaning louder and straining to push. "I think the baby is almost here" pronounced Asibi.

Lubna and I moved aside to see. With Memuna totally exposed now, we could see the head of the baby peeping from between her legs. She strained, groaned, and arched herself off the mat. Suddenly, there was the baby! It was a baby boy and did not make any noise at all as it slithered into the world. There was nothing to wrap him in, not even swaddling bands. Asibi brought some dry menstrual rags and cleaned him up. And then from the ever present bag of tricks in her robe, she brought out two thick cotton cords. She asked me to hold up the umbilical cord. With one of the cotton cords she tied off the umbilical cord close to the baby's tummy. She placed the second one on either side of it closer to the mother, flipped the umbilical cord over the cotton one and began a sawing motion.

This eventually cut through the umbilical cord. The baby was now separated from the mother. Asibi wrapped him in a corner of her robe but he was not breathing. She felt his heart was beating. I could feel it too but even as we tried to reason among ourselves what we should do next, his heartbeats became slower and more erratic. Finally, it stopped. The baby grew cold and stiff in Asibi's arms. None of us thought to cry. We were just too stunned by the ongoing events.

Memuna did not convulse anymore after the baby was born but she did not wake up either. She had stopped groaning and was just lying still. She shivered on the ground while her fever raged on. The placenta came out soon after the baby without much effort by Memuna, or assistance from anyone of us. Memuna bled a little but she did not look any worse than she was before the baby came out. Jehan used the soiled robe and the water she had been using to sponge her to clean up the whole mess. Lubna and I drew closer again to cradle her and cover her somewhat with our own robes.

From the noises outside, we knew when Morning Prayers were over. The sky grew brighter as a new day began. Jehan went out to get a fresh bucket of water. It was then that Ummi burst through the doors. She took a look at Asibi holding the lifeless baby, and Lubna and I cradling the unconscious mother and burst into a tirade. She cursed us for our ill luck. She cursed us for our incompetence and ineptitude. She accused us of being murderers and said so many other unpleasant things. Apparently she had looked forward to having this baby much more than any one of us had anticipated. Pointing her finger at Asibi she said, "Just make sure that gets buried." Asibi left with the tiny corpse.

After some time Ummi stormed out and Fawzia returned in her place. She brought another robe with which we dressed

Memuna. Wonder of wonders, she also brought a blanket! We had never seen a blanket in any of the camps we had been to since we were kidnapped, certainly not in our dormitories, nor with any of the men who had sex with us. This was really an unexpected kindness even though we did not know who was responsible for it, Fawzia, Ummi, or some other higher authority but we were grateful on Memuna's behalf.

Gratefully, we cleaned Memuna the best we could and wrapped her up. She did not convulse anymore but the fever kept going up and down. When she shivered with cold we covered her with the blanket, and when she burnt with fever, we exposed and sponged her. In her delirium, she talked to people we had never heard her talk about before. Lots of her talks were happy ones and we took note of the names and places she mentioned because we had nothing else to do. We tried to feed her *koshari* but she would just hold it in her mouth and not swallow. Fawzia supplied us with sugared tea. By wetting her lips and tongues with that, we actually got her to take up to a cup every two or three hours.

We all became quite exhausted caring for her. We took it in turns to stay by her side day and night, sponging her or feeding her with sugared tea. We thought that surely the nurse or whoever that was, who had given her the injections would come and do something. No one came. Even Ummi did not come back again. We gave it all we could under the circumstances. On the third day, just before the call to Morning Prayers, as I was taking my turn caring for her, Memuna suddenly opened her eyes. She looked directly at me with lucidity. I was trying to feed her the sugared tea. At my exclamation of surprise, the whole dormitory came awake and came to see what was happening. "Thank you" she said, "Thank you very much" and then she slept off.

Dust and Ashes

We could see this was now a more natural sleep. It was deeper than her sleep of the previous few days. We could not rouse her to feed her the sugared tea but her breathing was more even and the fever seemed to have broken. She sweated a lot. We kept sponging her just to keep her comfortable but she was no longer feverish. When she awoke again that evening, she asked for water and we were only too glad to give her both the sugared tea and plain cold water from the well. She appeared very weak but she seemed very eager to talk. "I am dying" she began, "but I am so glad to go."

She did not ask about the baby and no one volunteered any information about it. We were willing to talk of what she had put us through and the fears we had. Unlike her usual self however, she seemed more determined to talk than to listen. "I am willing to die and I am looking forward to it but you have to listen," she insisted. "I had a vision where some of you escaped. I don't know who will escape, and who will remain but you must never stop looking for a way of escape. When you escape, you must find my people and tell them what happened to me. Tell them that I died a very happy person and a believer in Jesus Christ."

"Don't talk like that!" We tried to chide her and make light of the matter. "You mean all our effort of the past few days would be in vain? Do you know what you put us through?"

But Memuna was more determined to talk than to listen. Throughout that night she talked almost nonstop. She would not allow the rest of us get any sleep either. She continued to encourage us not to give up hope of returning to our homes. She counseled us on what we should do if we escaped. "Don't wait to be rescued like we had been hoping. You must make your own plan to escape and tell the world what is happening."

Towards dawn, she began to look very tired and drained. I could imagine how she must have felt, having talked all night. I was just one of her listeners but I was feeling very drained of energy. She had consumed up to three gallons of water all the while she was awake and yet did not once talk of being pressed to urinate. Asibi and I had talked of what we would do if she needed to pee before the curfew was over. We agreed she could pee in a corner of the room if the need arose. She had been doing it on the floor all the days she had been unconscious anyway. However, the need never arose.

At last, she stopped talking and wearily closed her eyes. We were happy to be allowed to sleep at last. Soon afterwards, the call to Morning Prayers was made but Memuna never woke up again. When we finally realized she was not breathing and was growing stiff, we all let out an unplanned and collective howl. This had three of the kitchen women running in to see what was wrong. Unlike when Sara died, we were not asked to go to dig her grave and bury her. Fawzia came with two young men and they took her away, wrapped in her robe and the blanket. We were too stunned to even cry after that initial howl. Somehow, this death was different from Sara's. For a few days we were left to ourselves. We kept going over the sequence of events which had led to Memuna's death. We especially discussed her "Valediction". Hoda summarized it for all of us, "I don't want to die in captivity like this. If there is a way of escape, I am going to find it or die, trying to do so."

QASIM

The experience with Memuna was a first for me in many things. It was the very first time I had witnessed an actual childbirth process. It was also the first time of my watching a grownup die. Despite all these, the most outstanding thing in my memory at this time was that about seven days after Memuna died, a new batch of soldiers arrived and the marriages began again. This batch was more vicious than previous batches we had encountered. They were bloodthirsty! It was not so much as the pervert type of sex they wanted but that they seemed intent on drawing blood. The very act of drawing blood, and the very sight of blood really excited them. It actually drove them into frenzy. They preferred to be with all the girls together in a big lighted tent. They would all get naked and then begin the torture. They would bite us with their teeth, whip us with treated cowhide whips, and even beat us with knives and daggers. At the end, even Ummi had to step in and say "Enough!"

From subsequent talk, we understood they were coming from training camps in Yemen, and were on their way to different parts of the world to train Jihadists. I felt sorry for the parts of the world they were going to. All along, the focus of our prayers had been ourselves. We had prayed for sustenance, health, spiritual growth, comfort, a way of escape, and so on. For the first time, our prayers turned more fully outward. There was a whole unsuspecting world out there which did not know the evil that was about to be unleashed on it. This new brand of Islam was a far cry from the one we had known at Hosh Issa or even what we had thought of as radicalism at Damanhur. Even the born Moslems among us who were being indoctrinated to a stricter lifestyle before our kidnap were appalled. These men had no room for tolerance or being humane. In fact, they seemed hardly human. They radiated only intense hatred, even towards one another.

For weeks after they left, we were left strictly alone. I guess Ummi knew that we needed to recover from the shock and our injuries. A few weeks after this recovery period, came the next Ramadan. Again this happened at the camp with the sky view of many minarets and we knew we were close to Cairo. From our first Ramadan, we now knew what to expect. First and foremost, it was a time of reunion with those of our group who had gone in different directions. We had a lot of catching up to do. We told them about Memuna's death. It turned out Bama and Miriam had also become pregnant and been sent off to the camp of the mothers. Of the original twenty-two, thirteen of us were at the camp. Khadija had become pregnant and miscarried again. The rest had episodes of prolonged cycles and were relieved when their periods finally came, proving they were not pregnant.

There were also some other good things. Bashra, who had been so belligerent and was jealous of those girls that had special treatment, was now a baptized believer. She was an ardent disciple of Ester's. It was touching to see how she hung on every word the younger girl spoke. She was not just a vigorous crusader but also a very apt Bible teacher. She spoke to everyone who would listen, even the older women in the kitchen. She would not stop even when one of them threatened to report her to Ummi. "Oh, that is an opportunity I have been longing for" Bashra answered. "I really want to tell her why she had better believe that Jesus is the Messiah!"

She was never reported and we noticed that some of the women began to linger at the edges of our circle when we met. I like to think that Bashra's witness got to them and that the Holy Spirit would use it to work in their lives. In their own last camp, they had somehow managed to lay hold of a whole Bible. Every spare moment we had that Ramadan, we refreshed our memories on those beloved Old Testament stories and even discovered new ones which we had not known were there; like the story of Diana, the daughter of Jacob; and of Tamar, the sister of Absalom. We strongly identified with them in so many ways.

Hanan rediscovered her twin sister, Nadia, at that Ramadan camp. They wept in each other's arms to discover that they were both still alive. Each had given the other up for dead. We were glad to make Nadia's acquaintance. She and Hanan looked very much alike but not uncommonly identical. Just before the Ramadan camp broke up six weeks later, Nadia became one of those who got baptized.

A lot happened during our second Ramadan but the most interesting thing which happened to me was that I met Qasim. Perhaps because there were more girls or less number of soldiers, we were getting married at the most twice in a night and that, not every day of the week. We were not as busy as in the last Ramadan so we managed to get some sleep during

Al Kalima

the day when we were not occupied with talking with one another. It was during the third week of Ramadan that I met Qasim. As usual, I had not paid any attention at all during the marriage ceremony. When it was time to go and consummate the marriage, I followed him to one of the tents on the outer fringes of the camp and as soon as I got in, I whipped off my robe, lay on the thin mattress, opened wide my legs, closed my eyes and started thinking of the book of Esther which we had been reading earlier that day. It had become that automatic.

I expected him to descend on me and have his way and when he did not do so immediately, it did not occur to me to wonder why. I expected he was taking his time. Some came at it fast and hard, others took it slowly. Some men were slower than others. I was therefore startled when his voice brought me back to the present. Grunts, groans, the occasional expletives came with these liaisons but they often happened during the copulation, sometimes soon after but never before! I was even more startled by what the voice had to say. "Get up" he said, "And put on your robe."

What? I was not sure I had heard correctly. Still on my back with my knees pointing towards the poles of the tent, I cracked open an eyelid and squinted up at him. He repeated himself. "Get up and put on your robe. I want to talk to you."

Now, I had never heard of this happening. I had heard of men who had not been able to perform sexually. Some of them became brutal and used their hands, their feet or some other objects on the girls. I had also heard of those who totally ignored their wives and slept off until morning when Ummi came to witness the divorce. None of these had ever happened to me personally; but I had never heard of a man that simply wanted to talk instead of having sex! In fact, in these marriages, no talking was ever involved. I was dubious as to whether

Dust and Ashes

talking was even allowed. The men did not want to know our names even, and we certainly did not want to know theirs. I was therefore even more baffled after I had got up, put on my robe, and stood waiting for what would happen next when he then asked, "What is your name?"

I was about to open my mouth to answer when he interjected, "I don't want to know your real name of course. I just want to have something to call you by and to refer to you as, in my head. You may call me Qasim. That is not my real name either but it will serve its purpose for now."

The whole thing was too surreal. After what must have been an interminable silence, I blurted out, "Call me Sara. You may call me Sara, but my real name is Briska."

I do not know why I added that later part but what was I to lose? Perhaps he might mention it somewhere and my parents would hear that I was still alive. However he ignored it totally.

"Okay, Sara" he said. "I really do want to talk. Sit down and tell me what has been going on here."

That sounded suspicious to me. It might have been a long time since I read spy novels but I still had elements of it in my head. Besides, I had some native intelligence and natural instincts so I countered, "Perhaps it will help if you told me who you are, what you want to know and why you want to know it."

He smiled, inclined his head to one side and said, "Fair enough."

For the first time I looked him fully in the face. Although he was dark and handsome, his skin was quite light for an Egyptian. Broad-shouldered, with a head full of raven black hair and eyes to match, he also had a broad and intelligent forehead with strong brows. Unlike the other men we had seen so far since we had been kidnapped, his beard was rather tame and well-trimmed. He looked like the hero kind of a man we used to read about in those paperback romantic novels. He did not look dangerous enough like the Barbara Cartland heroes but possessed a firmness of the jaw beneath his beard which bespoke character. This contrasted with so much kindness that I saw in his eyes. Perhaps this was just my own imagination. At the moment, his lips were smiling benignly so I could not judge if they could be thinly cruel or sensuously full, according to the said novels. Later on, I did see another kind of look on his face which totally transformed it but I should not get ahead of myself. My first impressions could still do with a lot of wishful thinking. I probably desperately needed the proverbial knight in shining armor at that very moment.

Qasim's race was uncertain from his looks. He could have been Egyptian but then he could also have been Indo-Pakistani, Iraqi, an Afghan, or anything in between because of the lighter hue of his skin. When he spoke, he had a faint accent that sounded like someone educated abroad, probably in Britain. As I sized him up, he was obviously also sizing me up. Suddenly, I felt embarrassed. He had seen more of me than was decorous, even given the circumstances. But what were these circumstances anyway? I had come to be used as a sex object in a liaison that would end come morning or even before. I had not come to have a talk as if we were attending some English tea party.

"Fair enough" he repeated. "Now tell me what you would like to know."

"To begin with" I said, mustering all the courage I had, "Who are you and what do you want of me? How do I know you are not on a fact-finding mission which will get me punished by Ummi?"

And like that, we spent the whole night talking, just talking! He said his father was Egyptian, and his mother Jordanian. He

Dust and Ashes

was born in Alexandria but grew up in Aswan. He had done his post-secondary education in Britain and then worked in France and Britain for a few years before coming back to Egypt. He worked with a newspaper at Cairo, and at the same time was an international correspondent for a magazine based in New York. I asked him what he was doing in our camp then. He said that a friend had invited him for a Ramadan entertainment. Since he had nothing better to do he had come along. His curiosity had been aroused by the mass marriage. Even though he had been reluctant to participate at first, he saw the opportunity for a story and decided to interview whoever he was married to, and that was me. When I asked him if he was not married, he hesitated fractionally and then answered, "At the moment no, although technically speaking, I am married to you now. I was betrothed to a girl when I was a child but by the time I came back from Britain, the girl's family was having second thoughts. While I was in France, they returned her dowry to my family and told my father she had married someone else. When I was in France I also had a temporary marriage arrangement so I could decently share an apartment with two girls from Iraq. So yes, I have been married."

Qasim avoided specifics in answering many of my questions. He asked me to understand it was for security reasons. He told me he had three siblings but would not elaborate on whether they were brothers or sisters, older or younger. He just said that two of them were married with children and one was married without children yet, and so he had enough nephews and nieces to keep him occupied. On my part, I opened up to him and tried to be as specific as possible. I had the general hope that if it ever came up in conversation anywhere, my parents might hear, wonder, and hopefully be comforted. I told him a bit about my background, about my parents, siblings, grandparents, and cousins, especially Miriam. I told him how we had been kidnapped on our way to school two years before and how the other girls that were in camp with me all had similar stories. I told him how we thought we were entertaining just the soldiers of Jihad, not knowing the rest of the public were also involved at whim. I wondered how this could have made any possible difference.

I also told him about the special girls who were hired out for such high class entertainment. There was a lot to tell. We talked away the night. The tent was on the fringes enough that we did not hear the sounds from the other tents and hopefully disturbed no one by our conversation. As the call before the call to Morning Prayers began, I started summarizing frantically, knowing what was soon to happen. Even as I talked, we heard Ummi at the next tent brokering the divorce.

"Quick" said Qasim, "squat in that corner and don't say a word."

Even as I obeyed, I saw that Qasim had pulled off his tee shirt, loosed his belt and drawn his trouser low on his waist, looking for all the world as if he had been going at it the whole night. And he was just on time too. Ummi called out and then just entered the tent without waiting. She took in the scene at a glance and then turning to face Qasim she said "It's time for you to divorce the girl."

"O!" answered Qasim, "but I am not done with her yet. In fact, I want to keep her for the rest of the week. I understand I can even take her out of the camp."

"That is not how we do things here. If you want to have more time, there are other girls for that."

"But this is the one I want. I am already used to her. She pleases me well enough!"

Dust and Ashes

Ummi took a closer look at me. I just squatted in the corner, huddled in my robes, with my head bowed. I was praying for God's will to be done. She snorted. "Briska? I doubt if you will find this one totally pleasing. On the other hand, we have some girls who are specially groomed…"

And then Qasim's voice hardened. I stole a look at his face and saw him totally transformed. Whereas I had seen him as kind and benign, the man I saw now was hard-chiseled, authoritative, cruel, even bothering on the insane. His voice took on a sharp edge which seemed to cut the air in front of Ummi's face. It was like *Dr. Jekyll and Mr. Hyde*. "I say this is the girl I want. Would you want me to take this up with Mukhtar?"

I had no idea who Mukhtar was or what authority he had but either Qasim's words or his demeanor carried through to Ummi. "Very well," she said in an uncharacteristically meek voice. "We shall have it arranged. You can have her for the rest of the week."

"In fact" Qasim continued, "I am staying over at Mehmet's place for the rest of the week. I want her sent there."

"Okay. We shall get her ready." With that Ummi hurried away. She was already delayed in her rounds of brokering divorces.

As she left, Qasim turned to me and in that moment his face, his stance, his whole personality seemed to undergo another transformation. It occurred to me to wonder which one was his real personality, the one he showed to me or the one he showed to Ummi. He frightened me more than just a little but if I ever came close to really falling in love ever in my life up till then, this was it. All the infatuations we had as school girls in that other long ago life quite paled beside it.

"So" he now said, "we seem to have won a minor victory."

He dressed up again and left to join the other men in Morning Prayers while I was left in the tent not knowing what to do next. About thirty minutes later, Ummi came back with two other women. They had a medium-sized cellophane bag with them. She made me undress while they watched. Of course this simply involved pulling off my rough cotton robe. I would have liked to retrieve the things I had hidden in the secret pouches of the robe but I dared not do that while they were all looking on. She then brought out a similar robe from the bag they had come with and asked me to dress in it. This second robe was soft and silky and clung snugly to my body. There was also a separate lacy veil like Ameena and Beeba had. Now I belonged to the Classy Girls group. When Ummi's team had me fold up my discarded robe and put in the empty cellophane bag, I nursed the hope they would allow me go with it as a spare but this was not to be. They took it away with them. Ummi then gave me a brief lecture on what to do and what not to do while I was away from camp. I frankly heard nothing of all she said. I was wondering how to let the rest of the girls know that I was alright, and to give them a hint of this new adventure I was embarking on.

I thought we were going to wait in the tent for Qasim to come back from prayers to collect me but that was not what happened. As soon as Ummi concluded her lectures, I was hurried to a waiting car and made to get in behind the driver. To this day, Mike marvels at the fact that I did not know the model and make of the car I went in. All I could tell him was that it was a four-door sedan with a soft velvet interior, colored black on the outside and light grey on the inside. What did I know or care about cars?

There was no one else in the car. As soon as I got in, the driver started towards the minarets. We did not speak any word to each other, not even in greeting. I had never been to Cairo before but the signposts confirmed that indeed we were in the suburbs of the great city. Before we got into the city however, the car veered off the highway and we soon came to a luxurious hotel complex in a fairly built-up neighborhood. It was not yet broad daylight but it was already looking as if it would be another quiet Ramadan day. The car drove towards the back and I did not have time to catch a glimpse of the name of the hotel. As soon as it came to a complete stop, a man erupted from the doorway, cussing and almost hitting the driver. "Why didn't you blindfold her or at least make her lie down on the floor of the car? How can you bring her here just like that?"

In a frightened voice the driver answered, "I was not told to do any of those."

"Must you be told how to do everything? Don't you know how important these things are?"

Understanding the situation, I put my head back on the seat, closed my eyes and pretended to be asleep. This ruse helped because the next thing I knew the angry voice was almost in my ears as its owner bent down to look into the car. "Thank your stars at least that she is asleep. Don't ever make that kind of mistake again."

So saying, he shook me "awake", made me come out of the car and proceeded to blindfold me with a piece of cloth. I meekly allowed myself to be led into the doorway, up two flights of stairs and when we came into a room, my blindfold was taken off. He told me to wait there. It was a moderately large room with a big bed in the center. There were also an armchair, a desk, and a straight-backed chair in the corners. Two other doors opened off the sides of the room. The floor was covered by a thick Afghan rug. This was indeed a luxurious hotel.

Al Kalima

After standing near the door where I had been left for some time, I decided to explore. Moving away from the door I had come through, I moved to the one close to the head of the bed. It opened into a closet which was almost empty. A few shirts and trousers hung there, with a prayer mat and a briefcase on the floor beneath the clothes. I surmised these were Qasim's possessions. The other door led into a bathroom with a sparkling tub and a toilet bowl. There was also a wall to wall mirror. I surveyed myself in the mirror and then turned on the water. It was running! It was really running! I sat down on the bathroom floor and began to weep. I never imagined that I would ever see such luxuries again. It seemed like it was in another age that I had taken these simple comforts for granted. There was also a small window in the bathroom but it was quite high up. It had panes which made it even smaller. I could not possibly squeeze through there. However I noticed these only by the second or the third day.

The long night I spent awake must have taken its toll on me and I must have fallen asleep in the bathroom. The next thing I was aware of was the same irate voice which had berated the driver now sounding so syrupy and ingratiating. It was saying, "We put her in your room Sir. I hope that is okay. We locked the door from the outside, not knowing what you would want us to do, Sir."

And then Qasim's voice answered, "That is okay Hassan. You did the right thing. Thank you. I will take it from here."

I had not known I was locked in although that sounded very sensible. The key grated in the lock. A few seconds later, Qasim called out, "Sara! Sara! Where are you?"

I had forgotten my assumed name but then Qasim opened the bathroom door and said, "There you are! I'm glad they brought you over after all." He was dressed formally in suit and explained that he was on his way to work. He wanted to check that everything was okay with me.

"Where did you go to get ready?" I asked.

"I have a flat some distance from here. That is where I live. This place is like a bachelor pad which I come to when I am just in need of an escape. The hotel belongs to a friend of mine. Some of us get together here from time to time." That certainly explained a lot of things. He continued, "You will be okay here while I work, I hope. They will always keep the room locked though." He added this last bit as a matter of fact but also somewhat apologetically. "Is there anything you would like me to get for you?"

"I wondered if you could perhaps get me something to read" I asked.

He opened his briefcase and brought out two of the day's newspaper. "I'm sorry this is all I have as reading material now. I promise I'll bring more for you in the evening, okay?"

I was happy with this. "Please, can you also get me back editions?"

"Okay. I'll do that too. Would you like some novels as well?"

I could not immediately think of any novels I would like to read or reread. "Bring magazines instead" I requested. "I'd like Egyptian and foreign magazines please."

He left. I read those newspapers very thoroughly. I even read the cartoons, the advertisements, and the publisher's information. By the time I was reading them the fourth or fifth time I remembered my father and his daily habit with newspapers. I wondered if at that very moment he was reading the same newspapers I was. Filled with nostalgia I began to weep. I wept myself to sleep across the big bed. I was out to the world until Qasim was shaking me by the shoulders.

My days with Qasim became set into a pattern. He would sit in the armchair or stretch out on the thick carpet in front of the chair and I would recline or sit up in the big soft bed. We hardly slept at all at night but spent the whole time just talking. He always left as soon as Morning Prayers were called and went to work from his flat. I wondered when he slept but he assured me that being that the volume of work and office hours were reduced due to the Ramadan, he usually went straight home from his office to sleep before coming to the hotel. On my part, I spent the first part of the day poring over whatever materials he had brought back the previous day and then caught up on sleep for the second part before he came in the evening. Once I saw what might have been his real name on one of the papers but I never asked him about it so I never knew for sure. When he came in the evenings, he would bring food and I found myself tasting again the luxuries of bygone days. He brought deliciously spiced *koshari* with meat, ice cream, and even Coca Cola!

He would sometimes shower in the hotel bathroom, and then we would switch off all the lights except the bedside lamp. We left the rest of the world to wonder at what must be going on behind the locked doors and the drawn drapes. He would then tell me what happened at work and what was happening in the wider world. I would ask him questions about what I was reading. He said I had an incisive and analytical mind and would have made an excellent journalist. I told him that was what I had always wanted to be. Nobody ever disturbed us or tried to find out what we did all night, or what I did after he locked me in and left every morning. Not even once did he demand sex. I do not know what I would have done if he had. To all intents and purposes we were married, even if it was by Islamic rites. He was very kind and generous, and I liked him a lot! If I could do it with all those brutal men, how much more with this one with whom I was already half in love with anyway? But Qasim never asked, and this made me respect him even more.

In spite of it all, Qasim always had this air of wariness which seemed to roll off him like a huge burden once the main lights were off. One day he let me into his deepest secret. "Everyone sees me as the Playboy of Cairo, one of the most eligible bachelors, and growing older all the time. I do my best to live up to the image but the truth is that I actually lead a double, or maybe even a triple life. On the one hand, I have to be seen as an objective journalist. At the same time I am also a secretly committed member of a fundamentalist Islamic society. In another life, I am actually happily, if not contentedly married. All three lives must not mix or I will be destroyed, along with a lot of people for whom I care deeply."

Leaving out her name, he told me his wife was American. They had met during one of his trips to Britain. Taking a break at Cornwall where she was nursing her sick mother, they had fallen in love and been married there secretly. "We have two children now aged five and three. Thrice now, while I was out of the country I have seen them by some circuitous routes."

And then without even realizing it, her name slipped out. "It is no kind of life to be content with but Lisa is a unique woman with a very strong character and a steel backbone" he said. "She keeps telling me a half loaf is better than nothing at all. To her, she is glad to know she has me somewhere than not at all in her life. Yet my heart wrenches in my chest and I die a little more each time I have to re-introduce myself to my children and then disappear again a few days later; each time I hold Lisa and then have to say goodbye again; each time I catch a fleeting glimpse of what our life could have been.

Nobody else in my life knows of their existence or they would be in danger too. My parents are always trying to marry me off and get some more grandchildren. They don't know this set of grandchildren. My children do not know the joy of being doted on by such wonderful grandparents. Think of how I could have been proudly showing them off, doing useful family activities with them, and creating lasting memories. I see families like that and I envy them so much.

"I have tried but I cannot just be unfaithful to my wife. And so, my image is just that, an image. I found out it does not take a lot to uphold it especially since people want to believe it anyway. Even this liaison I have with you now will go out to the tabloids to enhance that image but it is so untrue!"

As the one week drew to a close, I wondered what would happen next. Should I grab the opportunity and attempt to escape like we had always discussed at camp? That was what Memuna had strenuously emphasized even as she drew her last breath. Should I ask Qasim to help me escape by looking the other way or even by providing the means, the transportation, or at least the connections? I had some relatives in Cairo but I was not sure of how to get to them. I did not even know the last names some of them used. On the sixth day, I let him broach the subject by himself but that very afternoon before he returned from work, I had the second of those my dream-wake visions.

Again, I was not fully awake but I was sure I was not asleep either. I was languidly looking at a shaft of evening light which showed through the drapes and thinking of pulling myself out of bed to the bathroom. The shaft of light seemed to grow in intensity and then suddenly turned dark as if there was a dust storm brewing. I felt myself floating up to the ceiling but the scene I was gazing at from above was not the luxurious hotel suite. Instead, I was in a sprawling camp in the desert and there

Dust and Ashes

were hundreds of girls milling about. It did not look like any of the camps I had been in so far. The biggest difference in this camp was that there were children running around, lots and lots of children, toddlers actually. The girls were busily engaged in different activities. Some were cooking, washing, attending the children, and so on. None of them, not even one person among them, looked happy. There were hundreds of them, and not one happy person! How I came about this number, I did not quite understand but what I saw were hundreds of girls. And then a voice spoke in my heart, "There is still much work for you to do!" Abruptly I woke up and found myself on the bed again. I was panting and felt disoriented but I was not confused at all about the meaning of this vision. The bottom line was that God did not want me to escape at this time. There was still much to be done. If I had enough presence of mind like Asibi, I should have asked questions like when, how, and so on but I did not. I was very sure of the meaning of the vision however, and with that I was content.

That evening as Qasim showered and changed, I laid out the things he had brought. He had visited the American canteen close to his workplace and brought hamburgers, packaged Cole slaw, ice cream, and a peculiar-looking meat pie. There were also some large bottles of Coca Cola. There was even a large package of a whole roasted chicken wrapped in an aluminum foil. It was quite a feast, even larger than was usual for the past few days. We usually ate as much as we could and then I would wrap up the rest and put away to nibble at while he was at work the following day but the following day was the *Eid*. It was a feast day to end the long days of fasting. If all went according to plan, this was also the day I was to return to camp.

I could see Qasim was very uncomfortable. He barely nibbled at his food. I waited for him to unburden his mind but

Al Kalima

he just could not get round to it. He did not recognize it but it was a basic character flaw which he had. That was why his life was in the mess it was. He took great risks all the time but he could not settle down to an ultimate risk that would make him say like Esther in the Bible, "if I die, I die!" He kept fidgeting and worrying his ankles with his feet.

At last I decided to help him out. "Something has been on your mind Qasim. Spill it out so we can have a peaceful last evening together."

He looked as if he wanted to deny that anything was on his mind but he must have seen something in my countenance that made him decide to level with me. "These last few days with you have been really blissful, Sara" he began. He still insisted on calling me Sara even though I had told him my real name. Ummi had mentioned my name in his hearing as well. I guess it was another form of denial to him. He needed such little things to keep things in focus in his convoluted thinking. "The most I can do is to offer you a way of escape. I have thought about it a lot. I could tell them that I wanted to keep you after all, pretend to travel with you to Damanhur, let down my guards and then allow you make your escape. That has seemed the most plausible plan to me so far." He paused but I was not letting him off the hook that easily and so I interjected "But…"

"I know that I am constantly under surveillance. Someone is always looking into my affairs to see if I am what I claim to be and you know I am far from that. I am always so close to being found out. If I followed that plan, as soon as I let you escape, the Islamic society is going to dig up anyone connected to me and make them pay for it in order to get back at me. The entire network I have painstakingly built up and worked for in the last two decades will not just collapse around me, it will explode with very dire consequences for everyone including you, the

Dust and Ashes

remaining girls at the camp, and probably also for your family." He would not look up. He would not meet my eyes. At last he said miserably, "I am sorry, Sara. I cannot just do it now. This is not just the right time. I am so sorry."

I took pity on him then and said, "I don't think this is the right time for me to escape either, Qasim. I owe it to the other girls to get back to them. If we ever escape, it would be nice if we could all do so together. Besides, I have a lot of unfinished business there still. But have you considered that you are as much of a captive as I am? Perhaps you are even more so because at least I have a cause. I believe in what I am fighting for but you have no cause that you are really living for. You have nothing that you consider worth dying for. You need to be freed from yourself above everything else. You know, Jesus said that you shall know the truth and the truth shall make you free. Do you know the Truth Qasim?"

I did not know where that one came from but I had ceased to be amazed at God. I had asked Him to use me and He let His word come up in me at unexpected times. I had spent nothing less than a hundred hours chatting with Qasim but we had never seriously talked of my faith and Whom I believed in until that night. With this opening I simply shared with him the reason for the hope I had, and which could be his as well. "That is the liberating Truth so even though I am in bondage, I am freer than my captors. It is a faith worth living for, Qasim, and also worth dying for."

Did I lead Qasim to Christ that night? Did I make any spiritual impact? Did I sow a seed which someone could water and maybe another person harvest someday? Did I water a seed which someone, somewhere had already sown? I really do not know the answer to any of these questions. I think I certainly led him closer to Christ that night. He made no verbal

Al Kalima

response at all. He had politely listened, and not interrupted me at all while I talked, not even by a nod or a shake of his head. At the end of my considerable monologue, he had an intense thoughtful look on his face.

When it was settled that I did not mind returning to camp the next day, we then freely discussed what he could do for me in lieu of helping me escape. We discussed what we could do, not if, but when we finally managed to escape. Qasim was up and coming with so many good ideas. "The first thing you should start doing is organizing a hoard otherwise you will escape from your captors and end up perishing in the desert, or worse still, recaptured by other people. You need to have contingency plans. Look for opportunities and be ready to seize the bull by the horn whenever the opportunity presents itself. If you ever have the opportunity, try not to escape alone. One person alone has almost no chance at all of survival. Believe me, this country is very hostile now to a lone wolf, not to talk of a lone vixen." His humor and the truth of the matter were not lost on me.

"On the other hand too, it might not be wise for more than a few people to escape at a time. Think of maybe groups of twos and threes. A larger group is more noticeable and easier to spot and recapture. A large group will always contain a weak person who will be drawing the others back. You must also consider that whenever anyone escapes, security will become tighter. The conditions will probably worsen for those who are remaining. Finally, there is always the chance that an escape bid would not succeed but never give up without trying."

He then told me what I have since considered a guiding principle in my life up till now, even spiritually. "Remember" said Qasim, "the best way to blindside your enemy is to keep him distracted from what you really intend to do. It works all the time even in the most organized and intelligent of units!"

Since then, I have used it on my opponents. I have also studied how the Enemy uses it on me. No matter how vigilant we are, we can all be blindsided and distracted at some point or the other in our lives. Qasim talked about this when we discussed how we may accumulate the hoard of money or food that would finally enable us escape. I told him we were only allowed to own one robe each, and the menstrual rags for our monthly menses. We had no way of saving up money or accumulating the needed resources. That was when he made the statement and then he added, "Use your imaginations. I am sure when you put your imaginations to work you will surely come up with something. Only remember to distract your enemy."

As a final concession to not aiding in my escape, he agreed that if I wrote a letter to my parents, he would find a way of getting it to them. This was a golden opportunity. Qasim had sheaves of plain paper in his briefcase. I sat down at that hotel desk to compose my letter. I had so much that I wanted to tell them. The whole night would not be enough to tell them half of it and it was already past midnight when I sat down to begin. However before I put pen to paper Qasim's voice intruded into my opening thoughts. "You know receiving the letter would spark a reopening of investigations into your kidnapping so you had better keep it as cryptic as possible."

He did not say more but I could imagine the end of the statement "…otherwise the letter will not reach them at all."

This was just as well because my first sentence after letting them know I was still alive was to tell them that for the past two years, we had spent Ramadan at a camp close to Cairo. Qasim said this would not do at all. Finally, after several drafts and redrafts, with Qasim telling me what to scratch out, what not

Al Kalima

to include, or even hint at in any way, I came up with a single page letter which sounded like, "*Dear Mum and Dad, a friend is allowing me to write this letter. This friend promises it will surely get to you. Of the nineteen of us who were kidnapped on our way to school, Sara is dead. We believe Rawya is dead too. She was taken away from us following an injury and she was then more dead than alive. She was never returned to us. We met so many other kidnapped girls in camp. Memuna Abdul from Asyut is dead also. Please let her parents know if you are able to. God is using me in camp here and many of the girls are repenting and being baptized. Please pray for us. We will keep looking for a way of returning to you. Much love, Priscilla.*"

Qasim had me remove all references to a Moslem camp, forced marriages or even how Memuna died in childbirth. Anything that could help a search, investigation of, or the identification of our real captors or similar groups was censored. At the end I felt I had said practically nothing in the letter other than to let my parents know that I was still alive. In fact, the letter sounded as if we had been kidnapped and were being held captive by one Christian sect which was forcing all of us to get baptized. It sounded as if we were enjoying our captivity too. I read it over and over. I comforted myself that at least, since it had passed censor, it would definitely be sent. I prayed they would read between the lines, understand, and more importantly pray for us.

Before the call to Morning Prayers was made, we could hear people already moving about. Wafts of delicious food aromas filled the air. Today was the *Eid*, the great feast to end the long days of Ramadan. Qasim did not go to work that day because it was a holiday. He went to visit his parents instead and returned in the afternoon with a large basket. Inside it was a very large tureen with delicious smells, two long loaves of

Dust and Ashes

bread, and a length of silk. Tongue in his cheek he explained, "The basket and the content are for Ummi. That is your 'dowry' for her letting me have you for this one week. In actual fact, it's the distraction I'm teaching you about." To me he presented a fanciful bangle, a necklace, and another length of silk. He also predicted that Ummi would take all of these at once. "Now this is my real gift to you." He then gave me a packet of stainless steel sewing needles which I had once mentioned would be a real asset in camp. And then he brought out a five pound note!

The denomination was still new in Egypt. I had never even seen one before then. I had read of its introduction to the country in some of the magazines and old newspapers Qasim had brought me. I had seen a colored picture of it but here was the real thing being offered to me! Five pounds was a lot of money in those days. We had never discussed how rich Qasim was or how much he earned but this was a lot of money to me who had exactly nothing at the time. Accepting it seemed somehow indecent to me and I hesitated. Seeming to read my thoughts, Qasim said, "It's not payment for your services or anything like that, Sara. I must say though that these few days have been not just very pleasant but probably the most refreshing time I have had in a very long time. You did me more service than you will ever know. You certainly put my life in perspective and I will definitely make a lot of changes in my life from this point on. We might never meet again but I want to be the first to contribute to your escape bid. Regard this money as your first step towards the escape which I could not get for you."

Put that way, I saw the money differently. It was more of a guilt offering. I began to think of what it could accomplish but Qasim had not finished. He showed me how to conceal the money. That man had a lot of imagination! Later, back at the camp, when I taught the girls how to steal, I used a lot of the lessons Qasim taught me that last afternoon we spent together. As dusk approached, Qasim embraced me. It was for the first, and the only time. It was a tight, desperate hug, so full of meanings that I could not decipher all at once. "Thank you, Briska" he said, using my real name for the very first time too, "Thank you." I could have sworn there was moisture in his eyes. He then picked up his briefcase and left. "Hassan will come for you" were the last words he said to me as he again locked me inside the hotel room and went out of my life forever.

Hassan, the angry man at the door came for me. I carried the heavy basket and went down the stairs after him. At the car, they again installed me behind the driver, gave me a blindfold to put on by myself, and drove me back. We went through noisy city celebrations. The noise receded as we reached the outskirts of town, and almost totally disappeared by the time we got to the camp. I removed my blindfold and gave it to the driver who leered at me knowingly. I refused to meet his eyes a second time.

It was as if Ummi was waiting for me at the door. She received the basket and ordered me to remove the silken robe immediately. I changed back into my previous coarse cotton robe while she and her assistants watched. Apparently my former robe had never been taken from the cellophane bag since the day I put it there. It had a musty odor but I was glad she had not searched it nor had it washed. In a certain attached pouch were the letters of Paul to the Philippians, Colossians and Ephesians. Just as Qasim had predicted, Ummi had shaken the robe I returned to be sure nothing was hidden in it. She did not order nor perform a body search. She took everything Qasim had given to me, including the ones which were ostensibly meant for me. Then, and only then was I allowed to join the other girls.

It was a joyful reunion as if I was returning from the dead or from an exotic tour as indeed I was, in a way. I recounted my tepid adventures to them and showed them the things that Ummi had missed. Taped to the inner side of my right thigh was the packet of needles. When I shook out my hair, out fell the new five pound note which was a real novelty for those of us who had been in captivity for over two years. They were all truly awed!

PREGNANT

The Ramadan camp broke up some two weeks after I returned. In the relative quiet which followed the *Eid*, I taught them what I had learned from Qasim. We also maximized our Bible teaching more effectively and got to know one another better. Many people were baptized including some of the older women that worked in the kitchen. We daubed them Bashra's disciples. Our movement became less secretive even though some of the diehard Moslem girls criticized our God as being impotent rather than omnipotent. "If he was as powerful as you say" they challenged, "why does he let you keep living in this terrible bondage?"

I never let myself be drawn into this kind of a debate but when it is a frank discussion I share with them again the assurance I had from God. With my last vision when I had actually thought of escaping, I was more assured this was where He wanted me to be for the moment. Some mocked us openly. Some snickered derisively, but politely. Quite a number went away thoughtfully.

Not everybody had my kind of inhibition, however. The previously-Moslem girls who had joined our movement were more vocal in their rebuttal of such challenges. Once I heard Hoda challenge one of the skeptics, "Okay, let us say He is impotent. How potent is your own Allah? He cannot even fight his own battles by himself. He has to employ such nefarious means like enslaving unwilling girls for the gratification of his soldiers!"

The only problem with such answers is that it sometimes caused a battle to ensue. Such battles were very often in words, but sometimes with blows and scratches. These would result in bumps and bruises which were not always easy to treat. I saw myself emerging as the leader who had to settle both sides. I sometimes resorted to salient quotations from the Bible such as "The servant of God must not strife", or "Leave vengeance to God". One could have said that I grew very mature in leaps and bounds. That was until my own trials came upon me!

When camp broke up, we found ourselves reshuffled again. This time I saw myself with Bashra, Zafya, Yasmeen, and a lot of other girls whom I met that second Ramadan for the very first time. Only Khadija from our original group came with my section. Seeing the remarkable resemblance between Hanan and Nadia, Ummi "promoted" them to the rank of the special girls. They were to work together. We understood that some men found this exciting. Asibi was in another camp with Ester and Jehan. The rest were all scattered. For my section, further good news was that Ummi was not in charge. She had developed a fierce dislike for me, especially after the Qasim incident.

As we broke camp and parted ways, we wondered if we would ever meet again. In anticipation of this sort of dispersal we had encouraged one another to be strong in the Lord and to never stop seeking a way of escape. I reminded them over and over about gathering and hoarding up loot against the day of escape. The packet of needles I had brought back had forty-eight pieces in it. We shared them all out. Asibi showed us how to sew secret pouches to our robes using pulled strips of thread from our robes and from our menstrual rags.

Chalk it up to the relaxed atmosphere, or to the good food I had eaten while with Qasim. For the first few months after Ramadan, my periods became regular. I became like those girls who could almost predict their periods by the fullness of the moon. The good thing about this was that while on my period, there would be no marriages until after I was purified.

After two months of this wonderful regularity however, I started feeling sick. The sight and smell of food nauseated me. I was not feverish nor vomiting even though I managed to just hold back on a few occasions. Originally slender, I began to lose weight to the point that even the kitchen women commented on it. Asibi was not there this time to give me the diagnosis. I arrived at it all by myself when I counted and noticed my period had been delayed by at least a month.

That was when I finally broke down. I, who had seemed to have all the answers... I, who had held it all together when the other girls went through their own crises..., I! I...

I did not want to be pregnant. It was enough that my body had been raped, abused, and violated. Why should I have a reminder of it? All the sermons I had preached to the other girls, all the encouragements I had given to Ester, Khadija, and Memuna came back to haunt me. None of these helped at all. Later in life, Mike taught me something about the stages of grief. I went through all of them: anger, denial, bargaining, depression, and finally acceptance.

Dust and Ashes

I was angry at myself for having a body which could get pregnant. I was angry at the men who raped me day after day. I was angry at the women who arranged for this to happen. I was angry at my co-captives for not being pregnant themselves. I was angry at them for pretending to understand what I was going through. I was angry at my parents for not looking hard enough to find me. Most of all I was angry at God! Was He asleep while all this was happening to me? Where was His promise to ALWAYS answer my prayers? Where was the joy in believing in Him? Where were all those miraculous events we read about in the Bible and even in the lives of contemporary Christians of wonderful and miraculous last minute deliverances and rescues? Why were we not seeing our signs? Did we not believe tenaciously enough even in the midst of all the difficulties we had faced so far? Was our faith not of a high enough quality? Had we not been through enough already? Why would God not give us any respite?

I went through denial. I refused to accept what my body was telling me. In the past, my periods had come eventually. Maybe this was a prolonged, prolonged delay. Maybe I had the flu or something like that. I continued to wear a menstrual rag every day, expecting my period to start unexpectedly. For almost a month there were no soldiers to service. By the time there were, I was so obviously sick that I was not pressed into service. Maybe if I was, I could have had a natural miscarriage as per Jehan's theory. I felt it was all so unfair.

And then I began to bargain with God. I reminded Him of all I was doing in His service. Would it not be inconvenient for me to become pregnant and have a baby at this time? I asked Him to somehow let me miscarry. If I did then I would double the energy I was investing in His service already. I must have spent a lot of time in prayers those days. Deep into the night, long after the other girls were softly snoring or whimpering in their sleeps, I would still be awake begging God to "Let this cup pass over me."

When it looked as if I was not going to get an answer to these prayers I became severely depressed. With my appetite already gone anyway, I would spend hours crying and praying. I tried to do this in private but somehow my mood seemed to affect all the girls. They tried to console me. Inevitably they used the same words I had used in the past especially to Memuna. I tried to be brave and smile at them but my very effort at smiling would cause even the most stoic of them to burst into tears, and then we would all weep together. In those days we spent quite some time in communal weeping more than we had ever done, even counting the early days of our captivity. Looking back now, it was all very funny in a sad kind of way.

This pit of depression must have lasted for about two weeks. Suddenly, one day God himself snapped me out of it. This time it was not another surreal dream or vision. I could have sworn that I audibly heard the voice of God. We had just endured another week of marriages and divorces and were allowed back to our dormitory after our purification baths. I was lying on a mat in the dormitory feeling listless and letting the tears slip down the corners of my eyes. I indulged in a feast of self-pity. I wondered why I had not seduced Qasim outright. At least if I had, I would have known or imagined that the father of my baby was an honorable man, someone who at least knew my name. Now, I could frankly not tell who the father of this baby was. I had no idea how he looked, how he thought, whether he was one of the nicer ones or one of the very brutal ones.

That afternoon, some of the girls were chatting while making pouches for their robes but the general mood was suppressed

Dust and Ashes

and gloomy. Suddenly, God said to me, "When are you going to snap out of this diet of self-pity?"

I was startled. I knew for sure who was addressing me. Before I could pull myself together to even decide whether it was my imagination playing tricks on me or not He went on. "So when you vow that you would give your all for my service it was only as far as it was at your own convenience, showed you in glowing lights and did not include some specific aspects of your life which you don't want me to touch? Have you considered this could all be part of my plan? When did you stop trusting me? When did you fancy that you could make a better plan than me? Since when did you make yourself my deputy to act when I am unable or indisposed? What sapped my strength? Answer me!!!"

I was dumbfounded. I knew then how Job must have felt towards the end of his ordeal. He too had complained that God was not answering him. And then God decided to answer him after all! He had then bombarded Job nonstop with questions which the poor man had no chance or hope of answering. He had not even attempted to answer any.

Like Job, I too was silent. I was covered in shame. I saw myself as I really was. I was mean, selfish, imperfect, whiny, groveling, condescending, hypocritical, arrogant, a dictator, and so on. What had I been teaching all these girls if I could not submit to God myself? Could I not personally trust God to know what was best for me; and that all things worked together for my own good? Could I not trust Him that nothing would happen to me by accident, any other person's choice, or the devil's design? If I could not trust Him, who was I to tell any other person otherwise?

I felt so ashamed and yet so liberated at the same time by the truth of this insight. I got up at that very moment and washed my face. From that point on, I began to find reasons to start accepting and being grateful for the condition I was in. I joined the other girls as they were sewing and reading the Bible. If they were surprised by my sudden transformation, they did not say so out loud. The general feeling was one of relief. They welcomed me back and tried to update me on everything as if I had been away on a long journey and was just returning. In a way this was indeed the case. Whatever happened, I was glad I was in the midst of friends who cared about me. This was my first baby step towards recovery so to say.

Khalifa was the leader of the camp I now belonged to. Unlike Ummi, she presented herself as very caring and gently assertive. She still saw to our marriages and divorces but in our hearing she would tell the men to "treat my girls kindly". Whenever possible, she would not allow more than one marriage per night. She took time to match fragile-looking girls to gentle-looking men. I never saw her lose her temper with any of the girls. Not so with the men, however! One day, Bashra came out looking battered by her erstwhile husband of the night. In our presence, Khalifa gave the man a thorough tongue lashing. "If I see this kind of thing again" she threatened, "if you ever abuse any of my girls like this again, I shall make sure Mukhtar hears about it. I will see to it that you receive forty lashes of the whip in public. Do I make myself clear?"

Our mouths were agape. It had been such a long time since anyone spoke up for us. We lapped up these crumbs of kindness like the Sahara desert sands soaked up rain. Even though we still remained slaves, kidnapped from our homes and held illegally against our wills and convenience, we began to feel that we belonged to someone who cared for us. If any of us looked or acted sick, Khalifa always showed concern. She tried to do something worthwhile, and as soon as possible, unlike

Dust and Ashes

Ummi. Even when there were no marriages, we still got to see her at least every other day. She would check that we were eating well, sleeping well, and so on. She knew of our underground Bible studies but did not confiscate our bits of the Bible. She allowed us take strings and threads from used sacks in the kitchen and asked the kitchen women to let us collect and keep empty plastic containers with which to store water for the night. Khalifa was too good to us, especially coming after Ummi.

Later in life, I would realize that sugar-coated evil was still evil nonetheless. As well-meaning as Khalifa seemed, we were still children kidnapped from loving homes. The common aim of our captors was not just to provide sexual entertainment for the soldiers (and sometimes the general public) but to also propagate children who would be used by the movement at a later stage, the baby girls for sex slavery, and the baby boys as cannon fodder. Children propagated this way were considered the property of the Jihad since the fathers were unknown. The mothers were mere slaves! Mike said that having practically no emotional attachments, they sometimes also lacked human feelings. They were indoctrinated and trained to undertake dangerous risks. They could blow themselves and others up in the cause of the Jihad.

Khalifa's sweeter approach got more results breeding babies than Ummi's combatant nature. It was just as honey more effectively attracted flies than vinegar. Khalifa had different and better techniques but both their aims were still exactly the same.

Khalifa took note of my condition almost as soon as I became sick. She asked what the matter was. When she heard I had not been eating my *koshari*, she asked Haleema, Asibi's counterpart for the camp, to make sure I got sugared tea from the kitchen until I could eat again. Haleema and Asibi were

Al Kalima

just longer-lasting slaves who acted as kind of housemothers or Big Sisters. I was also getting to be very good friends with Haleema as I was with Asibi. The tea from the kitchen was quite weak and more like sugared, colored water but it was such a luxury. For about a month, that, and the occasional mouthful of *koshari* was all that sustained me. For those few months, Khalifa observed me shrewdly. She would not let me be married to rough-looking men. She left me out of marriages altogether if it could be managed. This was another way in which she differed totally from Ummi. Once, she called me aside and tried to comfort me. "Things are not always as bad as they look. There is a saying that there is always some good in every bad thing; and some bad in every good thing. It might actually turn out that there would be a lot of good in this."

I was not greatly comforted at that time. However, just like Caiaphas at the time of Christ's betrayal and trial prophesied so accurately in his capacity as the ruling high priest, this woman's words held a lot of truth. She prophesied far beyond what she had imagined she was trying to communicate. Years later, Mike would tell me the same thing in other words. He said, "Things are never completely bleak. As the saying goes, there is always a silver lining to every cloud."

My depression passed when I was about three or four months pregnant. My appetite came back with a vengeance at about the same time. I was always volunteering for kitchen duties because then I could scrape and lick the pots and plates clean before washing them. We generally ate once a day between the normal hours for breakfast and lunch. When soldiers came, they ate twice a day. We were allowed to eat any of their leftovers before getting married to them. Working at the kitchen to clean up ensured this. Other times if one became friends with the kitchen women, one had access to a lot of leftover food, or food they put aside for some special reasons known only to themselves. This did not happen often, however. Of course there were incidences of thefts from the kitchen. We were really all growing children after all. In Ummi's camp, this could be punished by severe beating, but sometimes the basic drive of hunger overrode the fear of any beating. We tried very hard not to steal but once in a while, the *koshari* meant for the soldiers would inevitably diminish if left unattended.

Relatively tall and slender, I did not begin to show until I was into my sixth month. Now I got husbands who complained once in a while about how hard and lumpy I felt in the belly. A few naïve ones even assumed I was squirming when the baby moved. Back at the dormitory, we found the grace to laugh about these incidences. Technically in Islam, a woman was not supposed to be bedded if she was known to be carrying another man's child. However, in the sham marriage relationships we were into, who was to say whose child it was anyway? In any case the severe shortage of women caused that the holy verses and traditions had to necessarily be made to fit the prevailing situation.

Three of us were obviously pregnant by now. Two others were in the early stages. Those of us who were advanced enough were soon to be sent off to the camp of the mothers. I spent days preparing the girls for my soon departure. Unlike in the other camps where I had been, where there were some natural leaders, in this camp every other person seemed to me mediocre at best, even Khadija and Bashra. I fretted over this and frankly prayed about it until God asked me one day, "Whose flock are they anyway?"

I felt adequately rebuked. I was assuming that it was my own strength, my convictions, and my charisma that had been keeping them all along. This was pompous and hypocritical of me considering that if they had taken me at all seriously during my time of depression, they would all have dispersed a long time before. It was as if God had turned against me in those days. It seemed He was always harshly rebuking me. However those were perhaps the days I learned my most valuable lessons in captivity. Looking back now, I am very grateful for those days.

CAMP OF THE MOTHERS

But it was not all about rebukes. There were times I felt really close to God. I felt really cuddled by Him, just like my father cuddled me when I was still a little girl. One day, I was in that dreamy state, just before the call to Morning Prayers. I was feeling very languid and lax in all my limbs. And then I *felt* the voice of God again. "There is work ahead of you" He said. "You must not worry about this baby at all. Every baby is precious to me and this one even more so. You will have another Amira and she will NOT BE raised in captivity."

I was so reassured by this visitation that when Morning Prayers were eventually called I got up and excitedly announced to the girls, "I'm going to have a baby girl!"

There was still quite a number skeptics among us. The most cynical of these was Pasha. Pasha was a Moslem. She was not like any other opposition that I had known so far. She was neither belligerent nor openly critical. For every argument we advanced, she had some counter argument. She was very gentle in all her ways, and always maintained that our captors were

Al Kalima

not true Moslems. She always talked about how true and pure the Moslem Way was. Pasha maintained that Christians were the ones who were deluded and deceived. She even formed her own Moslem Fellowship and taught them from the Quran even as we tried to learn from the Bible. I believe it was because of her own Movement that Khalifa tolerated ours. When we resumed the habit of someone reading from the Bible while the rest of us sewed or knitted, Pasha insisted that those who did not want to listen to the reading of the Bible could gather around at the other end of the dormitory and listen to the reading of the Quran.

Pasha never denigrated Christianity. In fact she supported it but claimed that many of the things in the Bible were adjusted, misrepresented, misreported, or misinterpreted in translation. She had some staunch supporters. Many other girls vacillated between our two groups. The girls that went back and forth were always spoiling for Pasha and me to have a debate over our beliefs and convictions. I was not inclined to do this. In fact, I did my very best never to get into one. Quoting my grandfather Moussa, I always said, "The truth has a way of advertising itself; and the Holy Spirit is the one who gives light to the true seeker, not the clever words of any man."

This seemed very cowardly of me but I never had a strong desire to do otherwise. On the whole, everyone agreed that there were lots of similarities between the stories in the Bible and those in the Quran. The exception was that those in the Quran sounded more unrealistic and like touchups of the originals. Take for instance how Baby Jesus talked to defend himself from those who would have stoned his mother to death for adultery. The miraculous deliverance of Ishmael (not Isaac) from being sacrificed by Father Abraham was another dissension.

"Because" Pasha explained, "these stories have been modified by the British so they would sound more realistic but the Quran tells it as it was revealed to the prophet." That was an argument we had heard over and over before.

"But the Bible was not even written originally in English" Bashra refuted.

"And did you ever see the original Hebrew or Greek scripts?" Pasha asked. That was hitting below the belt for Bashra and some other girls like her in the camp. They had never read the Bible until this time in captivity. "The Quran on the other hand has always been in Arabic and no one can alter it" Pasha would continue. "The *Hadith* has it that someone once tried to add something to the revelation but he was exposed, punished, and damned for eternity. The Quran has never been altered but the Bible has been changed so many times especially in translation."

The *Hadith* were a collection of Moslem traditional lore of what the prophet or his close associates said or did. These were written down by those who heard and remembered them afterwards. The *Hadith* were kept as a supplement to the Quran. I am not an authority on these but there are different sources of, and different interpretations of these traditions. However, I always avoided public confrontations with Pasha. Later on, when there were no tensions, I explained to Bashra and the others that the Hebrews had even stricter checks and balances against alterations long before Christianity came to be, not to talk of Islam. Christianity, I explained again, was not a British religion but had also originated from the Middle East. If anything, the Egyptians had the old and the new testaments long before the English did. Our Coptic fathers had translated the Bible into our own language long before the English thought of translating it into their own language. How could it have been altered by the British?

In any case, the day I woke up and suddenly announced that God had told me I was going to have a baby girl, and her name was going to be Amira, my loudest critic was Pasha. "If that happens, I will start believing in your Jesus as God!" she said.

"I will remind you of what you said when the time comes" Yasmeen told her.

"O yes! And if it does not happen that way, you must stop believing in him!" Pasha rejoined.

"It will be a baby girl" Yasmeen assured her. "I believe that God said it to Briska. It will happen."

At other times perhaps I would have looked for ways to couch the situation in case it did not turn out exactly as expected. Unlike Zacharias and Mary in the Bible, or even Asibi in recent times, I had not thought to ask for a sign or clarification of understanding for my vision. If my baby turned out to be a boy, I had no leg to stand on and say, "O the Lord just assured me I was going to have a baby like Amira, He could have meant a baby boy and not necessarily a girl."

I could have said such things but I did not bother to do that. Deep in my heart I knew and understood exactly what the Lord had meant me to. Besides, the other girls, especially the Moslem converts to Christianity, had become infected with my happiness and assurance. I did not even need to talk or defend my stance. These other ardent believers talked on my behalf.

On the other hand, I subconsciously held back the rest of my conversation with God. If this baby was not to be raised in captivity, it meant that God had a plan for us to escape or be rescued. I was also reassured that this was indeed what He meant. Some instinct made me keep this bit to myself, at least for the time being. The day after this vision, we were moved to the camp of the mothers.

There were four of us who were obviously pregnant by this time, Pasha and I included. We reckoned that our pregnancies ranged from four months to six or seven months. One day, the four of us were woken up in the middle of the night and told to get into a mini bus. There we promptly fell asleep again. The bus drove throughout the night. Early the next morning when we were woken up and told to get out, we were at the camp of the mothers!

The camp was much larger than any other camps I had been in so far, even the Ramadan camp. The innermost compound was made up of eight long buildings arranged around a large rectangular courtyard. The two buildings which formed the shorter widths of the rectangle each opened to smaller compounds on either end. We soon came to discover that the outer compound was for the older women who were the administrators, organizers, officials or what-have-you of the camp. This area also housed "The Room". The Room was the labor room cum dispensary where the babies were delivered.

The smaller compound at the other end was the kitchen and sewage area at opposite ends. There were two water wells at both ends of the compound for the separate use of each of the facilities. The buildings themselves were limestone and wattle structures, interspersed with more modern concrete buildings. They all had small wooden window frames and shutters. When we got inside, we saw that they were all indeed long open dormitories with reed mats on the floor as in the other camps.

We arrived just before the call to Morning Prayers. As soon as we entered the outer court, prayers were called and people began to stir. By the time we were shown to our separate dormitories, the courtyard had turned into a veritable hive of activities. There were women calling out to one another, people going to the bathroom or some other assigned tasks, and babies crying! There were lots and lots of babies ranging in age from very newborns to about four-year old toddlers! I remembered the vision I had at Mehmet's hotel in the days of Qasim.

Having slept through the night, we were totally alert and curious about these new settings and the new people we were meeting. They were only a little less curious about us even though they knew what had brought us there. They were going through or had gone through it before us. We made some surprising re-acquaintances. There were people we had been with before in other camps. I rediscovered Bama and my cousin Miriam! Bama had delivered a baby girl who was then about nine months old. Miriam had a six month-old baby boy whom she had named Bitrus after her father. It was a joyful reunion. They shared with us their struggles with accepting the pregnancy, and their joy in the babies they then had.

"Labor was not a joke" Miriam said. "I've never experienced pain like that. The women who attend you only give you some foul-tasting brew and told you not to worry that the baby would soon come."

"The pain comes in waves. Just when you think it's over, another wave will start" Bama added. "And that is for a whole day or a whole night."

"Well, it's not really as bad as that the whole time" Miriam comforted us. "At first it comes like a stinging at your waist, or as if your bums are about to burst open. The most terrible pains are just towards the end when the baby is just about to come out."

"Speak for yourself, Miriam" Bama said. "From the first to the last I thought I was about to die with each pain."

"But you promptly forgot the pain once the baby was placed in your arms" Miriam countered.

We gazed at them with eyes made wide with curiosity and fear. The only delivery I had ever witnessed was Memuna's. She was unconscious most of the time and then she and her baby had died by the end of it. These descriptions were not just metaphorical in my imagination. My fear was real.

"Did the brew they gave you help you?" I asked.

"I refused to take it" Miriam said.

"I drank every last drop of it but I don't know that it helped me at all" Bama said.

"I think it helps a bit" said Fekria. Fekria was a new friend they had made in that camp. She was present at the discussion. "I took it and it did help with the thirst but I don't know that it helped with the pain."

Doria, yet another friend, told us, "From the screams that come from the place, I don't think many people are helped by the brew. Just go in armed with your faith. Believe that God will see you through, and He will."

This was comforting to me. I decided that when my time came, I was not going to take the brew. Eventually we got to know different angles to what went on in the Room, and what to expect when it would be our turn. This was a part of sex education which the barrier of civilization had not yet breached for us. Even if we had not been kidnapped, this was not what we would have known until we had our own first babies or if we had gone into nursing or a related course for a profession. In fact, traditionally, girls were prevented from watching or participating in the actual birth experience lest they became discouraged and decide never to become mothers. Men of course, were not supposed to participate in such things at all.

They went far away until it was all over and then they came to see their babies and to receive the congratulations.

There were over three hundred girls at that camp, besides their babies. Quite a number of us were still pregnant. The living arrangements were communal and very basic. Babies slept beside their mothers on their mats. Everyone's position was at least permanent while we were at the camp. One's allocated mat remained to one and her baby in their particular space amongst eighty or so other spaces in the dormitory. One could personalize her space with a decoration on the wall, the clothes on the mat, or the clothes piles by it. Apparently, we rated two robes here. The allocations made for each baby were three changes of clothes and half a dozen cloth napkins. Colorful lengths of cotton and old clothes were also brought into the camp from time to time. The women, for we could no longer be called girls, fought over who could get the best and the newest pieces. After all the fight and struggle, even the least aggressive still got some leftovers. From these we could make extra clothes for the children or pull threads from them to use for sewing. Nothing was ever wasted. When the supervising women were around, we were allowed the supervised use of two blunt pairs of scissor. We could be very creative. I have seen a beautiful multicolored frock made out of several pieces of rags. In time I managed to make a decorated pillowcase which I used for storing all the other clothes we were not wearing. I also used this as a pillow at night.

On the first day, we were given our two new robes and told we could do whatever we wanted with the old ones. After almost three years of continuous usage – sleeping, bathing, copulating in my robe, it was almost falling to pieces. That robe was more than just apparel to me. It had so many secret pouches in it and had also seen some patches of good time with me. I kept it and used it as a sheet on my mat. Remembering how useful the pieces of Rawya's robe had been, I decided it might come in useful someday. Apart from this though, it really was the only possession I had. I just could not bring myself to throw it away. We were told we would get the cloth napkins, baby clothes, and extra menstrual rags after we delivered our babies.

Supervising the use of the scissors was very, very necessary. Apparently some girls had tried to kill themselves or one another with the instrument before. Most of these happened while the girls were still pregnant. Apparently, a protective maternal instinct came upon everyone after labor. Even this was not universal. Some girls still tried to kill their babies after birth. About two weeks before we came, one of the girls had deliberately suffocated her week-old son. If a baby did not survive, the mother would be matched to another baby whose mother had died, if there was one. If there was no "spare baby", the mother was returned to the general circulation of wives, or more correctly, sex slaves.

With the limitation of clothes, laundry had to be done almost every day. There were many plastic buckets and basins for this but not nearly enough. Soap also, was a rare luxury. Again, battles were fought over the use of the few vessels. More often than not, it was the vessel which ended up ruined. Back at Hosh Issa, my grandmother despised plastic vessels as too expensive and not long-lasting enough. She would rather invest in cheaper clay vessels or better still in costlier but longer-lasting iron vessels. Miriam told me about the pieces of a clay pot that two girls used to seriously wound each other a few weeks before we arrived. Based on this tale, I could imagine how much damage a metal bucket would cause.

Fights broke out often over the use of these vessels, whose turn it was to use the buckets, use the basins, draw water from the well, and so on. Fights about the children also broke out from time to time. It was usually over whose child was trying to beat up another's among the mothers of the toddlers. People also fought over who stole whose laundry which was spread out to dry. These fights were just in addition to the usual fights over the rags that were given out from time to time, and the daily fight over food. It was quite a life!

That first day, I saw that the Christians met to pray and read the Bible together after supper before the compound settled down to sleep. Miriam, of course, was the leader. Counting Hami and I who came to join that very day, there were twenty-eight Christians in the camp. On the first day, we prayed that God would give us His grace to shine forth His light in the midst of the camp. I said additional prayers for myself concerning the vision which God had given me. "Please Lord, help me know where to start and how to proceed. I leave the results in Your hands. Help me not to be discouraged with the results that my eyes see."

I was allocated to the same dormitory as Miriam by chance but I knew God had a plan. The next night two of the girls closest to her quarreled with each other and did not want to stay near each other anymore. I offered to exchange places with one of them and she was more than willing to trade. This was how Miriam and I became neighbors. We spent the night catching up on what had been happening to us since we last saw each other almost two years before. We reminisced about home and what our beloveds must be doing. "They must have given up on us by now. They must believe we're dead."

"Maybe; but would they in their wildest imaginations, believe what we're going through now?"

"Will they believe there is a little boy in a captive Moslem camp named Bitrus?"

And then we were silent for a long while. At last I asked, "Are you asleep Miriam?"

"No" she answered and from the catch in her voice I could tell she had been weeping silently.

"Before she died, Memuna had a vision that we would one day escape from our captors and go home. Before we came here, God gave me a confirming vision."

There in the midst of the dormitory as people slumbered, I went on to tell her all about the vision as quietly as I could. She was silent until I finished, and then also for a while afterwards. Finally she said, "Briska you must not breathe a word of this to anyone, no one, until the time is right."

"So you believe me?" I asked.

"Every single word" she answered, "everything you said. However, like you said, there is work for us to do here before then."

I was so relieved to have now shared this vision with someone. Thereafter we spent night after night talking and praying and taking care of baby Bitrus.

MOTHERS AND BABIES

Motherhood! The very word evokes visions of love and softness; of tenderness and protectiveness. I know now that it is all of these and more! There are also pains and tears; bitterness, disappointments, and so on. I saw all of these in concentrated proportions in the camp of the mothers. I learned that a mother's protectiveness could be expressed in so many and amazingly sometimes contradictory ways. Mike has a favorite expression for how angry one's words or actions were. He would say the person became like a mother bear robbed of her cubs.

It was a very apt description. The same could also be said of a lioness robbed of her cubs, or a cow of her calves. I am most intimate with a hen robbed of her chicks or even feeling her chicks were threatened. At Hosh Issa, domestic animals were often not penned up. They were allowed to wander around the compounds and streets searching for food, as long as they returned to their owners' each night to roost. When we were about three and seven years old, Yohana and I saw some fluffy

Dust and Ashes

yellow chicks marching in line with their siblings behind their clucking mother. We tried to pick them up because they looked so cute and cuddly. Immediately, the mother hen turned around with the feathers around her neck puffed out. Her wings were also puffed out. She seemed to grow to a multiple times her original size. With what sounded to us like a vicious roar, she attacked Yohana and me. We let out howls and shrieks. We cried aloud in our distress. This brought our parents, grandparents, and every other adult and child in the house running to us all at once. They rescued us but both of us sustained painful scratches and bruises. From that day onward, we learned to respect hens and to keep our distance from cute chicks.

In the same way, Motherhood had the power to transform even the mildest mannered person into a vicious beast. Somehow these fights were something more than the fights for survival. Let a little child cry out in pain; immediately all the mothers who thought the cry was familiar would be in the area asking what happened. If the child's mother thought the child was being unfairly treated, she simply went to war, provoking the anger of another mother. Sometimes, other mothers joined the fight and before long it could be a one-for-all and all-for-one melee. This was somehow different from what we used to know at home. Back at Damanhur or even Hosh Issa, we all played together as children. Our mothers were protective too but they did not go batting for us without fairly judging an issue. In fact, one was likely to be disciplined by an adult who was not one's parents as an adult who was. In the event that discipline had to be meted out by one's own parents, it was likely to be harsher and so discipline by another adult was much more welcome.

In the camp of the mothers, it was not so. I attributed this mostly to mutual suspicion of one another. We did not know one another nor trust one another. Circumstances which were less than ideal had thrown us together. These circumstances were also amongst the harshest a human being should ever face. Again, I think the fact that we did not have much else to do was also responsible for the animosity which came through in our mothering of these children. Finally, these babies were about the only precious possessions we ever had, nothing else. They could neither compare to the rags we were given, nor the other little things we pilfered and hoarded. These were our only precious possessions and so we protected them with all the passion we had, the passion which we could not disperse to other things or in any other form.

Before my own baby was born, I shared Bitrus with Miriam. He was such a precious chubby fellow with a very cheerful disposition. He looked very much like Miriam's little brother. I understood the homesickness that made Miriam name him for her father. Miriam allowed me to bath him occasionally. He really loved being tickled in the tummy. He would kick his chubby legs and gurgle with laughter. I watched in fascination as Miriam breastfed him. I think our captors worked out that breastfeeding was not only cheap but was the best for the baby. All the girls hung on to the practice until the child was taken away. It was not unusual to see a three-year old toddler walking over to his or her mother to be cuddled and breastfed. Once every year, people came and "harvested" all the babies which were over three years old. That night there would be real wailing among the mothers until they were taken away the next day to go to join the general pool of wives again. For the distress this abrupt separation caused the mothers, one could only imagine what it did to the babies. With the resulting emotional trauma, one could also only imagine what they end up becoming later in life. Asibi had told me the boys would be trained to become

Jihad solders while the girls ended up becoming slave-wives as early as when they turned six or seven years old.

The day of taking away the babies was never known for sure but after a child turned three, their mothers began to live in apprehension. It was usually at this stage that mothers tried to escape with their children. They were usually inevitably recaptured and brought back in shame and even deeper depression. I heard some mothers threatening to kill themselves and their babies than give them up. I saw this harvesting and its consequences happen only once. I soon discovered this touchy issue could be a point of contact with everyone in the group. I shared this insight with Miriam and we began to pray about it.

The large courtyard was where the babies were taken care of. The dormitories were crowded. The windows were tiny, and indoors were always so hot and stuffy during the day but quite comfortably cool at night. Most of the time we found ourselves outside in the courtyard during the day except if there was a windstorm or driving rain, or if one felt sick or something. In that courtyard we talked, sang, and engaged in different types of activities.

In the camp of the mothers, *koshari* was served twice a day. We had to prepare the meals ourselves. This was about the only organized activity we had. Each dormitory took it in turn to prepare the meal so that it got to be our turn every eight days. Whichever team got kitchen duty started immediately after Morning Prayers. They served the first meal just before midday. The remnant in the pot was served just as the sun fell. In actual fact, the meal was cooked in forty large pots. Each pot was for a dormitory. When it was done, each dormitory was served in about ten communal trays. It was up to each dormitory to finish the entire pot at one fell swoop or stretch it out till the evening. For this, the ten longest-dwelling members in each dormitory went to dole out their dormitory's portion. I guess over time, and with experience, each succeeding group had found out that it was good to show restraint in the morning so there would be something left over for the evening. The real work of the kitchen crew after cooking was to keep watch over the pots in the kitchen so that hungry people overcome with temptation do not go to pilfer from the kitchen. Despite this, it still happened anyway, often by the kitchen crew which was trying to keep the watch.

When one was not on kitchen duty, was the time to sew, bath the babies, do laundry, or engage in any other activity. With the shortage of buckets and basins, washing was the greatest temptation of all. People were always fighting over buckets and basins. When we came, the solution had been to divide up all the available buckets between dormitories. There was always pilfering between the dormitories with accusations and counter-accusations resulting in fight outbreaks. The first disagreement I had with someone at the camp of the mothers was with Pasha! It was over a bucket, or rather over the remnant of a piece of bucket.

Miriam had managed to get hold of a bucket and a piece of soap and I agreed to help her wash Bitrus' clothes. I was washing the clothes inside this bucket and putting the ones I had finished washing inside the scrap of a bucket. This scrap was at one time a whole bucket but had been fought over in the past and had broken into pieces. The piece I was then using was not large enough to hold much water. It managed to just keep my laundry off the sandy ground. Lost in my thoughts, I had done up to half of the laundry when someone said belligerently in my ear, "Why are you being so selfish Briska? How can you hoard two buckets when some other people do not have even one for other needs?"

Dust and Ashes

Startled out of my reverie, I jumped upright. "My God, Pasha! You really frightened me" I said.

"Is that so? In any case, why should you be so selfish? Some of us want to wash too."

"But... but..." I stammered. Then at that moment I had a flash of insight. Pasha was either trying to pick a fight or to prove a point. She could not possibly wash even a handkerchief inside the scrap I was using. She watched my eyes warily to see what excuse I would give. Cautiously therefore, I replied, "Okay. I am nearly done with these anyway. If you can have a little patience I will give the two buckets to you as soon as I am done." She opened her mouth to argue but on another flash of inspiration I found myself quickly adding, "If you want, you also could add your laundry to mine. I will help you wash them."

This was a showstopper. Whatever else she had expected me to say, she had not been prepared for this. "But..." she started, and then the full realization of my offer dawned on her. "Are you really serious? Do you mean what you're saying?" she asked incredulous.

"Yes" I answered. "It's not as if I have something else to do. I will be willing to help you wash what you want washed."

I was surprising even myself. Even in my parent's house, washing clothes had never been my favorite activity. Under the strenuous circumstances I found myself in, I certainly did not enjoy it but the die was cast. I was determined to go through with it. As if to test it out, Pasha went and brought over the bundle of clothes she wanted to be washed. It was just one robe and a few baby clothes. There were about five pieces in all. We counted them together. "Okay," I said, "I will let you know when they're done."

She looked at my face searchingly one more time and then walked away. She walked away backwards, as if expecting me to take back my offer at any time. I just bent down and got back to washing again. Miriam was nearby nursing Bitrus and had watched the entire exchange. "I notice she did not give you any soap to wash her clothes with. Are you planning to use my soap?" she asked. "Yes" I answered simply. "We shall trust God for the provision of another piece of soap when we need it. I have been praying to be able to reach that girl for a long time. This might be an open door to her soul."

"Humph" Miriam snorted, "Humph" but she did not argue the point.

I finished washing, spread out our own clothes on the lines and the rocks around. I took Pasha's own to her, still wet, inside the whole bucket. I left the scrap bucket where I had washed for anyone else who might need it. Pasha took the bucket from my proffered hand. She continued to search my face, I guess for any hidden tricks. "Lord Jesus" I prayed in my heart, "Let her see only the love of God shining through."

From that day, Pasha never taunted or challenged me again. She never asked me to wash her clothes again. However, when she had her baby a few weeks later, I went to stay a bit with her. I offered to do all her laundry and she was grateful for this. Her labor had been long and hard. She had also lost a lot of blood. Her immediate friends were ready to help her bath, bring her food, and take care of her baby. None of them offered to do her laundry. She was always so grateful for my services in this area and for just staying nearby. One day she asked me, "Why are you doing these things for me Briska?"

I could have given any number of answers but again I asked inspiration of the Holy Spirit. Instead of any of the stock answers I could have given, I found myself saying, "Because someone needs to do them, and I can. I am that someone and I am glad to do them for you."

She was touched. I thought I saw tears in her eyes. Immediately after her delivery, she had stopped holding her own classes. Before I had my own baby, I began to see her on the fringes of our own meetings. She eventually openly confessed her faith in Jesus Christ as Savior by the time I had my baby. She attacked Bible study and Bible defense with the same kind of zeal with which she had previously tried to discredit it. We certainly did not have any baptisms after we came to the camp of the mothers but I am glad Pasha was one of those who came to believe. That story also has another place.

MIRIAM

Until I came to the camp of the mothers, the only experience of labor I had to go by was Memuna's. Usually, last thing at night, one of the supervising women would come to ask if any of us was feeling "queer". I later understood this term to connote any unusual feeling which might signify that someone was in labor. Anyone who was feeling queer was taken to the outer yard for the night. The person returned the next morning if undelivered. If she delivered, then she returned a few days later with her baby to tell us her own version of what labor was like. That is, until Reba. Reba came to the camp of the mothers about a month after I did. One could see straightaway that she was still very young. She said she had been kidnapped soon after her eleventh birthday and had been in captivity for about two years. This made her only about thirteen years old, certainly less than fourteen.

The next thing one noticed about Reba was that she looked white all over. She was not white as Caucasian-white; she was white as someone who was extremely anemic! And then one noticed the puffiness. She was swollen in every part of her body. Her hands, her feet, her face, and of course her tummy were all overtly swollen. Her face was so puffy that her eyelids were turned outwards and red. In fact, they were the only part of her which seemed to have any color. She confirmed that seeing out of her eyes was a real problem then. She said that she saw everything bathed in queer yellow lights.

Her tummy, on the other hand was not as big as we thought it should be. In fact, when she said she thought she was about eight or nine months pregnant, we seriously doubted her. She looked just about six months pregnant or so. She moved very carefully like someone in great pains. Bristling with protectiveness Miriam adopted her immediately. Reba on her part happily leaned on Miriam. She informed us that she had an older sister also named Miriam.

She admitted that her feet were aching. Her tummy was aching. Most of all, her head was aching all the time! She said that her head felt as if there was a tight band around it. We prayed for her and swathed her head with wet clothes. She said she found this soothing. There was nothing else we could do for her especially about her continuous tummy aches. We did most of her duties for her. Most of the time she preferred to just lie down quietly inside the dark dormitory while the rest of us were outside in the courtyard.

Three times in the past Reba had slept out at the dispensary because she was feeling queer. The last time she had stayed there for three days in a row. Since she was always reporting that she was feeling queer and had not delivered her baby, they had stopped asking her altogether. About two weeks after she came we came into the dormitory one night and found her moaning softly, twisting and turning on her mat. At first we thought little of it. We felt she might just be having a bad dream. Miriam tried to waken her gently but to no avail. We tried harder but she only moaned louder. Suddenly, she started convulsing. Certainly, nobody had asked her that very night if she was feeling queer. She had not even been in the courtyard when someone came around to ask and nobody had thought to go in and ask her. When we had sized up the situation, two girls ran to the front huts for help. That was the day I realized that we were actually locked in at night. The two girls continued to hammer frantically at the doors but nobody came to answer them. Throughout the night Reba kept convulsing and moaning loudly intermittently. Towards dawn, she scrunched her knees right up to her chin, gave a really long strain and groan. Out, burst her baby and the placenta with a gush of blood and fluid all at a go! Just like Memuna, the convulsions ceased thereafter. Like Memuna, she did not wake up either.

The baby was a girl. She was queerly-shaped but she was alive. Miriam took the baby, stripped away the membrane which was covering her, separated her from the placenta, tied off the cord using one of our twirled threads for knitting and cleaned her up. We thought of what to use to cut the umbilical cord. We did not have even the crudest of any cutting instruments but then I told Miriam how Asibi had used a thickened cord to do this bit for Memuna's baby. We did not have any such cord handy but using the remnant of the twirled thread we had used to tie off the cord, I began sawing and eventually managed to separate the baby from the placenta.

The baby looked rather ugly. She had a wizened face like a picture of Gagool that I had once seen in an illustrated and abridged edition of *King Solomon's Mines*. Her head was at least three times the size of the rest of her body. All her ribs stood out like someone who was at the last stages of a terrible disease like tuberculosis or cancer, or otherwise had been starving

Dust and Ashes

for a very long time. Her eyes! Her eyes were something else! They were wide open and too big, even for her big head. They shone and sparkled right from the first day like an aged wily woman's. They seemed to either be telling us something or hiding something from us. All in all, the baby looked more like a lizard or a monkey than a human being. As soon as Miriam exposed the baby's face she started whimpering weakly. By the time Miriam finished cleaning her up she was mewling like a drenched kitten.

I had most of my attention on Reba though. None of the other girls in our dormitory had slept that night but they were not being very helpful either. Some had joined us in our mumbled prayers throughout the night. Most, however, having never seen someone convulse before, were too afraid to come near. They were not sure it was not infectious. The others kept their distance except for Bama, Fekria and Doria. By the time she expelled her baby amidst the mess of blood and fluid, even Doria fled. Surprisingly, the amount of blood and fluid was not much. The mess she made at delivery was certainly less than Memuna had. Bama and I tried to clean her up but by this time I was very pregnant. Bending over had become a real problem for me. Nevertheless, I tried my clumsy best until Miriam handed the wrapped baby over to me. "Here" she said, "let me take over the mother."

Just then, Morning Prayers were called. Miriam sent Fekria for some water to use to clean Reba up. She sent Doria to see if the outer hut had been opened so they could be informed about Reba. She had Bama hold her in position or roll her over while she cleaned. Just as they were finishing with the cleaning, and covered her with an old robe, Bitrus decided he wanted his mother's attention. He and the other babies had been mercifully quiet the whole night. This was just as well but it was morning now. The drama was virtually over. It was time to get back to a normal day.

Two women came from the outer hut. They examined Reba cursorily. The examination of her baby was even more perfunctory. They then told us there was nothing they could do. We had thought the outer court was a kind of clinic or hospital complex. We were bewildered that they would not take Reba over but the women insisted they could not look after her. "Call us if she wakes up" one of them said as they turned to leave.

"If, or when?" Miriam demanded angrily. In Egyptian Arabic, the two words sound very much alike and I guess she wanted to be sure she had heard correctly.

The woman shrugged. "She will probably not wake up. We have seen this kind of thing before. That baby will die soon anyway. Just keep it in a corner to die peacefully" and they walked away.

Miriam was so angry. She snatched the baby from me. The misshapen creature had stopped her piteous mewling but had not fallen asleep. She was rooting at my chest hungrily but I had nothing to offer her. Miriam knelt on the floor and tried to put her to Reba's nipple. Reba was still unconscious but even then the baby could not latch on to the nipple. Huffing angrily still, Miriam tried to put the baby to her own nipple but the baby could not grasp it. It mewled even more piteously. By now, Miriam was weeping angry and frustrated tears. I pried the baby free from her hands, cuddled her to my chest and rubbed her back until she became quiet. After about an hour she started mewling again.

Finally, we had the idea to go to the kitchen area and collect one of the tin cups. There were about a dozen rubber spoons for adding ingredients to the cooking pots in the kitchen. We borrowed one of them. Miriam expressed some of her breast

Dust and Ashes

milk into the cup and we fed the baby this with the spoon. She drank every drop of it. After she burped, we tried some warm water. She took this eagerly also. After this she fell asleep till afternoon. We had no idea if what we were doing was correct or not but at least it bought us some peace of mind to be doing something. The alternative was just to leave the baby abandoned as we had been told and watch her die. We could also go to throw her into the pit latrine with the placenta as one of the other girls had suggested.

Reba remained unconscious for that whole day and night. Like Memuna, she woke up the following day but was too tired to move or to even talk. I went to inform the supervising women at the front that she was awake. "Good" said the woman I met there. She was not among the ones who had come to see Reba the previous day.

"Should we bring her over here?" I asked.

"Come here to do what?" she asked me irritably. "There is nothing we can do here for her. She should stay where she is."

I stood there for some time but she did not pay me any more attention. I finally went back to the dormitory discouraged, to report to the others. We realized then that we had to be the ones who would take care of Reba and nurse her back to health if she had any chances of surviving at all. We fed her *koshari* and sugared water. Her appetite was very poor at first but it improved gradually. She wanted to see her baby but lacked the energy to hold her for any amount of time. Sometimes she would not mind the baby lying down beside her. Some other times she would turn away and push the baby away from her. The day after she woke up, Miriam encouraged her to put the baby to breast but Reba refused. However, since she really did not have the energy to fight, Miriam put the baby to her breast anyway. The baby could not latch unto Reba's nipple. She would mewl inconsolably whenever Miriam tried to leave her with Reba. At last, we gave up. We just kept feeding her with warm water and whatever Miriam could express from her own breast. Fortunately, she had already introduced Bitrus to *koshari* and the boy liked it. He still preferred his mother's arm and comfort though, and he still liked to breastfeed.

Three days after she woke up, I asked Reba if she would not name the baby so we could stop calling her "Reba's baby".

"She's so ugly" Reba said. "She will soon die anyway. Why bother?"

But the baby did not die. Once we got the hang of feeding and changing her, she was actually not much bother. She was always strapped to Miriam's chest unless she was being fed or changed. Other mothers were now eager to contribute breast milk. For such a tiny human being she had a really big appetite. She began to gain weight. Her ribs were no longer so prominent. Her huge eyes seemed to shrink as the rest of her face caught up. The rest of her body began to catch up with her huge head. She slept often and only woke up to eat or to be changed. For those first few weeks, we dared not bath her. She was so tiny.

Reba on the other hand began to shrink. At first she was too weak to even get up. We realized we had a problem when she tried to get up to go to ease herself. She could not. She ended up urinating all over the mat and weeping in humiliation. We tried to reassure her and clean her up but thereafter she would weep and weep but could not drag herself up to go to the bathroom area. At last, after she had wept and soiled herself for two days, Miriam devised some menstrual rags for her to wear as diapers and to pee in. "Don't worry" Miriam told her, "I will wash them for you for now. Eat and get strong then you can pay me back by doing my laundry for the rest of this year."

Dust and Ashes

The promise or threat seemed to work like a charm. It seemed to make the young girl more determined to get well, and as soon as possible. She did her best to eat better. Every day she attempted to rise from her mat. A week after she delivered, she was up to sitting at the door of the dormitory. A few days later she did not need the improvised diaper anymore. She peed often and seemed to lose all her accumulated puffiness in the process. Slowly but surely, a slim and very beautiful girl emerged from the bloated and ungainly ugly duckling we had known for the past few weeks.

Reba survived and her baby thrived. The baby grew beautiful too. She began to look very much like her mother. Reba finally accepted to start breastfeeding. Miriam explained to her that if she did not, her breast milk would dry up and then the women would immediately come to take her away and return her to the general circulation of wives. Once she got the hang of breastfeeding Reba became really good at it. She loved it, and her baby loved it too.

The women in the outer hut came to see them about a month later and to bring the baby her allocation of clothes. Up till then she had been using borrowed clothes from all the other mothers. They were very surprised at how healthy the mother and daughter looked. Miriam proudly displayed both of them. She had a glint in her eyes that hinted at how much more she would have liked to say to the women but was barely holding back.

"Remarkable!" said one of the women, "Very remarkable!"

"Yes" Reba agreed. "That is why her name is Miriam, Baby Miriam, my very remarkable baby girl!"

AMIRA II

My tummy had been growing bigger. I found myself clumsier in everything. Pasha delivered her baby soon after Reba. I found myself the unofficial laundress for myself, Miriam, Pasha, and Reba. Laundry was not a chore I ordinarily enjoyed but the people I did these for were so appreciative. Besides, while doing laundry I found time to daydream and to pray. However, I found it more and more difficult to lean over from the waist. Fortunately, there were a few scattered big rocks in the compound and some left over slabs from some previous constructions. I found it easier to put the bucket on these and not have to lean over so much in order to wash. Although some other people were always ready at the well to help me draw water, I sometimes found myself at the well drawing the water myself. This was becoming increasingly more difficult too.

I had noticed other changes in my body as the pregnancy advanced. I had unsightly stretch marks on my tummy, thighs, and buttocks. My breasts had enlarged and were sometimes tender. I noticed that if I pressed the nipples in a certain way, slimy, colorless fluid came from them. Once in a while, while bending over, my tummy would grow as hard as a rock, my waist would tighten, and I would not be able to straighten up immediately. As soon as I stood upright or relaxed from what I was doing, these discomforts would pass. Bama and Miriam reassured me these were normal. It did not mean that I was in labor.

I was glad to let the other members of my dormitory assume my kitchen duties. It was a sure way of getting extra scraps but I was not one for eating much anymore. I had noticed that some of the girls became increasingly lethargic as their time approached to deliver. I was not feeling tired and had as much energy as I always did.

One day, after our usual activities, the women from the front came and completed their rounds. They went back with two girls who were feeling queer. We held our devotions. We prayed, read the Bible, and reminisced with one another. Feeling tired, I went to my mat and slept off. Miriam, Reba, and a few others stayed out later in the courtyard. They were just talking and putting their babies to sleep. It was a warm night and there was no hurry to get into the stuffy dormitories. When they finally came in, I was roused and found it difficult to go back to sleep. I twisted and turned and found my mat uncharacteristically uncomfortable. I could not pinpoint the source of my discomfort. At last, I found out that if I sat up, resting my back against the wall, with my shoulders and hip braced up against the wall, I had some measure of comfort. If there was some light source, I would have found some scraps of the Bible to read but we did not possess any such luxuries. Silently, I recited Bible verses I had memorized to myself. I tried to remember books I had read. I did mental sums and went through the multiplication tables. At last I found myself nodding off. I slid down unto the mat to be more comfortable. Hardly had I done that when the discomfort started again. My only relief was to sit up and brace myself against the wall again. I sat up and began my mental exercises again until I found myself nodding off. I would slide down unto the mat and it would start all over.

I had no idea how long this went on but at last Miriam, sleeping on the next mat, woke up and asked, "Are you okay Briska?"

"I think so" I whispered. "I am just unable to stay asleep for long."

"Is anything bothering you?" she asked.

"Nothing more than usual" I replied.

"In that case, go to sleep. Some of us are trying to enjoy our sleep here."

We both laughed softly and she went right back to sleep. I tried to sleep but I just could not. After some time she woke up again and asked, "You are still not asleep. Are you sure you're not in labor?"

"I don't think so" I replied.

"Well, put your wakefulness to some use. Pray for us."

Again we laughed and she went back to sleep. Prompted by her suggestion, I tried to analyze my discomfort. Yes, it seemed to be coming from my tummy and my hips. It was not like anything that had been described to me, or that I had witnessed as labor. I was certainly telling the truth when I did not come forth as feeling queer earlier that night but I was now feeling very queer indeed. I could really be in labor. With this realization I started praying for myself and for the baby. I told God that I was committing the process of labor into His hands. He knew that the two deliveries I had attended had been very frightening. I don't know for how long I dwelt in my private musings. At last I determined that I had to wake Miriam to have someone to share this experience with. As I leaned forward to do so I was suddenly assailed by an unaccountable and overwhelming nausea. I tried to swallow a few times but I found myself retching instead. I shook Miriam by the shoulder urgently. She came awake instantly. "What is it? What is it Briska?" she asked.

"I'm feeling sick" I gasped." I think I'm going to vomit."

By now I had managed to stand up and was making my way as quickly as I could towards the door. We were allowed to wander in the courtyard at night here unlike in other camps we had been in. I had one step out into the courtyard when I was assailed by a hot wave of pain at my back and upper thighs. I doubled over and felt hot fluid pouring down my legs. "Lie down! Lie down now!" Miriam commanded sharply, and a bit too loudly.

She did not really need to tell me that. My legs could no longer support me. I just lay where I was, half in and half out of the dormitory. Quick-thinking Miriam grabbed the old cloak on my mat. She stepped over me and came to look between my legs. I was still retching but not bringing up anything. "I feel like shitting" I gasped. "My hips are tearing apart."

"Then shit" she said. "Give it everything you've got! It's your baby coming."

Whatever she meant, I was not hearing her properly at all. Some forces which were greater than me had taken over my body. I could not, not push even if I had tried to. The pain was unbearable. It was like one trying to pass very hard stool. I could not just hold back. I wanted to cry out. I wanted to shout but I thought of all the other girls who were still sleep. I took a deep breath but it caught in my throat. I found myself straining very hard. I felt all my abdominal and back muscles contract and hold. They were not relaxing. With my third push, Amira slipped into the world. Miriam caught her. As soon as her face was wiped, she gave one very loud and healthy cry. She announced her arrival into the world even before the umbilical cord was tied and cut. The call for Morning Prayer was made just at that moment and the compound began to come awake. A new day had dawned! She was so perfect and healthy in every way. I held her close to my chest and could not stop praising the Lord. "God, You are so good! Thank You Father! Thank You, Jesus! Oh Father, I thank You!"

Miriam scrambled to find a thick thread to tie off the umbilical cord, and then she began to saw through. This time she was more expert at it than she had been with Reba's baby. The thought raced through my mind that they probably had scissors to neatly cut the umbilical cord at the outer compound. They certainly had a more secluded place to deliver. Maybe they even had a bed with a mattress and a few other conveniences. But Miriam would not have been allowed to come with me. I would have had my baby in the midst of uncaring strangers. To them this precious moment would have been just a part of their baby-making industry. Under open skies, literally, God helped me to have my baby girl, attended by a friend and a relative. I felt really blessed. I had every cause to praise Him!

The placenta came out without rancor as the other girls now came to watch. My bum felt as if it was on fire but I was not paying it much attention. I was too fascinated by my perfect baby. She was so small but perfect in every way. She had brownish red fuzz on her head that portended deep russet-colored hair like my mother's. Her face was pixie-like. It ended in a pointed chin like my sister's. She had a dimple at each corner of her mouth like Yohana's. As I gazed at her she opened her eyes and stared

Dust and Ashes

right back at me with light brown eyes that reminded one of melted honey. They were so much like my father's and Gamal's. She was so beautiful. She reminded me about all those people I left at home, who must have been mourning for me. Miriam said she looked a lot like me but I did not really see anything of myself in her. I did not spare a thought for whoever might have fathered her. I felt choked by mixed feelings of joy and sadness. Overriding all these was praise. I was so grateful to God. I praised Him with all my heart that morning.

I thought I should go and have my bath but one of the supervising women, probably called by one of the other girls, came to take Amira and me away to the outer compound. I felt very tired but content. I was more than willing to be bossed around. I followed the woman that was carrying Amira with her crudely cut and tied umbilical cord. At that moment I looked into the crowd of the girls gathered and looking on with awe. The face of Pasha stood out prominently among all the others. As we went through the door, I distinctly heard her say, "So it is true. Now, I believe."

My baby girl was not even up to an hour old yet and she was already a soul winner.

The labor room was a real eye opener. These people really did have fairly modern facilities. Why were they not making them available to us even in times of crisis like in Reba's case? There were gleaming stainless steel basins and surgical instruments. Amira and I even had proper beds with mattresses. They checked my blood pressure and temperature with equipment similar to what I had seen at my mother's work place. I even saw vaccination cold boxes. I had heard that once every two or three months, someone came to vaccinate the babies en masse. I saw now that this was so. The realization that they could have given us these modern conveniences but deliberately withheld them from us only made me sadder than ever. We were human carnage and they tried to protect their interest but not our humanity.

The two girls who had felt queer the previous night were still there. One was groaning intermittently in pain while the other one was sleeping fitfully. The women examined Amira and me. They fed me tea with milk and *koshari* with meat two times each day. Amira got her allocation of baby clothes. By the time my breasts were secreting milk fully on the second day, we were allowed to return to the general compound and be reunited with the other girls.

It is true that the first thing Amira did was to cause Pasha to give her life to Christ. But Pasha did not come alone. She came with all her disciples in the Other Way. She had the most forceful and convincing arguments. She talked about how there was so much about Jesus in the Quran and so little about Mohammed. I had never heard of that before. Apparently the Holy Spirit had been working in her heart even more than I had imagined. Amira's birth was just the proverbial last straw which broke the camel's back.

This new set of converts threw themselves into serving the Lord with the zeal with which they had opposed Him before. It was so touching to behold. Once, I told this story and someone asked me if I did not feel like gloating. Not at all! I felt so thoroughly humbled by it. This was what only God could do and it made me believe in Him even more. I was thankful that my baby and I had even the smallest part to play in it all. I was also very grateful that I had not misled or been an obstacle in any way, maybe by one act of thoughtlessness. God had been, is, and always will be so good. I am ever so glad I am on the same team with Him.

WINDS OF CHANGE

Amira thrived. I learned all I needed to learn about motherhood by instinct, trial and error, and from all the others who had been there shortly before me. I learned about breastfeeding, burping after feeds, the meaning of different types of baby cry, changing shitty napkins, bathing her, putting her to sleep, and so on. Amira was a very easy baby. She always had a reason if she cried. She was also easy to console and pacify. Even at her birth, as soon as she was cleaned and swaddled, she stopped crying and looked about with a curious but unfocused gaze.

I loved it when she would firmly grip my fingers as if she would not let go. Even in the early days, she smiled a lot even in her sleep. Miriam assured me that she was smiling at angels. In time she learned to smile at me and then at every friendly face. She was a very friendly baby. I loved it when she smiled. Her "Yohana" dimples appeared and disappeared and made me miss home so much. Like her older namesake, she chose me above every other person. I could sit for hours just gazing at her or playing with her. Like all the other mothers in the compound, I fashioned a sling from my old robe so I could carry her close to my body when I went about my chores. At night, even though we slept on a mat on the floor, we cuddled close to each other. No palatial divan could have beaten our cozy nest. Apart from the clothes I had received for her, she inspired my imagination to sew and knit pretty things from the rags and sacks we received. I remade and adjusted them as she grew in size. By inspiration, I made her a sort of girdle and again began marking the passage of time. I added a knot to it every seven days from the day she was born.

She was present at every fellowship we had. I sang all the ditties and choruses I could remember from my childhood to her and made up new ones as the fancy took me. I began to constantly remind God of His promise that she would not be brought up in bondage. In loving Amira, I began to appreciate how my parents must have felt about me. Further than that, I began to appreciate how God must feel about me.

The babies thrived in that camp of the mothers. We had the occasional bouts of mild fever, cough and cold, diarrhea, and vomiting. Considering the population of mothers and babies in that camp, we had only a few deaths. We learned the importance of fresh air and sunshine even during bitterly cold weather, sandstorms, or rainstorms. We learned the value of clean drinking water, sugar, and salt solutions. We even learned the use of cornmeal for treating diarrhea. Of course we never overlooked the importance of prayers. When all else failed, there was that. Most of our babies survived and thrived.

Amira was a lovely, chubby baby. The combination of my mother's russet hair, and my father's golden eyes sat very well on her. She could hold up her head without support at five weeks. She could sit without support at three months. At five and a half months she could crawl. By nine months she was attempting to stand with support while trying to take a few steps. It took her two more months to start walking and running independently however. Even in the chubbiness of her baby fat, her face still looked elfin with the pointed chin and dimples that kept appearing and disappearing according to her mood. Everyone loved her. She quickly learned that she could settle quarrels by simply hugging opposing parties.

When Amira was about six to seven months old, she became very sick. Her little body was very hot. Whereas she had started accepting small bits of *koshari*, she now simply refused to eat anything, not even breast milk. And then she started having diarrhea. Two children had died the previous week of similar symptoms. Their mothers had been taken away just the day before Amira became sick. Rumor had it that the mothers had been returned to the general pool of wives for the incessant cycle of marriage and remarriage. About two months before, another child had died of the same symptoms. The inconsolable mother "fortunately" acquired another infant whose mother had died soon after childbirth. The pair was matched up and they were still in the camp. I was therefore understandably frantic, for many reasons. Now I knew firsthand what all the other girls suffered whenever their children became sick.

Amira refused everything we gave her except for plain water. She would not even take the water if there was any hint of sugar or salt in it. She refused the corn meal that had treated other children successfully in the past. She would not even be suckled and I guess the breast milk soured. By the third day, she had become very, very weak. I tried to forcibly feed her expressed breast milk with cup and spoon but then she started vomiting in addition to every other thing. After the first few bouts of vomiting, she just lay there gasping like fish that had been thrown out of water. She looked like a shadow of her former self, and without doubt at the very doors of death. I realized firsthand what Hagar must have felt in the Bible when she thought her son was about to die. Leaving her with Miriam, I went behind the toilet hut to weep in private.

"Lord" I pleaded, "I am in Your hands, every shattered bit of me. I cannot hold myself together. I don't know how I can take it if she dies. I am sorry for ever saying I did not want her. Did You not promise that she would live and not be raised in bondage? Please spare her, spare her Lord and heal her. Lord, I don't know what to do, I don't know what to do, O Lord..."

I prayed and wept until there was nothing left in me. I had no more words, no tears, no expectations, nothing at all. I just lay there, vacant and cold until Miriam found me in the evening. She asked me if I could come to breastfeed Amira.

Amira had not died after all! Apparently, after cleaning her up, her temperature had come down to normal. Miriam had tried giving her plain water again. She not only accepted it but continued to crave it in small quantities. By that evening she had started crying inconsolably. She did not want to be touched by anyone and so Miriam had come for me. As soon as she saw me, Amira opened her arms wide. She even greeted me with a shadow of her former smiles. I hugged her tight and indulged in a few tears. Afterwards, she was content to just cuddle in my arms. She suckled a bit, and fell asleep holding tightly to my fingers. She did not vomit again. The fever waned. Throughout the night she needed to be changed only twice. From this point on, she rallied and slowly recovered until she again became her usual chubby, bubbly self. Immediately after that ordeal, she produced two shiny teeth on her lower gum that she seemed to always be proudly displaying in generous smiles.

Dust and Ashes

When Amira was about a year old, we began to notice subtle changes in the camp. Children were due to be harvested again. Those whose children were over three years old were naturally apprehensive. Having Amira now, I could easily imagine how scary this prospect was. There were renewed talks of defiance and escape. Our fellowship swelled in number. There were always talks and prayers for Divine rescue, portals of escape, and so forth. Naturally, I joined in all such talks and prayers but somehow I found myself very reluctant to share the vision I had. By some unspoken agreement, neither did Miriam.

The other change however was in the activity of the captors around us. We had always been given the basic ingredients for making our *koshari*. Now, we were being given dry corn in its rawest form. We were supposed to de-husk, shell, and then grind the corn into the finished product before making up the *koshari*. At first this generated a lot of complaints among the girls, not that anyone gave us any choice in the matter. We just did what we were told. However, we did wonder if our captors did not regard the millstones as potential weapons. Perhaps they hoped we would fight and kill one another to spare them the trouble of having to kill us themselves. Nobody used the millstones as weapons however. Some of us had never used, or even seen millstones used but we quickly caught on. After the initial complaints, we found out that we actually liked the break in our monotonous lives. We were quite proud of the finished products too. Besides, grinding our own corn somehow increased the quantity if not the quality of our meals. At the end of each day, we were always all too tied to fight one another or to even argue.

We must have become very proficient at grinding corn because we began to receive more and more corn to de-husk and grind. Some of it was being taken away from the compound at the end of each day so we soon got to understand that we were not grinding for our compound only. We were probably also grinding for other camps in the network unless they were selling off the finished products for gain or to fund their projects.

The next change was not so subtle. Pregnant and breastfeeding women were sometimes permitted not to fast but we calculated from the passage of time that another season of Ramadan had come round again. Just as we were settling down to speculating what might be going on in the other camps we had been to, we woke up one day to unusual noise and disturbance outside the compound. At first it was a hiss, and then whispers, and then it became the titter and giggles of many girls together. In a matter of minutes, they burst into the courtyard and we saw that it was a group of about twelve girls. Among them was Khadija with whom we had been kidnapped, Bashra, Hanan, Nadia, and other girls I had met at other camps. We hugged them and they introduced us to all the other girls they had come with. Some of those girls were also being joyfully reunited with other acquaintances too. We wondered how far along their pregnancies were but they informed us that only Mulyat was just about three months pregnant as far as they knew. What were they doing in the camp of the mothers then?

"Who knows?" Khadija asked with exaggerated bewilderment. "Someone woke us up in the middle of the night, ordered us to get into a truck where I promptly fell asleep again. Now here we are! Who ever said they owed us any explanations for the things which had been happening to us?" She asked, trying to mimic Ummi.

We were still talking when with another burst of noise and screeches another group of girls arrived. They told much the same tale. After this, truckload after truckload of girls began

Dust and Ashes

to arrive to our camp. By the end of a six-day period, the population of the girls in the camp of the mothers had more than doubled! Only a few girls among these recent arrivals were apparently or even covertly pregnant.

It was a time of joyful reunion for many of us. People who were kidnapped together were reunited. Of the original nineteen of us, seventeen were now in the camp. All of us were there except for Sara and Rawya of course. We kept count with the very first trucks that arrived, and had brought Khadija. We did not let up until another truck discharged Asibi, Hoda, and Ester on the evening of the third day. Hoda was very obviously pregnant. She was about five or six months along.

Despite the overcrowding and the overstretching of resources, it was a joyful reunion all around. Some other groups had a mixture of joys and sorrows. Deaths and disappearances were discussed or disclosed as we exchanged news and experiences. In one isolated case, a girl who had been kidnapped five years earlier discovered that her younger sister and her cousin had been kidnapped four years later. Her younger sister had died after the first round of marriages. Each day, we stayed late into the night trying to catch up with one another. By the time Morning Prayers were called the next morning, none of us would have slept a wink.

We speculated on what this abnormal congregation meant. We still did not know where we were but from the lack of minarets on the skyline, we were sure we were not near Cairo. Someone speculated that we were in one of the oases close to Alexandria and there was a direct train route from there to Damanhur. She also quickly informed us that she had only visited the area a long time before and had only dim childhood memories of it. The new arrivals admired our babies. We talked of lost pregnancies and babies. I shared with our original group the vision I had of our redemption. It turned out that Asibi and Hoda also had similar revelations with only a few differences. Asibi described the escape as "Freedom, without pain" while Hoda described hers as a time of confused family reunion. "My parents were rejoicing that I had been released but my brothers were beating me for talking about Jesus as Messiah. I just knew it meant that I was going home."

For all we knew, these visions (or dream, in Hoda's case) could have been nothing more than expressions of wishful thinking but we were either too far gone in our delusions and needed such hopes to hold on to, or we really had the assurance from God. Whatever they were, we knew deep down in our hearts that they were genuine. Besides, the part about the birth of Amira in the vision more than enhanced our confidence. This at least had already been fulfilled.

When we talked of our pooled resources however, they were very meager indeed, to say the least. Apart from some needles, buttons, scraps of clothing, pencils and paper, all the money we had was a few pilfered coins and two bank notes. This was including the original five pound note which Qasim had given me. Our total cash resources came to about twelve Egyptian pounds. Besides, none of us had ever independently ridden on a train or a public bus in all our lives. We always had parents, teachers, Aunts, Uncles, older cousins, and such guardians to take us on such trips and pay for the transportation on our behalf in transit. Even with all our resources pooled together, we did not know if we could so much as send one person into the outer world to tell our stories. Qasim had also advised that if, and when we escaped, we should do so in twos or threes but not solo.

"This is where God comes in" Miriam said reasonably. "This is where He proves to us if this is from Him or just merely wishful thinking."

"And this sudden move to bring everybody together might have a lot to do with God's escape plans" said Asibi. "In all my years of captivity, such a thing has never happened. I tell you, God must be up to something."

Somehow Asibi had gravitated to, and stayed with our group. By rights she actually belonged to the outer camp of the "Officials" having been with the group for so long and no longer possessing any cohorts so to speak. Two of us were especially drawn to each other also. We just resumed our friendship. After the novelty of being all together had worn off and we were more or less back to established routines, albeit with swollen numbers, Asibi and I still found time to just sit and talk, catching up with each other. She had grown tremendously in her faith. The times I spent with her greatly refreshed and shored me up. Amira took to her even more than she had taken to Miriam. The two of them bonded so tightly that it was a wonder to behold. I was torn between jealousy and amusement.

One day, Asibi shared with me her vision of our redemption in a greater detail than she had with the rest of our group. We had been talking as usual and I started speculating on how she might find her way home when we escaped. Would she remember the way to, and recognize her home after all these years? How would her people accept her? Would she not be like one resurrected from the dead? That was when she told me. "In my vision Briska, I was with you. I tried to get you to introduce me to your immediate and extended family. You were eager to do so but somehow while I was looking at them they were looking through me. I would talk to them but they could not hear me. They were totally ignoring me."

"Oh Asibi!" I exclaimed "That is a very wonderful idea. Of course I would love to take you home with me. I'm sure my parents would just love to have you as a daughter!"

"So, how do you explain the fact that they were all looking through me and not paying attention to what I said? They might not want me. I don't know what that means but it does not signify their total acceptance to me."

"Oh Asibi, no member of my family is a snob. Of course they will welcome you just as much as they would welcome me." Teasingly I added, "I might even arrange for my elder brother Gamal to marry you then you will truly and legally be part of my family! We will be both sisters and sisters-in-law!"

I expected Asibi to be enthusiastic or laugh with me. Rather she replied somberly, "I will never, ever marry anyone if I ever get out of this mess, Briska. If I ever get my freedom, I shall remain celibate for the rest of my life! It is a vow I have made to God."

"Not even for the sake of a precious baby like this my Amira" I asked. I tugged at Amira's legs as she determinedly tried to poke her little fingers into Asibi's eyes.

"Not even to have a baby" Asibi answered. "If God wants me to have a baby, He must have to arrange it by some other means because I am very serious about this vow to Him. I will never marry or ever have sex again once we get out of this ordeal." After a brief pause she added, "But of course, as His obedient child, I should add, 'Lord, let Your will, and not mine be done.'"

Later, I will remember this conversation as well as her summary of it to the bigger group. She had said that for her, escape would mean Freedom without Pain. On that day, however, we just went on to discuss something else and forgot all about our escape for the time being. The germ of the idea took root in my mind. I decided that when we escaped, I was going to go home with Asibi. After we were fully recovered, if she was minded to, we could travel to Nigeria and try to find her family.

HOPE

The biggest change of all was that we were no longer as isolated as we had hitherto been. Instead of a soothing quietness except for the hum of activity among ourselves, there was now a lot of noise from outside our compound. This was noticeable despite the increased volume of the noise from within our compound. Asibi, who was freer to come and go between our courtyard and the outer courtyards, reported that lots of serving women had also come with the influx of girls. They were quartered in nearby compounds. On top of this, one day we heard male voices. Bass and tenor voices were chanting Islamic prayers in the early morning. Throughout the rest of the day, they chanted Arabic war slogans. Two days after we heard them, the marriages began again.

Ummi came into our courtyard! We could almost all pinpoint the moment she entered from wherever we were in our own compound. From the courtyard, to the dormitories, to the kitchen, and even to the toilets, there seemed to be a sudden chill. It entered the courtyard with Ummi and affected the air from the very entrance of the courtyard to the backs of the kitchen and the toilets. With the chill, spread an abnormal quietness. With one accord, we all stopped what we were doing and turned to gaze at her apprehensively. Mothers instinctively drew their children closer and hugged them protectively. Ummi stared right back at us with a cold, cruel smile. She just took a general look at those of us in the courtyard. She let her gaze linger at our various activities, and then she turned and left. We let out a collective gasp of relief. That night however, at about the time when the caretakers came to see who was feeling queer, Ummi returned with her whip and four assistants. She went into the first dormitory and began to select girls by simply pointing her whip at them. Whoever she pointed at was set aside and guarded by the four women. When she had enough girls, she turned around and left the compound with them. We all knew what this meant.

The next day, she came and repeated the exercise in the next dormitory, and the next and the next. Once we figured out her pattern, girls took to squatting in other dormitories if they knew their dormitory was going to be the next. Ummi changed her tactics. She would go into all the dormitories and then start selecting from the dormitory which seemed to have the most girls. We tried hiding in the kitchen and the toilets. Again she caught on. She would sometimes start from those areas and take all the girls not in a dormitory before filling up her quota for that day with those still in the dormitories.

When we figured that pregnant girls and nursing mothers were exempt, baby-stealing became a real problem, at least for the night. Smart babies clung tightly to their mothers but daylight usually revealed which baby belonged to whom. Some girls ingeniously made up cloth bundles and tied it to their middles so as to look pregnant. Ummi still had a way of sniffing

Dust and Ashes

out such tricks. Those who were caught were whipped first and then still selected for marriage.

After about a month of this we just gave up. We resigned ourselves to whatever happened. Soon enough, we realized that no one was really exempt. Whoever was selected still went through about seven to ten days of marriages and divorces before returning to the compound. I was selected on one occasion and worried about what was to become of Amira. The previous three days I had to tend her as well as Bitrus when Miriam was selected. Miriam had not returned yet. Although I knew the other girls would step in and help, it was with a great deal of relief that I saw the two babies, Bitrus and Amira, clinging to Asibi in the shadows as I departed.

The marriages and divorces were no different from how it had been before. There was still the ritual bath and then the sham *Nikkah* during Evening Prayers. Then came the dark booths and the sweaty men, ranging from those who fell asleep even before consummating the marriage to those who were so vicious they were not content with just having ordinary sex. There was still the sham divorce witnessed by Ummi or any of her representative before Morning Prayers were called. After that came the ritual bath and then the daily *koshari* while we waited for evening to start the cycle again.

This time around, it was a bit more difficult to get into the rhythm again. The first few nights I felt the pains very keenly. They were not just in my body but also in my soul. After the men were asleep, I wept myself to sleep until it was time for them to divorce me the next morning. By the third night I got my "rhythm" back. I was again able to escape to a place of Bible verses and church choruses while they did their business. After seven days I returned to the inner compound and found out that virtually all the girls had been "married out". Asibi and

Haleema were left in charge of a large nursery of babies. They were assisted by only about a dozen other serving women and the few very pregnant girls like Hoda.

For about a month, the marriages slowed down. We had a few days of respite. We shared our experiences, prayed for one another, and renewed talks of escape and freedom. We reminded ourselves of what we had said we should do, like going through the clothes of our rapists to see if we could get anything of value to help us escape. I, personally had not remembered all these, and neither had a good number of us. Some of the other girls were hearing about these for the very first time.

It was good we had this time of respite because the marriages again started and intensified. The second time I was selected, I saw that I was among the last to be selected. In fact, I was probably the very last because as I left, I noticed that only Asibi and the pregnant girls were left in the courtyard. Even Haleema seemed to have been pressed into service. Hoda had just had her baby and was still too weak to care for even herself. I wept as I left Amira yet again. This time however, I also had a different prayer. "Lord, cause this to come to an end; please cause this to end!" I pleaded with Him.

The ritual bath... the marriage... and then I followed my "husband" into his selected booth. In the gloom, I saw the thin mattress in the corner. I whipped my robe over my head, arranged it as a pillow for my head, lay down, pointed my knees at the ceiling, spread my legs and began to recite Psalm 121 in my head with my eyes closed.

I had come to the end of the last verse: "The Lord shall preserve your going out and your coming in from this time and forevermore..." when I realized there was no "action". I cautiously squeezed open an eye and realized there was a lit candle, held by a hand. Beyond the hand was a face. The mouth belonging to the face spoke. "Get up and put on your robe, I want to talk to you."

Déjà-vu! This kind of scene had happened to me before. I sat up quickly, recovered my robe and wore it back. I was now keenly conscious of my nakedness and exposure. Even though the voice had not sounded familiar, in my joyous disbelief, I began to exclaim "Qasim". At the last moment, I swallowed the word in a choke. It came out like a sob instead.

"Pardon?" said the voice.

It was just a male voice. It was not Qasim's. It had no particular characteristic either. It was neither kindly nor cruel. It was neither authoritative nor indulgent. It did not even sound amused or sad. It was just bland. The man had the advantage over me in that while he studied my face with the lighted candle, I could not make out any more than a vague outline beyond the hand which held out the candle. He might have realized this discrepancy but he made no move to correct it. He placed the candle on the floor near where my head had been and retreated even deeper into the shadows around the door of the booth. I thought I saw the glow of the tip of a cigarette but I did not perceive the foul odor that should usually accompany this. That, and the sound of his breathing, was the only indication of his whereabouts in the room. Some people liked to smoke before they had sex. Perhaps this was the prelude and he was trying to relax before getting down to business. As my eyes adjusted to the gloom, I saw that his shadow stayed near the door. He sat with his legs folded beneath him, lotus style. He ordered me to snuff out the candle if I was comfortable enough. I did so immediately. Only then did he begin to talk.

"Your name is Briska" he said. It was a statement, not a question. "Never mind how I got to know that. You may call me

Sa'ad. I am here to organize a rescue for you and your people so you must work in collaboration with me."

"I don't know you" I replied. "I've never met you. How do I know you are not deceiving me; that you are not spying for our captors?"

He kept quiet for about two minutes and then asked, "What does your heart tell you?"

Truly, in that short period of time, my heart had carried out a complicated debate with my head. It started with how he could have known my name. Who could have sent him? Did he have anything to do with Qasim? Was he truly a friend or a foe? Even if he was a foe, could we be in any worse position than we currently were? Was it by coincidence that I got "married" to him that night or did he somehow prearrange it? Most importantly, what was the Spirit of God whispering to my heart about this situation? What I felt above all was, "Did you not pray earnestly this evening expecting an answer or is this too soon for you?" I asked myself over and over, "what do I have to lose by trusting this man?" Absurdly, in the midst of all these arguments, the story of Peter's rescue from the prison popped into my head. What would have happened if Peter had spent valuable time arguing with the angel sent to deliver him? What if he was debating whether the angel was from Jesus or from Beelzebub?

"Okay" I answered Sa'ad, "What do you want me to do?"

"After you return to the courtyards, organize leaders over groups of twenties. Next time you find yourselves in these courtyards, at the time of the ritual baths, go to the corner of the dispensary where you will find trucks. These trucks will take you to a place at Alexandria. From there you will know what to do."

I had questions. I wanted details, especially about our babies but Sa'ad did not encourage any discussions. In fact, I bowed my head to digest what he had just said. By the time I raised my head, I saw his shadow going out of the booth, into the night. "Perhaps" I thought, "he has gone out to smoke after all". Some of the men did that. I waited for him to come back but he did not return shortly, and maybe not at all. I must have slept off because the next thing I knew, Ummi was shaking me by the shoulders and asking where my husband was. I had no answer to this. She huffed angrily. This meant I could not be "properly divorced" and remarried on Ummi's schedule. She kept me in that hut till afternoon, probably asking around for whomever my husband of the previous night was. By late evening, she told me to return to the inner courtyard. I had to wait for a formal declaration of abandonment before I could be married to another person. This was a clog in the wheel of Ummi's procedures and it had her really hopping mad. When she eventually returned by midafternoon, she punished me with a dozen lashes to my back as if I was entirely responsible for the disappearance of my husband but I did not mind at all. My mind was engrossed with so many other things. After the whipping she ordered me to return to the courtyard with the babies until she had figured what to do with me. I was going to see my baby! I was going back to Amira!

I was glad to return to Asibi and the babies. That night, Amira went to sleep in my arms. I saw that having to tend over two hundred babies was not a holiday, even with about twenty helpers. By the time all the babies were finally fed and persuaded to sleep, we were all fit to drop. Instead of sleeping, however, I wanted to talk with Asibi. "Hush" she said, indicating with her eyes that I should listen to more than her words. "Wait till the babies are soundly asleep before you think of going to ease yourself."

I understood then that we should not talk in the dormitory in the presence of the other girls and attendants. As tired as I was,

Al Kalima

I could not fall asleep. Late in the night, when everywhere was quiet and snores had become regular, I got up to go to the toilet. On my way back to the dormitory, I saw Asibi. She waved me over to a portion beside the kitchen area. Even before I opened my mouth she said, "When did you get to tell this Sa'ad about me?"

"Tell Sa'ad about you? I was thinking you were the one who told him about me! Didn't you?" I asked.

"No", she said. She too had met Sa'ad for the first time only the previous night. "It was really late in the night and I was returning from the toilets. I was at this very place we are standing right now when a figure detached itself from the shadows and saluted me with peace. I was startled. He didn't even apologize. He simply introduced himself. He said to me, 'My name is Sa'ad. I am here to help you escape, You and Briska must organize the girls into parties of twenty with leaders. We will arrange to get all of you to Alexandria. From there you will know what to do.'"

"Did you believe him?" I asked.

"Yes" Asibi answered simply. "I believe he was sent by God."

I nodded. "Did he give you further instructions? Did he tell you the details?"

"No" Asibi answered. "I understood you would know what to do. He did not linger. He told me what I just told you now and he left. Our conversation lasted less than two minutes."

This man could have been a phantom. He could have been a figment of our imaginations except that two of us could not have been deluded at different times, or approximately the same time in different ways. I then described my own encounter with Sa'ad to Asibi, up to and including the fact that I was still married to him because Ummi could not find him to broker the divorce. Asibi was impressed most by the latter portion of my tale. "Nobody has ever done anything like that before! Maybe going to hide before a divorce could achieve the same thing; but then Ummi would have flogged the foolishness out of the girl's head. You just wait. They will soon find a way around that very soon as well. Someone must be studying the *Hadith* even now, to find something relating to how to shorten the effects of wife abandonment."

But I was more concerned about the problem at hand. "How on earth are we going to find the right leaders? What is going to happen once we get to Alexandria? What of the babies? They are never with us during, before, or after the ritual baths. How are we going to bring them along? Some of these girls don't even know the nearest town to where they were kidnapped. How are we going to get them from Alexandria to their homes? I have two uncles and an aunt at Alexandria but I've never gone to visit them alone. I don't even remember where they were living or if they are still at that same address? How much time do you imagine that we have before the plan is set into motion? ..." I had so many questions!

"I wouldn't worry about all those if I were you" said Asibi equably. "If Sa'ad thought you could do it, then he must know what he is saying. Besides, if this is of God, He will make out the ways and the means. It's like a winding road. Until you come to the bend in the road you may not see how it continues. It could also be like a good book, as you used to say. The plot will unfold as you turn the pages, one step at a time. I think we should just pray about it and wait on God to show us what comes next."

I ought to have told Asibi that it was easy for her to say so. I did not do this because her words not only made sense, they somehow comforted and reassured me. Besides, both of us were every bit as involved in this project together. Jesus must have had very good reasons for sending out His disciples two by two, even in the days we were living in. It felt good to have her not as worried as I was. Her calmness began to calm me

Al Kalima

down too. I then asked about why she did not want us to talk in the dormitory.

"Ummi has planted spies everywhere" Asibi told me. "Virtually all these people here, selected to assist me with the babies, have some sort of obligation to her."

"Even the pregnant girls?"

"...Especially the pregnant girls! Noha told me in confidence that Ummi threatened to take away her baby once it was born, and return her to the general circulation of wives immediately if she does not agree to be her eyes and ears among the dormitory girls. Every day Ummi keeps telling her that she is not doing very well on the job. Noha is now always pressed to find a way to impress Ummi."

"Aha!" I now understood a lot, and just in time too. I had been thinking of putting Noha in charge of the girls who had come from her hometown of Cairo. I saw now that what Sa'ad was asking of us was a very great responsibility. As such, I needed to spend more time in prayers than in planning. What better time to start praying but immediately? Kneeling there at the corner of the toilet and the dormitories, Asibi and I held hands and prayed fervently for wisdom and minute directions. I asked God to please take a hand, especially if this thing was not of Him. Asibi added emphatically, "Especially since this thing is of You, Lord, Amen."

While we were praying, someone crossed to go to the toilet, and then crossed back again. The next day, Ummi called Asibi and cautioned her to remember that she was "a cut above the common dormitory girls". She was not be seen in the dark cavorting with someone who was in a marriage. She meant me! At least, nothing had been reported of what we had been discussing and praying about. We probably had not been overheard as well.

ESCAPE

That cycle of marriages ended about a week after we met Sa'ad. Sa'ad was never found. Since I was never formally divorced, I was not let back into the pool of wives for that period. Normally, after a period of abandonment, a wife could then choose to formally divorce her husband. I was not sure of what was considered a suitable period. I also knew I was not going to be given the choice of divorcing "my husband". The process was out of my hands. The decision was going to be taken by Ummi, or someone like her, on my behalf. I was very sure I was going to be available for the next spate of marriages but for then, we all had a respite.

Another outcome of that spate of marriages was that three of the girls, Ester, Jehan, and Hanan came back with lots of money. Ester said her "husband" had given it to her. "I think he was drunk or something. After the first round, he just took out this wad of notes, called me a harlot, asked how much I was worth and then threw it all over me. When he slept off, I

Al Kalima

got up and gathered the money. I figured I had earned it. In the morning, he divorced me and went his way and I went mine."

Jehan had come about hers when Ummi ordered her to clean up the booths. Two of the men had returned while she was doing so. When one of them remarked that cleaning girls might steal their belongings the other one had said, "Let them keep whatever they want. They are usually searched and they're not going anywhere far. Whatever they have still belongs to us." The man had laughed and then shouted to Jehan, "Hey Slave Girl, whatever you find and like, you may keep it!"

Jehan had found the wad of money, liked it, and kept it. After the cleaning, Ummi had searched her and gone through her clothing but had not discovered the money.

Hanan said she had boldly taken her own off her sleeping "husband". He had been quick about consummating the marriage and had fallen asleep immediately afterwards with a satisfied grunt. "I had amused myself by going through his clothes and had discovered wads of money. I was very nice about it. I took only half of what he had. After all, I am entitled to half of my husband's belonging especially following a divorce. Maybe I should have taken everything but I decided not to be too greedy."

It was quite a windfall for us. Some of the other girls had also come back with money. Some brought ten pounds here, twenty pounds there, a few coins, small change, and large denominations. Nothing was as much as Ester, Jehan, and Hanan had brought back with them though. Something must have been afoot for the Jihadists to be carrying around so much money, and to be careless about it. We had never had such a windfall before even when we had been diligently searching all those months after Qasim put the idea in my head. It was quite remarkable. Asibi and I saw it as a sign from God. At the end of

Dust and Ashes

the day, when we pooled everything together and counted, we found out we had quite a bit more than five thousand Egyptian pounds! And this was just among the fellowship members who trusted us enough to tell us about what they had. These were those who knew about, and strongly supported our escape plans. We agreed it was not safe for the money to stay all together. We distributed the resources in such a way that everyone had a cache in case of escape.

We discussed Sa'ad's visit first among the inner core of those we had been kidnapped with. We then discussed it with the inner core of those we had fellowshipped with and we were sure of their loyalties. The general consensus was that we should play it close to our chests because not everyone was to be trusted. Nearly everyone in the courtyard was then coming for our fellowship meetings but we knew that not everyone had the same level of commitment. We were truly a mixed multitude. By mere estimate alone, we were over a thousand girls in the compound. This meant that we needed more than fifty leaders. On what were we to base our choice of leaders? Should we base leadership on age and maturity, commitment to Christ, geographical origins, or perhaps cohorts of captives? Besides, there were pregnant girls and nursing mothers with very young babies to be considered also. And what was to become of our babies? Not one girl was willing to go and leave her baby behind. "I'd rather stay back or kill her myself before I leave" said Reba, speaking for most of us.

With all the whispered meetings going on, naturally interests were piqued. People began to ask what was going on. One girl eventually asked outright if there were escape plans afoot. We gave them vague answers which must have been very unsatisfactory. One day, Ummi came into the yard. She rounded up about twelve of us including Miriam, Hoda, Jehan, and me and asked what was happening. We feigned ignorance and stupidity. She kept us standing under the hot sun and the cutting wind at the center of the courtyard the whole day with nothing to eat or drink. Hoda fainted and had to be carried into the dormitory. When the rest of us were still not forthcoming, she whipped us by evening, screaming all the while, "I will kill you! I will kill you if you spearhead any revolution or uprising. If you cause anyone to become stubborn and disobedient, I will kill you! I will kill you!"

 We were all too tired to even whimper while she whipped us. From her ranting however, we gained a very great idea. A revolution! We could make it look as if we were organizing a revolution. That kind of activity would cause natural leaders to emerge. Sa'ad had not said the rescue was for only the Christians among us. It was supposed to be for all the captives. Put that way, we all had very common points on which to revolt. From then on, we determined that we would talk openly about the possibility of escape without giving the specifics. The danger, of course, would be that we would again be scattered to different camps. We felt that something was happening which made these other camps out of commission for the time being at least. We were all confined to this one remote camp together for now, but we were not sure of how long this would continue. This was probably our one good chance of escape. Whether we botched it or not, we were never going to get such a good chance ever again. We might as well give it our all and risk everything on it.

 To cover up the escape plan, we also protested about our feeding arrangements. Since our numbers swelled, we were having to process much more corn as well as rice. We ate only once a day, except for expectant and new mothers. These ones got "half a meal" extra at the end of each day. We were going to

Dust and Ashes

boldly present our complaints and demands to Ummi the next time she showed her face in the courtyard.

But Ummi did not show her face there the next day. Maybe she had also been affected by the suffering she made us pass through the previous day. The report we got from Asibi was that Ummi was ill. We could afford to wait. That day, we would more carefully refine our plans and presentations. Those of us who had gone through the ordeal of Ummi's whip were seen as natural ring leaders. In essence, Ummi had really helped us begin to solve our problems. As we began to meet and talk, other leaders emerged. About twenty-five of these, I would have actually chosen myself. Most of the others, I would have seriously considered. However there were quite a few surprises, especially among those who did not fellowship with us. All of the leaders had great suggestions as we plotted along. They thought of the nitty-gritty. They came up with contingency plans I had not even thought about myself.

Apart from the demand of improved living conditions, I suggested it would be a good idea if each of these leaders selected twenty people each to specially relate with and speak up for, like in a house of parliament. This would be like reverse elections where the leaders chose their voters instead of the other way round. And then someone else came up with the suggestion that if we ever escaped, this kind of division would give us a basic unit of operations. Everyone was enthusiastic about the idea of an escape. It sounded more improbable than the idea of a revolt but we delved into it. If these talks ever reached Ummi, we knew we would all be considered a very serious threat, but we hoped.

We came up with secret codes and "Double talk" where saying one thing could actually mean another thing altogether. To those of us in the know, we would recognize the double talk by a preceding phrase or a phrase that was cleverly concealed in the middle of the sentence. Ironically, one such phrase had to do with Ummi. For instance, if one said, "As Ummi would say, having your bath is better done in the evening..." it would mean, "Do not bath in the evening!"

Such devious minds! The nation was definitely deprived of some advancement as a result of our incarcerations. We had loads of fun even as some of us knew that these meetings served a much more serious purpose. We prayed as usual in our fellowship meetings. Afterwards, those of us in the know still met to continue to pray. On top of this, Asibi and I still spent snatches of time late into the night to pray together for God's guidance. We were apprehensive but we had also begun to feel hopeful again.

Four days after Ummi punished us, we still continued to seek audience with her. We asked every morning and every afternoon. When the women came in the evenings to look for those feeling queer, we again asked for audience with Ummi. According to Asibi's report, Ummi got only sicker and sicker. By the fifth day we heard she had ostensibly been taken away to a hospital. We never saw Ummi again! Our last encounter with her was that day of punishment in which she had unknowingly given us our great idea for an escape plan. I was not sorry to see her go, but I kept wondering if all the prayers we made for her had made any impact at all.

After Ummi left, there was no other spate of marriages again for about two more weeks. The day this respite ended, it was Khalifa who came to select the girls that would go. Many people felt good to see her again, especially as a replacement for Ummi. I, personally, was almost sorry she was going to be the one who would bear the punishment for our escape. By this time, we had greatly honed, and thought we had refined our

Dust and Ashes

plans. All the leaders were to be on the alert at every instance, whether for a revolt, an escape, or even a windstorm. All we had from Sa'ad was that we should have groups of twenties, each with a leader. When we got the signal, we were to go to the corner of the dispensary. From there we would be picked up and taken to Alexandria.

We determined that Asibi's part in the matter was to make sure that the babies were eventually reunited with their mothers. In our choosing of leaders, we had also managed to have at least one obviously pregnant girl or a very new mother attached to each group of twenty. This was because from what had occurred so far, such girls were not usually in the general pool of wives and were appointed to be aides to Asibi while the other girls were going through the spate of marriages. We explained to the group leaders that the pregnant girls and new mothers in their midst was for community responsibility. All the group members took care of such girls, and they on their part rendered such duties as they were suited for, such as caring for the babies in that group while the mothers were busy. Asibi cared for them all. This seemed good to everyone and was unconditionally accepted.

Secretly inserted into each group too, was someone who was given the task of hiding the money for that group. Each of these had enough money to be able to disburse about five pounds to each group member in the event of an escape but this was not general knowledge. Only those of us in the inner circles knew this. The "Treasurer" in some cases was also the group leader, the "fragile member", or neither. Every organized group of twenty had such a treasurer, and enough money. It seemed like a good set up so far.

Sa'ad had also said we were to escape around the time of our ritual baths. Ritual baths happened twice, before and after the marriages. We were not sure of which one he referred to but we were ready for either.

As before, the next spate of marriages was preceded by the increase in the sound of male voices filtering into our compound. Late in the night we had heard their trucks arriving. The next morning we heard their voices at Morning Prayers. By midmorning we heard them chanting Arabic war slogans and so it went on, prayers and war chants, prayers and war chants, the whole day long. From the volume of voices, they were not few in number either. We expected the marriages to start that first day but it did not. It did not start for the next one week. Life went on as usual for us despite our apprehension. And then one day, Asibi went to the outer compound as usual and did not return! She did not return that day, that night, nor the following morning. That morning, Khalifa came instead.

When Khalifa came to begin selecting the people who would be married, unlike Ummi, she did not come bearing whips. She came with assistants, alright. As ever, she was smiling and friendly. Again, unlike Ummi she did not seem to be selecting "Fit girls". She just went into the nearest dormitory and politely asked them to take all their things and clear out.

"To where?" the girls asked, bewildered.

"Oh, just find places in the other dormitories. It is only a very temporary arrangement, I promise you."

"But all the other dormitories are full" they protested.

"It's going to be very temporary" she said again with a very sweet smile.

And so the girls took their things and moved out.

Khalifa then went into the next dormitory. With the help of her assistants, she began to select the obviously pregnant girls. She ordered these to go into the emptied dormitories and wait there.

Systematically she went through all the other dormitories, separating the pregnant from the non-pregnant. The non-pregnant she ordered taken out of the compound. We soon realized that "wait there" for the pregnant really meant going there to wait. Unlike Ummi, Khalifa did not seem to have the diabolical ability of telling people who were faking pregnancy, on sight. Every two hours or so, she went back to the first dormitory and began to press on the tummies of the girls waiting there. Still smiling benignly, she would compel those who were just stuffing clothes under their robes in order to look pregnant to go to where the non-pregnant went. Unlike Ummi too, her assistants did not go about their jobs brutally. They were nevertheless more thorough than Ummi and her group. Like well-trained guard dogs, they stood at the doors making sure people went where they were asked to go and do what they were supposed to do.

She entered our dormitory last. Earlier, when we had realized what was happening, we had rehashed in hushed voices what we had agreed to do. We were desperately worried about where Asibi could possibly be. On the surface, I knew Khalifa seemed good but she was actually more dangerous than Ummi in many ways. On top of having a very organized and thorough mind, she was more likely to sniff out plans and dash our hopes than Ummi ever could. Where Ummi was at least predictable, Khalifa had a devious and twisted mind. I did not put it beyond Khalifa to have sent Asibi away. This alone had put a big clog in the wheels of all our plans. I reminded myself sternly to stop worrying and to trust in God, especially in contingencies. I handed Amira over to Hoda whose baby was still about a month old, and went out of the compound with the rest of the non-pregnant girls.

The selection exercise had taken the whole day. By the time Khalifa came to the dormitory in the other compound where over eight hundred of us were waiting, it was already dark. Evening Prayers were long over. She told us we were to have our ritual baths that night, and she would address us the next day. I guess she was very tired and wrung out herself too.

The bathrooms were too small for even a large fraction of us at the same time so we went in small numbers. I squatted outside the doors waiting for my own turn when I heard a voice. "Now is the time, NOW!"

People have asked since, if I could describe the voice which spoke to me and who I thought it was that spoke. Was it Sa'ad's voice? Was it male or female, deep-toned or soft, shrill or grating? For the life of me, I cannot even now say if it was even a physical voice. I did not even think about it, nor question what I heard. All I know was that I was suddenly galvanized into action. Of course this was the instruction Sa'ad had given me. It was the time for the ritual baths! This was also an ideal time. We were all together outside the courtyard. It was a dark night and our guards were worn out after a hard day's work.

I was not sure of what the groups of twenties should do but I ran into the bathroom. I identified four of the leaders trying to have a bath. "Rally your girls now and meet me outside" I said. I then ran into the dormitories, identifying all the leaders I could find. Some were still wet from their ritual baths. Some were still very dry, not ready to take their turns in the bathroom yet. About three were asleep already and I had to wake them up. I did not have to do all the work by myself. Those to whom I spoke first helped me to wake the others. Word spread like wild fire. Everybody knew something was afoot but nobody quite knew what.

Dust and Ashes

By the time I got outside again, some groups were already waiting. The night was very dark and our black robes made it difficult for us to see one another. I went to the head of the line. We held hands and moved in a single file. I went more or less by instinct towards the place where we had heard the chants of the men earlier in the day. The others followed me without hesitation. The path led us towards the dispensary and the other dormitories. This was also the path towards the roads which had brought us to the compounds on that long-ago day when we had arrived. Close to the road, I saw the shadowy outlines of some trucks. Someone materialized from the dark startling me. He asked, "Did Sa'ad send you?"

This must have been the test question and even though I knew I should have answered in a coded way, I had no forewarning of this so I simply answered, "Yes."

"And your name is…" enquired the voice.

"Briska" I said.

"Okay" said the voice, and that was enough. "Come this way."

We filed after him until we were a little way from the compound. There were more trucks. When we came to the lead truck, he simply said, "Get in."

I gestured to the girls behind me and told the leaders "See that as many of you as possible can get into the truck. And please be quiet about it."

I had never seen girls behave so quietly. With round, startled eyes, they started boosting and pulling one another onto the trucks. By starlight I could see that some of the girls looked frightened and bemused. Some others had the amused glint of adventure in their eyes. Every one of them was getting in. Leaving them at it, I went back for the next batch, and the next… and the next…

In all, I do not know how many times I went back and forth from those trucks that night. I lost count after the first few times. I never took stock of how many girls were in each truck but they must have been packed tight like sardines. The groupings did not figure at all in this process. People just kept getting on until each truck was filled up and moved off then they began getting into the next truck in line. Each time I returned I would hear the faint sound of a truck in the distance. By the third truck, one of the girls exclaimed, "My baby! What of the babies?"

I had thought of it after the first truckload but I now went to the courtyard where the children were kept. That was when I discovered that the doors could be very easily unbolted from the outside. Everyone seemed not only to be awake but also to be alert and tense. Something or someone must have woken them up or maybe they had yet to fall asleep. "Quick!" I told them, "Gather up the babies. We're leaving."

They just obeyed me without questions. Each girl with her big belly and about two babies under each arm just followed me. Some babies walked along, urged on by their minders. The next five or so trucks were dedicated to these. More trucks of non-pregnant girls came after. I was able to reassure mothers that the babies had already left. By the time there were no more girls to be found in the inner dormitories, the outer dormitories, or in the bathrooms, I went to look in the dispensary. There was one girl there. She was not really in labor. I woke her up and she came along with the last truckload.

Amazingly, as quiet as we had been, there was still some measure of abnormal noises and commotion for that time of the night but nobody else seemed to have been aroused by it. No one else seemed to be awake. No one came to challenge or talk to us. There were supposed to be guards patrolling the

Dust and Ashes

camp and who shot on sight after curfew but we met no one, not one person. No shots rang out. Even doors which we knew were usually locked at night were unlocked. People who were supposed to be watching out, at least at the dispensary were not even there! Later Mike would tell me that God sent a divine drowsiness upon our captors while we escaped. Up till today, I do not doubt this. There might be other explanations but I knew God arranged whatever it was.

Last of all, I had to climb into a truck but I thought of Asibi up to the very last moment. It would be tragic if she was in one of those buildings, perhaps even held captive or serving a punishment and we left without her. On a last sweep, I dared to look into the buildings in the outer court but I saw just men sleeping in most of the huts. I also came across a few huts with the women that worked at the kitchen and the dispensary but no trace of Asibi! I knew I should not continue my search. I knew I should not linger anymore. I said a quick prayer for finding her and reminded God of His promises. I decided to do one more last sweep in the toilets and kitchens. Before I set off the same man who had met me at the trucks at the beginning of the evacuation came up to me and said, "You have to leave now. We cannot delay any more."

"I know" I answered. "I still have one person missing. I have to be very sure Asibi is not here."

"I can assure you" said the man, "Asibi is not here."

I did not see his face at all. I could not gauge from his voice whether he was telling the truth or not. I wanted to be definitely sure I had done all I could but he practically grasped me under the arms and heaved me unto the last truck. The last of the girls stretched their arms and pulled me in. The driver shifted the gears and the truck glided forward. We had all escaped. I should have been exhilarated but I wailed inwardly, "Oh Asibi, where are you?"

Apart from the man who had shown us the way to the lead truck, we did not meet the drivers of the trucks. We did not set eyes on any other person who had helped us in our escape, not even one. We had not spoken with anyone else except for whispered questions, responses, and directions among ourselves. The truck went on in the night. The road was rough at first but grew less so. Eventually it became quite smooth. I did not hear the sound of any other vehicles, not even the ones which must have gone before us, or any that might be returning after dropping off the first batches. I had no way of keeping track of time. It seemed to me like two hours. It could have been much more or much less than this but we soon began to see more lights and more buildings that showed we were approaching a city. Eventually we came to a stop. It was in front of a big cathedral, on a street we knew would be quite busy when day broke. At that time of the night however, it was totally deserted. Not even a watchman was in sight. Through the door we saw other black-robed girls milling about in the dimly-lit interior.

When we saw we had come to the end of our journey, we began to jump down from the truck. As soon as the last person came down, the truck simply drove off. There were no instructions, no suggestions of what we should do next. As we turned to go into the church and join the others, I saw Asibi! With a strangled cry we fell into each other's arms and hugged tight. With a finger to her lips she signed us to hush. We crept into the church auditorium and saw that it was uncomfortably warm with so many of us packed in there. At the same time, it was also so eerily quiet given the number of girls and children there. We were happy, we were bewildered, and we were awed! Even the babies felt the excitement. They were still impossibly awake at that time of the night.

"So what do we do next?" I whispered to Asibi.

"That is what I've been asking myself since yesterday" said Asibi. "Believe me, this situation is not easy at all. I will tell you."

Eventually I realized that like me, she had also heard a mysterious voice in the night. She had turned aside, been directed into the back of a truck and been brought here. By daytime, she had scouted out the place. She knew there were coffee shops and a railway station close by. She knew that the curator of the church was not only very unfriendly but was especially inhospitable to people dressed as Moslems. At night however, this was the only door which was left open whether by accident or by design. Realizing this, she had snuck into the church to wait for the dawn of a new day. She had been woken just a few winks later by the arrival of the first truckload of girls. She had brought them into the auditorium but then realized that truckload after truckload kept coming. She had hoped I would be in the first ones that would arrive but had instinctively also known I would probably be in the last. She had worried about me being left behind even as I had worried about her!

THE COST OF FREEDOM

We did not sleep for what was left of the night. By the time I was all caught up with Asibi, the morning call to prayers was already resounding from many minarets. The very first thing was finding a way to hide over a thousand girls and a few hundred babies. We had a meeting with the designated group leaders and determined that the various groups of twenties should spread out into different nooks and corners of the cathedral, try to stay out of sight and keep as quiet as possible.

The very first problem with our newfound freedom was how to get food. In captivity, even though we had been fed sparingly, we never had to think of going to get the food. There had always been food, even in the month of Ramadan. None of us had an idea about the current cost of foodstuff. Most of us had accompanied our mothers or other guardians to the shops or market a lifetime ago but had never been very intimately involved with transactions except for maybe a very few of us. Even if we had obtained ingredients, we had no way of cooking

Dust and Ashes

them. Asibi assured us that our best bet was to find hawkers of already-made food who abounded around there during the day time. We knew about these vendors. They were ever present near our schools, at parades, ceremonies, and other outdoor and even indoor gatherings. They could also be found in markets, near stadia, bus stations, train stations, and so on. The prices of their wares were usually fixed and often temptingly affordable. Right then we had so many mouths to fend for. We agreed that having the leaders scout for twenty people each made it much easier than thinking of how to feed over a thousand people.

That morning we also agreed on several other things. First and foremost, we agreed that we should find a way to provide food for everyone immediately. We thought of food like a loaf of bread and a water bottle for water. Thereafter we would split all the money among all the girls in readiness for emergency evacuation. Following this, if people chose to team up or go their separate ways it was entirely up to them. We agreed that first, the leaders would all go out together and find out as much of the lay of the land as possible. We would stay hidden in the church for that day and maybe the night but plan to evacuate latest by the next morning. Some of the girls were understandably scared and hesitant but we all agreed that we could not continue to stay together in one place. Finally we agreed that the girls who did not know their way home would pair with those who did, especially those who were from around Alexandria. Getting to somewhere safe, we would all work our ways home from there, helping one another as much as possible.

People have pointed out to me since then that there could have been better plans. We could have marched to the police station en masse. One or a few of us could have gone to talk to the police or government officials. We could have taken those whose homes were nearby home first, and then have

Al Kalima

their parents ask for help for the rest of us. We could have... I do not remember now why we did not do any of these. We were just children and had been incarcerated from the general society for so long. We were doing the best we could with what little experience we had. Having said this however, we soon discovered by bitter experience, proven again many decades later by the analysis of one of Mike's Egyptian friends, who was also a historian, that Sadat had by then established The Sharia Legal System as the official law of the land. We were just girls or women and we were right in being very cautious and stealthy at this stage.

We had also asked some of the girls from Alexandria if they could go home and get help for us. The majority of them said they were not sure of where we were in Alexandria. They were not sure of how to get to their homes from there. Many of us, including me, had relatives in Alexandria but we had no idea of how to go about contacting them. Most, though, were frankly too scared to leave the security of the main group. We felt that if anyone blundered before the rest of us were ready to move, it would give away our positions and endanger the rest of us very seriously. We decided to wait till that evening therefore before making any definite moves.

We had no illusions about other troubles which might be awaiting us. Our captors were probably in an uproar by now, looking for us. Who knew that Alexandria might not be the first place they would turn to look? We agreed that if any one of us was caught, we would not tell on the others. We would try to divert attention from where the rest of the girls were camped. If even a few of us got away, these ones might be able to get help for those who might be recaptured. Finally we agreed on a sign, something which would let the people inside know a friendly party was approaching. Ironically, what we settled on was a native ditty with Ummi's name in it. It was not exactly the Ummi we knew, but the fond name a child called its mother. The chorus went, "*Who will ever love me like my mother? O my mother! O my mother! Who will ever love me like my mother? O my mother! O my mother, I love you!*"

The ditty repeated once meant "A friend is nearby"; sung fast, it meant "Run and hide"; sung in breathless snatches, it meant "Danger is really very near!"

At dawn, the group leaders, Asibi and I went out in twos and threes to scout for food, determine the lay of the land, and find out about transportation and train schedules. Across from the side door of the church were several coffee shops. Some of these backed onto the street from right across the road. We agreed to meet there by the call of the noon prayer and discuss what we had discovered. We would then return to the church to talk to our different groups.

God directed our steps. That early morning, before we had gone far from the church or truly dispersed, we ran into a vendor selling bread "wholesale" from the back of a van. This meant that he was selling about a dozen loaves of bread at the cost of ten loaves. His target was the retailers who made their gains of the cost of those two extra loaves by the time they had sold all their lot. When we stumbled on the vendor, he did not seem to be having a great day. Although a lot of people were gathered around him including our own girls, only one or two people were making actual purchases. The rest were complaining about how expensive his wares were. "How can the price of a loaf of bread almost double overnight?" they were asking him.

"Blame it on the new government policies" the vendor protested. "We're hardly breaking even as it is." And then he added in the wheedling voice of a salesman, "But look, these loaves are bigger than the usual size. We still want our customers to be happy."

We stood back wondering what to do. We did not know what the price of bread had been recently but the loaves he was displaying, cut in two could actually sustain each girl for about two days until they reached their destination, found some other means of sustenance, or were recaptured. We quickly conferred among ourselves. We decided on the spot that we would give it a go. We went close to the vendor with the leaders of the twenties and bargained for thirteen loaves at the cost of ten. In conventional bargaining, this was a timid move but it was also unusual to bargain for wares with such fixed prices. However, considering where we were coming from, it was an audacious move.

The vendor hesitated but seeing as there were many of us, and no one else was buying, he reluctantly agreed to sell to us on those terms. By this time of the day, he should have sold off all his wares. Obviously it was being a bad day. The most he could do in order to cut his losses was to make the best out of a bad situation. We had happened on him at just the right time. The offer we were making him could yet save the day for him.

We wanted fifty sets but as we bought and paid for each set we found out he had only thirty-four sets, and six single loaves left over. We asked for those six loaves at a reduced cost too but he adamantly refused. He insisted that he had already lost his profits as it were. He insisted that if we wanted those six loaves he would only sell them to us at the usual price, and as a half set. We paid and took them. We had come out with enough money to pay for the bread and we still had some money left over. The leaders had paid for each set separately so as to get change. We needed smaller denominations of money to make sharing easier.

The people who were gathered around the vendor heckled us as we bought. They called us suckers, losers, disloyal citizens, and so on. They did not understand where we were coming from. They did not understand their heckling was the least of our worries. Our immediate worry at the time was how to transport all the bread back to the church. In the end, we had the girls carry about ten loaves each and we went back the way we had come, heckled all the way by the crowd. They did not try to physically attack or stop us in any other way. We realized that the loaves were really heavy. Carrying them back was quite a chore. We managed it however. Those who were not carrying any loaves at all spelled those who were tired from time to time. Back at the overhang of the coffee shop, we sat down and thought of what to do. There were also other black-robed figures hanging around the coffee shops and station. They looked remarkably like us. They were hawking different wares ranging from fresh fruits to prepared meals so we did not look out of place at all.

I worried that we would not have enough bread for all the groups but Asibi said reasonably, "If Jesus fed over five thousand people with only five loaves of bread, don't you think we already have too much bread even now?"

We laughed, breaking the tension for the first time since we set out that morning. I thought we should go around and see if we could get lucky and buy about four more dozen loaves or so just to be on the safe side. Asibi thought this was not a very good idea. "Let some of the leaders go back in with the bread we have now while the rest of us go to scout for water bottles. That is another very urgent need."

This also sounded very, very reasonable. We kept watch. In twos and threes, thirty of the leaders, laden with loaves of bread, went in through the side doors of the cathedral to the frightened girls waiting inside.

By then the day was progressing. The market place was filling up. We mingled with the crowd and tried to look as much a part of the scenery as possible while watching our backs for anyone who might be on our tails. A few at a time, from various shops and hawkers, we bought plastic water bottles. We exchanged our money all the time and broke it down to get change. The girls hid the water bottles under their robes to avoid attracting attention. Once each girl had up to twenty or so bottles, we started lading another girl. When two girls had enough bottles, we asked them to sneak back to the church. We aimed for five hundred water bottles but when we ran out of carriers, we had to go back to the coffee shop. From there, we carefully snuck back into the church.

Everyone was in good spirits considering the circumstances. There was a general buzz of hushed voices and activity in the church. Surprisingly, no one had come to the church and so we were still undiscovered. Rather, the girls themselves had discovered a water faucet at a side lawn, as well as an outhouse with bathrooms for the parishioners with real indoor plumbing. Organized by the leaders, they had gone in batches to ease themselves. They had however withheld the sharing of the loaves of bread until we returned. Now, we asked that all the bread and the water bottles be brought to the center of the aisle where there was enough room. We then had each group leader take five water bottles and five loaves of bread each. By the end of the first round, the water bottles were noticeably diminished but the bread still remained a lot.

We went a second round, having them take three loaves and two water bottles each. By the end of that round, a lot of bread was still remaining, and only a very few water bottles. We had the leaders take two loaves of bread each for the third round but even then, there was significantly still some left over. By now,

Asibi was shaking her head. "I think the miracle has happened again" she said.

I had always preferred reading to Mathematics but ever since the Times table incident with my father, I had become very good at multiplication and division. Yes, the number of loaves we bought should have been finished a long time before that point. After the third round however, we decided we should leave all the remaining loaves right where they were. We encouraged the leaders to allocate half a loaf to each person in her group but that if anybody felt a need for more, they were welcome to the extra which was there in the middle. As for the water bottles, we asked that the pregnant girls and the people with little children get theirs first until we had more to go round. I took one because of Amira, and some of the girls went to fill them all up from the lawn faucet. I collected my own half loaf and put it away in a pouch in my robe. Asibi collected hers but chose to leave it in the church until later on. She was however not allocated a water bottle yet.

We turned our attention to sharing the money after we were done with the bread and water bottles. The situation was not quite as easy as the bread situation. Thanks to the morning's exercise, we now had more change. We pooled all the money together, and with the change we had, allocated about a hundred pounds to each group. We asked that each person got about five pounds each. Some people were going further than others but we did not want to go into the nitty-gritty just then. We were not sure of how far five pounds would go, but it was a start. We still had some lump sum and a few groups that had not received any money at all. Later that morning therefore, we decided to go out again to buy more water bottles and hopefully bring back more change.

Before we left, we quietly prayed together. We thanked God for what we had achieved so far. We confessed our inadequacies to Him and asked Him for guidance in what we had yet to do. I held Amira in my arms for what I did not know would be the very last time. She had missed me. She wrapped her chubby arms around my neck chortling happily and blowing bubbly wet kisses at me. Just two days before, I had tied what was the seventy-ninth knot into her girdle. She had twelve teeth including four back teeth. When she smiled, she seemed to want to display all of them at once. Her vocabulary at this time included two-syllable words like Ma-ma-ma and Ba-ba-ba. I hugged her and told her "Be good to Aunty Miriam or Mummy will spank you when I return." She laughed and gave me another wet kiss. I then left her with Miriam to go and confer with the other leaders that were going out.

We encouraged just a few of the leaders to go out in twos, and return as stealthily as they could. The others were to stay back with the rest of the group and be on the alert, as well as be ready to move as soon as possible. We rehearsed our signals again. While the other leaders were to try to buy us more water bottles and get more change, Asibi and I were to go to enquire about train fares and directions. We knew we were at Alexandria. We had people travelling as far and wide as to Cairo, Asyut, Aswan, Damanhur, and so on. We agreed we could not afford to spend on luxuries like changes of clothes and foot wears even though these would have afforded us much-needed disguises if our captors were hot on our tails. "Let us aim to spend at most one more night in this place because they might be closing in on us. It is better if we all went in different directions sooner, rather than later. This way, at least some of us will escape."

Ten of the leaders went out in twos. Asibi and I were the last to leave. As we emerged from the side door of the cathedral, the sight which met our eyes was something else! Gone was

Dust and Ashes

the sedate tranquility of earlier that morning. The thick walls of the cathedral had insulated us from the noises in the street. The market place seemed busier but not in the normal way. There were now the roars of angry voices. As we went towards the railway station, we met most of our girls coming back. They reported that they had successfully purchased more water bottles and obtained more change "but there seems to be a street protest going on."

"Over what? On which street?" I asked.

The girls were not quite sure. They reported that it seemed to be over the price of bread, rice, or foodstuff in general. As for where, they reported it seemed to have originated near the government house, but that it was spreading. As they went back into the cathedral, Asibi and I hastened towards the train station. We hoped the riot had not reached there. We never made it. By the time we rounded the corner of the street which should have led up to the station, an angry mob swept by us. Shop owners were hastily trying to close up but some of them were already too late. The mob swept down the street, destroying and looting. They smashed store windows and vehicles which were parked on the street. They even smashed trash cans, lampposts, and other public fixtures on the street. They chanted slogans like "We are hungry! Give us bread!" "Death to the bread thieves, death to Sadat!" "Bring back Nasser! Give us Nasser!"

We took shelter in a doorway at first but someone put out a hand and shooed us away. Helpless, we were swept along by the crowd until we were near the church again. Desperately, we tried to get behind the coffee shop where we had met in the morning. We were inadvertently pushed into a dry gutter by the side of the road. We got under the culvert to hide. This was probably what saved us from being trampled by the angry mob. None of our girls was in sight. We prayed the leaders who had gone out earlier had all safely got into the church before the uprising became this bad. We lay there winded and scared out of our wits. Was this what we had been missing all the time we were in captivity?

The side door of the church was within our sight but nobody came out or went in there. As dusk approached and the noise of the rioting grew distant, we saw that some hefty men seemed to be patrolling the church premises. Their presence might have been what deterred the rioters and looters. Asibi and I discussed in whispers about going to these men for help. As we watched, two figures that were black-robed like us hurried by carrying empty basins with which they might have been hawking wares earlier that day. We did not recognize them as among our numbers. The church patrollers challenged them and asked them to turn back the way they had come. We heard the girls pleading to be allowed to cut through the churchyard so they would not run into the rioters. The men refused.

"Not tonight" one of the men replied. "We cannot afford to have Moslems tramping through these premises tonight. You might be innocent but God alone knows what mischief might be coming after you."

We realized then that our own help would not be forthcoming from that angle. If this was their reaction to a pair of harmless-looking girls, what would they do at the sight of over a thousand more, all dressed in black robes? Our captors were ingenious. People often identified others just by what they were wearing. Convincing people that the wrapping was totally different from what was inside was often a very arduous task. Dressed as we were, we could not possibly get past those guards. We prayed instead that the girls inside would know enough not to break their cover.

Dust and Ashes

As the dusk deepened and became night, the men did not leave their posts. Even after everywhere had grown quiet, they were still very vigilant. I must have slept because the next thing I became aware of was how uncomfortably cold I was. Asibi and I were leaning against each other. From her even breathing I could deduce that she was still asleep. I could hear the distant sound of passing vehicles. I peeped over the side of the gutter and saw that the patrollers were still there. Some were sleeping, slumped in awkward positions but a few were still vigilantly walking up and down. We could not even then sneak into that side door. If they had been there when we arrived by truckloads the previous night, we could not have possibly got past them. What were we to do? Only God who had arranged the previous miracles could possibly arrange this one too. I started praying harder.

As if on cue, the call for Morning Prayers began. It sounded rather subdued and hesitant compared to the one of the previous day. Asibi woke up and began to rub her arms to dispel some of the cold. She too peeped over the edge of the gutter and saw the patrollers. Those of them that had been asleep were now also waking up and stretching. We heard them organizing the watch for the day. For brief periods they actually left the door unguarded but such moments were too brief for us to make a dash for it. As we waited and watched, the street around us began to come awake. People emerged from their houses to gaze at the previous day's damages. The sun soon rose to reveal these damages in their ugly details. As more people began to move about, we felt safe enough to emerge from our hiding place. We dared not return to the church to blow the cover of the rest of the girls.

We decided to go to the train station anyway. Perhaps we could complete the task we had begun the previous day. On the way we came across a mosque. There were various taps, bowls, and kettles for the faithful to use in their ablutions. We stood there for a moment just watching. A few men still lingered after Morning Prayers. "The women section is on the other side" Asibi said at my shoulder. "We could use the bathrooms there." I had not even thought of easing myself but as she mentioned it, I realized that I was indeed pressed. We wandered over to the women's section and true enough, we found a bathroom and we went in and used it. No one challenged us. Even as tattered and as dirty as we looked, we fitted right in. I thought, "Perhaps if we had hidden in a mosque rather than in a church we would have been less conspicuous and more welcome."

The thought had barely taken form in my head when I saw what looked like a familiar face. I could have sworn that I saw Khalifa. Not far behind her, I also thought that I saw one of her lieutenants. I grabbed Asibi's arm and darted into the street. We walked off hurriedly towards the station as I explained what I thought I had seen. Asibi said she had not seen them but we walked on as fast as we could without actually running and drawing attention to ourselves. We still went towards the station but now with hearts pounding with fear. Only a few shops were fit to open or had dared to open after the previous day's riots. The crowd on the street was not much. We could have hidden in a crowd.

Since the previous day, neither of us had eaten anything. I was not sure Asibi had even eaten for over two days. As we passed a small restaurant, the aroma of well-spiced *koshari* wafted to our nostrils. My stomach lurched and rumbled loudly. I still had my own half loaf within the pouch of my robe but Asibi had left hers behind. We stopped under the awning of a shop. I drew the bread out and broke off a bit for each of us. We tried to eat it slowly and stretch it out as long as possible but we

Dust and Ashes

were really famished. I still had my own water bottle, filled with water. I drank some and passed it on to Asibi. She took a gulp, lowered the bottle and jerked at my arm. She pulled me up and virtually dragged me along the street. I followed her, bewildered and kept asking "What? What? What is it?"

We had turned two or three corners before she finally released me. "I saw them!" she gasped. "I saw Khalifa and Rashidat. They were walking down the street peering into faces and through shop windows!"

So it was not my imagination after all. Our captors were on our tail. If they had spotted us, we dared not lead them back to the others or let them suspect what our plans were. It made sense that they would search for us in the market place and near the train station. What were we to do?

With Asibi's mad dash, we had become disoriented. We were now on totally unfamiliar grounds. We were far from the church and the train station. We tried to find our way back by fixing our eyes on a minaret which we thought was close to the train station. As we wound our way down streets and corners, we realized we were getting more lost. The streets were very confusing to us. At one point, we found ourselves in what appeared to be an affluent residential district. It still had lots of coffee shops but the fronts of the few shops we saw were more shored up. The area seemed not to have suffered any damage from the riots. We were weary and footsore. At least we had not caught sight of our captors again. We stopped under a lamp post and sat down, leaning against it. I thought of the situation we had found ourselves in. I thought of how far we were from the others, including Amira. I thought of the men who were determinedly patrolling their church, effectively trapping the other girls inside the church. I thought of our being lost in a strange big city, pursued by people who had the most malevolent intentions towards us. I thought of the total hopelessness of our situation and I sat down on the ground and began to cry. Asibi put her arms around me. She tried to console me through her own tears. As we sat and wept, two young men came towards us and dropped some coins in our laps. I looked up startled. The young men just rushed on looking abashed, not even wanting to meet our eyes. That was when I realized what had just happened. They thought we were beggars and they were doing *Zakat*! We looked dirty and ragged enough. Our tears must have made us look very piteous indeed. We sat there wavering between surprise, amusement, and gratitude. We really needed the money though. Between Asibi and me, we had just what was left of that half loaf of bread, our bottle of water and the robes on our back. We had not yet received our own share of money. Whatever pittance we received as beggars might actually augment what we had and make the difference between death and survival for us.

We must have sat there over an hour and been given close to five pounds in coins when I suddenly jerked upwards and then surged to my feet. The coins on my laps all scattered. "What is it?" Asibi asked jumping right up with me, except that she had the presence of mind to clutch on to her own coins. "Khalifa? Is it Khalifa? Did you see Rashidat? Where are they? Where are they?" She looked about wildly.

Mutely I pointed. Across from where we sat were a group of young men emerging from a coffee shop. One of the young men looked uncannily like Gamal, my big brother.

"Who? What?" Asibi asked, now looking with bewilderment at the direction I was pointing.

"It's... It's... It's my brother" I managed to stammer out in a strangled voice.

Dust and Ashes

"Your brother?" asked Asibi still bewildered.

"Ga... Gamal" I said.

"Are you sure?" Asibi asked. "Are you sure it's your brother?"

Of course I was not sure. What would Gamal be doing at Alexandria, so far away from home? I rubbed my dazed eyes and then looked again. The young man was still there. He still looked like Gamal more than ever. This person was a little heavier than when I saw him last. He was somehow fuller and had a more mature face but he looked like Gamal all the same.

"I am fairly sure it's him" I told Asibi.

"Then you have to talk to him" Asibi said urgently, "Maybe he can help us."

We dashed across the road without thinking. How could a dirty, ragged beggar girl approach a well-dressed university student? As we closed in on the group I hesitated. It might be all right for Gamal to see me the way I was but was it all right for him if the rest of his friends saw me this way too? I remembered how particular he was about our keeping out of his affairs. I had been kidnapped at the phase where he was still not comfortable enough to introduce me to his friends. All these thoughts were overshadowed by the nostalgia which filled my heart, almost smothering me. This was the chance for a rescue. This was my brother. We belonged together! He was a breath of home, a glimpse of the life which had been. We ran after them.

As we got nearer I whispered, "Gamal." He turned and looked through me, looked through Asibi and looked as if he wondered where the voice that called his name could have been coming from. Urgently I whispered again, a bit more loudly. This time he did look at me, but then so did two other young men in the group. He looked more closely and then with surprise exclaimed "Briska?"

"Yes" I answered. "We need to talk. This is very urgent."

By now all the young men in the group had also become interested. With a good presence of mind, one of the young men moved us back into the coffee shop so as not to attract a crowd. He was fuller and somehow more mature than the rest. He appeared to be a leader in the group. He spoke to them with a quiet and assured authority. Another young man asked, "Is this your sister? Is she the one who was missing?"

"Yes" answered Gamal, still looking very dazed. "This is Briska."

We had not made a move to hug each other or to make any form of bodily contact. His eyes filled with tears and he began to shake with sobs. He whispered over and over again, "This is God's doing... Thank You, God... God, I thank you... This is God... This is God..."

On my part, I don't know now if I could have withstood a hug at that moment. I did grip his hands tightly and began to talk urgently in his face. "Listen Gamal, we are trying to escape from our kidnappers but Miriam and all the other girls are trapped in the church. Khalifa and the others are after us."

There was now no chance of telling Gamal the story in private. All the young men with him were very much interested. They fired questions at me. They wanted me to start with what had happened to us after we were kidnapped up to the moment when we found Gamal in front of the coffee shop. Again, it was the authoritative young man who had steered us inside that had the same presence of mind to call them to order. He asked them to wait while I told them why we needed help so urgently. I never learned his name that day. It was years later I discovered his name was Ayman. If not for his presence of mind, this chance meeting would have been more chaotic and probably wasted. Again, years later I would get to understand that the reason for their stupefaction was amazement at God's awesomeness. They

Dust and Ashes

had just come from a prayer retreat in which they had been pleading earnestly with God that I, and all those missing with me, should be found. My sudden appearance at that moment was therefore more than a minor miracle. To them it was a cataclysmic answer to prayers and they could not get over it.

But we were in dire and immediate need! Starting backwards, I told them of how we had got lost. I talked of how we had seen Khalifa and Rashidat in the crowd peering into faces and doorways. I told them of how we could not get in to over a thousand other girls hiding out at the cathedral near the train station because some men were patrolling the doors. I told them how discouraging this was after we had gone to such a great length to escape from our kidnappers, coming in the trucks by batches throughout the night.

At this stage I realized I could not be making much sense to them. I was not making much sense even to myself! I started weeping in frustration. Asibi tried to pick up the fractured tale but they either did not understand her or they did not really want to listen to her. I was the star of the moment because I was Gamal's sister. It was their leader, Ayman, who came to the rescue again. "I think I know the church she's talking about. Let us look at the problems at hand and see how we can help. First, you say there are over a thousand girls who have lived quietly in a church for nearly two days. These girls escaped from their captors who have kept them for a very long time."

I nodded, while Asibi answered "Yes." At least my tale had not been that completely senseless.

"These girls are from all over Egypt and beyond?"

We affirmed this again.

"Do they have money to return to their various homes?" He asked; and then immediately countered his own question. "Of course they would not. How stupid of me to ask that!"

"But they do!" I exclaimed. I then briefly explained how we had come about some of the money, to the avid interest of my listeners.

"That would help" the young man confirmed "but we might need to cough up a little more to add to it depending on where they're travelling to." All the other young men nodded and he continued, "The major problem now is that these girls in hiding might soon be discovered either by the church parishioners or those who are after you..."

At this, we looked up and I thought I caught a glimpse of Khalifa passing on the street. I knew this was not a figment of my imagination when Asibi also stifled a cry and dashed under a table. She butted heads with me because I was there already. Both of us were literally shaking with fear. The young men looked up at the same time. They saw nothing abnormal because she was gone. People milled outside on the street normally, going about their businesses. They were unconcerned by the drama which unfolded within the coffee shop. One of the young men dashed outside and came back to report that he had not seen anything unusual. How could he see anything unusual when he did not know what, or for whom he was really looking?

"Okay," said the leader, as I thought of him then. "Now that we know where the other girls are, I suggest we get these two to somewhere safe and then plan on how we're going to rescue the rest. Who is up for an adventure guys?"

He made it sound very exciting. Of course all the young men were up for an adventure, even Gamal whose reddened eyes had never left my face. The leader now addressed Gamal. "Gamal, I think you ought to take your sister and her friend to your Uncle Youssef's house. She can be safe there until we bring out the rest of the girls."

Dust and Ashes

Gamal opened his mouth to argue but Ayman said, "Just think about it, Gamal."

Of course this was a very excellent plan. It was the best there was, under the circumstances especially if Khalifa and Rashidat had really pinpointed us and were following us. We did not want to lead them back to the hiding place of the others. I raised my eyes to Gamal's at about the same time he must have come to the same conclusion. "Of course" he agreed.

"Yes, that is the best plan" Ayman concurred. "I suggest you call a taxi now to take you to the house. As soon as you get there, start telling your uncle the story and of our plans. He might have means and suggestions which would help us. The rest of us will go to the university hostels and fellowships to canvass for clothes and other things that would help us disguise the girls and make them look more like churchgoers than Moslem girls hiding out in a Christian church. Let's go. We will split up and decide the most effective ways of canvassing as well as where and when to meet. Time is of great essence.

"One final question, Briska, how will the girls know we are friends and not foes?"

An excellent question! Now we were glad for our prearranged signals even though they had seemed silly when we were hatching them. We told them about the ditty and using it as a signal. Asibi added, "It might be best for you to approach them with ladies. These girls have an understandably deep mistrust of men right now."

The leader looked at Asibi with renewed interest and respect. "That makes a lot of sense" he agreed. Humbly he added, "Thank you for sharing these with us."

We paused to see if there was anything we were forgetting. Nobody seemed to be remembering anything. After about a minute of silence the leader laughed a bit self-consciously and

Al Kalima

said, "Well, we are just coming from a prayer meeting. It makes sense that we should say a prayer, no matter how briefly, before we move on again." He called on someone to pray.

I know it must have been a brief prayer but it seemed to last for a long time in my own estimate. I know he thanked God for answer to prayers that I would be found. He thanked God that I was found not just alone, but with so many others. He asked for God to direct and guide us in what we were to do next and to throw off the scent of those trying to recapture us. Sincerely, I did not really listen to the prayer. I was too busy watching out for Khalifa and Rashidat. At last he ended the prayers and we all said "Amen".

Leaving Asibi and I with Gamal and one other young man, the rest got up and crossed the road to where Asibi and I had been sitting begging. We saw for the first time that we had been sitting at the gate of The University of Alexandria. I wanted to ask Gamal what he was doing far from his own school at Tanta. Did he finally manage to switch schools? However, also uppermost in my mind at that moment was the fact that Khalifa and Rashidat might be just around the next corner closing in on us. Asibi and I hid behind the door of the shop, away from any window. Gamal kept a close watch on us. His friend stepped outside to get a taxi. He came back a few minutes later and we then went out to join him on the street. He asked us to get into the back of the taxi. All three of us did so while he himself got into the front passenger seat. For the first time since that morning, I began to relax. I remembered something and sprang upright. "Asibi!" I exclaimed, "we forgot to tell them about the babies and the pregnant ones."

"What babies?" Gamal asked, "What pregnant ones?"

"There are babies too. Some of the girls are pregnant" I tried to explain inadequately.

Dust and Ashes

"Oh" said Asibi very calmly, "they are very intelligent and resourceful young men. They will know what to do to help everyone suitably."

Gamal's friend turned back to face us from the front seat. His eyes brimming with curiosity he repeated, "Yes, what babies and what pregnant ones?"

Before we had a chance to figure out how to begin to explain the answer to the questions, the taxi came to a screeching halt. "Out! Out!" shouted the taxi driver, jumping out himself. "The riots have begun again."

We hopped down from the taxi, hot on his heels. We could see from the cross street that there was a mob of people moving through the street pillaging, looting, and chanting slogans just like the day before. Already the taxi driver was running down a side street. We followed him. We dashed down narrow alleys between buildings and cluttered backyards. When we looked back we could see cars burning and hear shop windows being smashed. We crouched low and kept running. Asibi and I held hands as we ran. We could hear Gamal and his friend running right behind us.

And then it happened. We were coming out of one alley to go into another alley when inadvertently we ran into a mob. Just like the day before, we could not go against the tide so we got swept right along with the mass of humanity. I held Asibi's hand tightly. I knew her heart was pounding just as furiously as mine. Did we escape from our kidnappers just to be killed with the mob or by the mob? We kept on going until there was a little nook where the corners of two buildings met. We were able to squeeze into this nook while the crowd swept on. We crouched there, holding each other tightly and sobbing.

And then suddenly the noise of the crowd changed. They were no longer chanting war slogans. The noise turned to cries of distress. We dared to peep out of our nook and saw armored tanks. They were surrounded by soldiers holding guns. They were holding their guns as if they meant business too. There were a few loud shots and suddenly the crowd scattered, running helter-skelter in all directions. We looked around but could see neither Gamal nor his friend. In fact, it seemed that a few minutes after the gunshots, we were the only ones left in that large expanse except for the soldiers and their armored vehicles. Asibi and I looked at each other. We did not know what to do. We squatted on our haunches and hoped fervently that Gamal would come to find us. I was tired and at my wits end. My eyes felt gritty and too dried up to cry. I let my head sink onto my chest and I simply blanked out.

END OF THE ROAD

I came to, with Asibi shaking me violently by the shoulder and calling urgently, "Briska! Briska! Get up! We have to get out of here!"

"Mmm!" I answered at first. I resented being pulled back from a pleasant dream. In the dream I was sitting at home, at a decorated table. On top of the table was a huge celebration cake. I sat sandwiched between my father and my mother while everybody welcomed me and told me how much they had been praying for me.

As soon as my addled brain realized what Asibi was saying I went "Mm-mm" meaning No, No. "I'm not going. How will Gamal know where to find us? I'm not going. No! NO!"

"We have to go" Asibi insisted. "I think I saw Khalifa and Rashidat again."

"I don't care. Gamal knows where we are. He will come back for us."

"What if Khalifa finds us first?"

"Then she finds us! I have to wait for Gamal here. This is where we lost each other. He will know to come looking here for me. I have to believe Gamal will find us first."

"We don't know it was at this point Gamal lost us. He might have lost us earlier and might not know to search this far for us. I know where we might go to wait for them, Briska. His friends were going to help the girls at the church. I think I see the train station from here. If we find the train station, we might find the church. We will then be there waiting when the young men come."

Suddenly, my depression lifted. This was Asibi to the rescue again. How on earth could I have come this far without her good common sense? Of course her suggestion made a lot of sense. If we could find our way to the church, we would be rescued right along with the rest. I got up immediately, reinvigorated. We started to walk towards the station. It was now late afternoon by the position of the sun. The streets were still fairly deserted after the soldiers showed up but there were a few people moving around. We all avoided the roads as much as possible, staying very close to the shadows of the houses and shops on either side. We were using the alleys as much as possible. There was army presence at every street corner. Even though they leered at us, their presence somehow made us feel more secure than when the rioters were in control.

Tacitly, we avoided going straight to the church. We did not know who was following us or keeping an eye out for us. We were hoping that given some time Gamal's friends would at least arrive at the church before or at the most about the same time as Khalifa and her team if they were following us. We passed the mosque where we had gone to ease ourselves that morning. On an impulse we decided to sit on the step of a shop opposite it and just observe what was going on around us.

Dust and Ashes

There were more people on the streets now, still moving around cautiously. Asibi asked if I still had some bread. I did. I brought it out and gave her. She broke some off and gave me.

"No," I said, "I'm not hungry."

"I know," Asibi said. "I'm not hungry either but we have to keep up our strength so we can think and act rationally when we need to."

I took a bite but found it very difficult to chew and swallow. I took a mouthful of water to help it down. It tasted like sawdust in my mouth. As for Asibi, I doubt if she took much more than I did. What she returned to me was very much like what I had given to her. If we had not encountered the rioters, we would then have been comfortably eating a well-prepared meal in my uncle's house. I would probably be on the phone to my parents if not actually in their arms already. How could God have brought us this close to freedom and then let it slip away again?

I don't know how long we sat at those steps. The shadows deepened. It was dusk when a kindly woman came out of the shop and told us to go home. "There's a curfew. Nobody knows what the army will start doing by then. Just go home, girls."

We got up, looked around and saw that the streets were indeed getting deserted. We started going towards the station again. On the way I looked over my shoulder and saw Khalifa, Rashidat, and about two more of her people come out of the mosque and start following us. I grabbed Asibi's arm and pointed. She saw them too and we took off running. They ran after us. We ran straight into an alley beside the shop and plunged wildly on. They were hard on our heels. They made no pretense of pursuing us. Again, we lost all sense of direction. We dared not run towards the road for fear of the soldiers with the guns. We had since lost sight of the station and had no idea where the church might be. Fear lent wings to our feet but

Al Kalima

after some time we became too fatigued to run. We slowed to a jog; and then to no more than a stumbling walk. We both had stitches in our sides. It became darker and darker. All the while as we ran, we had not fallen but now I tripped over something on the ground and fell headlong into a ditch. Asibi, going ahead of me must have heard me fall. She turned back frantically whispering "Briska! Briska..."

"Right here" I whispered back.

She jumped into the ditch beside me, and just in time. We heard the sound of running feet. Our pursuers had not been far behind us. They ran past the ditch and went on into the night. We released our breaths together at the same time. I had not even realized I had been holding mine. We stretched out in the ditch, not caring how dirty it was, what, or whom we were sharing the ditch with. We lay absolutely still, too tired to even move. If they had come back and recaptured us then, we would not have been able to as much as put up a fight. We lay there breathing as quietly as we could. We waited to see if they would come back but they did not.

"Are you hurt?" Asibi whispered at last.

I did a mental check of myself. I carefully moved my head and my limbs. There was no abnormal pain or sting. "I don't think so" I whispered back. "My chest just hurts from all the running."

"Mine too" Asibi said. "Thank God we're okay and at least out of the cold."

Yes, thank God for little mercies, anyway. I was sure I would not be able to sleep that night for fear of Khalifa and her lieutenants but before I knew it, I was woken by the call to Morning Prayers. The chill of the night seemed to have penetrated to my very bones. This time of the year was the worst for sleeping outside and we had done just that now for two

Dust and Ashes

nights in a row. Every part of my body ached. Asibi's enthusiasm also seemed to have been dampened. She coughed every now and then, clutching her chest, and she would not move. When I propped myself on my elbow to look at her I saw that her eyes were open and staring straight ahead into the sky. I gazed at her and expected her to move her gaze to meet mine but she avoided my eyes. As I looked, two great pools of tears formed in her eyes and gently rolled down the corners towards her ears. Just yesterday she had been the stronger, wiser one. Was she giving up now? I would not have it. "Get up, Asibi" I said. "We're going to see the end of this!"

"I don't know Briska," she sobbed, "I don't know if I can go on."

"Of course we can go on. Come on." I insisted with sudden authority which I did not quite feel. I pushed and prodded until I got her onto her feet and moving. In the night, our pursuers could not have known where we went but they could be pretty sure we were in that general area. I too was tired of running. I decided it was time we changed tactics and went on the offensive. We climbed out of the ditch and I looked around. I determined that we were probably on the outskirts of Alexandria. The buildings were smaller and less crowded than where we were the previous day. Nevertheless we could see it was metropolitan enough to have street lights, lampposts, and lots of shops interspersed with what looked like residential quarters. Forests of signposts advertised many businesses, nearby and far away. At the next corner from where we were, there was a filling station. Opposite that, on the other side of the road was what obviously was a very important government building. Even as I looked, I saw that it was a police station, probably also housing a magistrate court and a jail.

Briefly, I outlined to Asibi what I intended to do. "We'll go across to that police station. I will give them my uncle's name, tell them we were lost and that some people are after us. I will then ask them for police protection."

It sounded so simple that I wondered why we had never thought of doing this before. Asibi was uncharacteristically unresponsive. She neither approved nor disapproved of the plan. She made no suggestions to either encourage or to discourage me. She just looked on morosely and was more or less expressionless. We sat back in the ditch and waited while the sun rose and the street became busier. I kept my eyes on the building across the road until I saw that business had picked up. Lots of people were going in and out of the building. Many more people were on the street. I was confident that our safety lay in the number of people who were around. Khalifa and her team would not dare kidnap us in the presence of so many witnesses. Pulling Asibi by the arm, I boldly went up the steps and in through the front door of the police station. The duty office at the desk asked what I wanted. "My name is Briska" I said. "I am lost and I want you to make contact with my uncle because I saw some people pursuing us."

The duty officer looked up and said, "Just a minute. I will get a pen and take your statement."

He already had a sheaf of papers in front of him. He reached across the desk for a pen. In that instant, Khalifa blew in through the door like a stiff wind and grabbed me by the elbow. "Ehen Briska, there you are" she said with a lot of spirit. "And you, Asibi... Can you imagine what we've been through trying to find you for the past two days? Thank you Officer. We'll take it from here."

For a minute I was nonplussed and then I began to struggle. "No! No!" I tried to tell the officer. "This woman is a kidnapper.

Dust and Ashes

Please don't let her take us. Help us return to my uncle" I pleaded.

"Don't mind her, Officer", Khalifa said smoothly. "These are my husband's younger wives. You know how foolish these girls are these days. They used the opportunity of the Bread Riot to escape and we have been searching for them these two days." Ingenious! Asibi and I looked dirty, tattered, and starved enough to fill the part she had just described to the officer. Besides, she called us by name, the same name I had just given the officer. But I did not pause long enough to reflect on this.

"That's not true! That's not true" I insisted. "She kidnapped us. Don't let her take us away again. Help us! Please help us!"

By now I was screaming like a mad woman and making quite a scene. Asibi stood beside me weeping quietly. Khalifa remained as calm as a lake on a breezeless morning. She turned to Rashidat and said, "Go and get Razaq."

The man at the desk paused in what he was doing and regarded all of us. A surge of uniforms came from the door behind him and gawked at us. Other people coming into the building paused to stare just as much. I kept screaming. At this stage I figured I was better off making a scene. If I had to go, better to go with a bang than to fall just meekly. Who knows, someone from the audience might recognize me and come to our rescue. A portly middle-aged man now forced his way through the crowd at the entrance. He looked very dignified, dressed in Western style suit and a turban. Khalifa salaamed and bowed to him. She called him "Sayeed" which more or less meant "Our Lord" or "Our husband". "We've found Asibi and Briska" purred Khalifa in a very syrupy voice "but they are not coming quietly. They are making a scene."

"Of course they will make a scene" the man said. I had never seen him before in my life and I knew for sure I had never,

ever been married to him. He turned to the officer at the desk and said, "Officer is there a problem here? I will like to take my wives home."

Flustered, the duty officer now turned inquiringly to one of the other officers who had come through the inner door. "What should I do, Sir?"

I calmed down my hysterics long enough to notice that some of the people gathered looked as if they believed me more than they believed Khalifa. I was also interested in what the superior officer had to say. He shrugged and said, "Why don't you refer the case to the magistrate court and let him settle it for them. In the meantime, keep the two girls in jail until we know more."

I figured that at least Khalifa would not be able to get her hands on us if we were in jail. During that time, maybe some sort of miraculous deliverance could happen for us. Being in the jail could not be worse than being recaptured. To my surprise, the man called Razaq was agreeable to the plan. We allowed ourselves to be led off to jail.

There were four other women already in the jail cell. The quarters were cramped but relatively clean. It was certainly no worse than what we had endured in captivity. It was much better than where we had slept for the past two days. There were mats laid out on the floor. Asibi curled up into a fetal position on one of these in a corner and I thought she had gone to sleep. I stubbornly stuck near the bars, sobbing and looking around for a means of deliverance. One of the female guards came towards us. I had seen her out of the corner of my eye when I was having my hysterics. She had not uttered a word of support to either side but I felt she was on our side and against Khalifa. "Quickly, Girl" she whispered, "What is your uncle's name and what is his address?"

"Yousseff Yahya. I don't know his house address but he works with University of Alexandria" I whispered back.

"In which department is he?" She asked.

And to my shame, I did not know. I had never even visited his house. I had not paid attention to a great deal in the past because someone else had been taking those decisions for me as a child. No one had imagined I would ever be in this type of situation I found myself in. Frantically I began to describe all I could remember of my uncle and his family to the guard. Someone from down the hall shouted something about the office being shorthanded. The female guard hurried off. I was relieved that at least someone knew my story. There was a very slim chance we might yet be rescued.

The guards brought us bland *koshari* and water around midday. Other than that, they left us strictly alone while the buzz of their activities went on round us. The other occupants of the cell did not talk to us and we did not talk to them. There were no visitors. Asibi remained uncommunicative and in the state of stupor she had slipped into. When I went near her, I discovered she was not asleep. Her eyes were wide open and occasionally filled with tears. They silently rolled down from the corners. As I watched, her whole body began to shake. When I touched her to console her, I found she was really burning up with fever. She had taken just a mouthful of *koshari* when the meal came. I offered her some of our hidden bread and water. She rejected the former and had just a sip of the latter.

Just before the call to Evening Prayers, the guards came for two of the women. The rest of us continued to wait, girded with silence. Dusk came and the noise within the complex dwindled gradually to almost utter silence. Another guard brought us some more *koshari* that evening. I told her my sister was feverish. "Please, is there any way you can help us?"

She went and came back with some pills and more water. Asibi sat up and took these and then lay down again. She continued to cough intermittently. I was becoming really worried about her. I placed my palm on her forehead and prayed. She covered my hand with hers and held it there to her head. About an hour later she started sweating profusely. She began fanning herself with the edge of her robe. The fever went down and we slept on the mat on the hard cold jail floor. Considering that we were even shielded from the elements, especially the biting cold, this was sheer luxury compared to what we had for the previous two days.

The call to Morning Prayers signified the beginning of another new day. It was now four days since our monumental escape from captivity. I wondered how the rest of the girls were faring. Were they rescued? Were they recaptured? I had regretted our waiting on the steps of the mosque but with the power of hindsight, Khalifa already had her eyes on us even then. If we had not waited, we would have led them straight back to the other girls. Who knows what the consequences would have then been? I could not underestimate her devious mind.

The next morning, the office complex also woke up around us as people came in to work. Gradually the din increased until the place was buzzing like a beehive. Maybe this would be the day I would be reunited with my family after more than four years in captivity. Hopefully we would get help for Asibi because she was now so obviously sick. The night guard gave her more of the pills which made her sweat and get better for a brief period but she obviously needed more help and medical attention.

The guards did not come for us that morning. Later in the morning, they came for the other two women who had shared the cell with us in the night. We were the only ones left in the cell. By noon they brought in four more women. It was not until late afternoon that our case was called and we went before the court.

The magistrate court was small and overcrowded. The people in the previous case were just going out as we came in. There were weepy women, smug-looking men, and various other people in different states of satisfaction. Hopefully, I looked around for a familiar face or at least even a friendly one. There was none. Khalifa and her lieutenants were on the second row. On the first row were the man called Razaq and a few other strange men. Asibi and I were led to the dock. A male court clerk appeared and told us that we were now in the family court of the distinguished justice "Somebody". I did not quite catch his name. I continued to crane my neck towards the door in case my uncle or Gamal would make a late appearance. They then asked us if we swore by God to tell the whole truth to the court. Asibi and I nodded. Our accusers were then asked to state the case against us. Razaq came forward and told a load of lies. The essence of his tale was that we were his lawfully wedded wives. We had taken advantage of the riots of the past few days to run away and that he would like to please have us back.

"I see" the judge said, "And what do the families of the defendants say?"

Someone who had been sitting beside Razaq on the front bench, whom we had never, ever seen before that day came forward. He stated that I was his daughter. Asibi was his niece whom he had also adopted as a daughter ever since her own parents died. He said that both of us had been happily married to Razaq for the past three years until he was informed two days before that we had run away from our matrimonial home and turned up here yesterday morning.

Al Kalima

To the questioning of the judge the man replied that yes, our bridal gifts had been received in full.

"Was *Nikka* properly performed for the two of them?"

"Yes" replied the man, "three years ago."

"Has there ever been any report of a mistreatment by their husband before this time in all these three years?" asked the judge.

"No, as far as I know" answered the man. "My family and I have nothing to complain about Razaq. He has been an ideal and a generous in-law. However, he has reported that his younger wives have become very impertinent and insolent. He said they have developed wandering feet."

"So you think they are guilty in this circumstance?" asked the judge.

"I see no reason why my daughters should not be lawfully punished for trying to run away; and returned to their lawfully wedded husband" the man answered.

After this exchange, the magistrate kept quiet and looked down on the papers in front of him as if he was trying to make up his mind about something. I hoped he was getting ready to question us and hear our own side of the story. When he looked up therefore, I was ready to begin our defense. I had got ready to deny everything all these people were saying since no other person had appeared on our behalf. Instead, the magistrate looked towards us but not at us. He fixed his gaze at a point between Asibi and me, and beyond our ears as he began to pronounce sentence. "According to the *Sharia* Law governing this land, a woman who has been married should remain under the protective custody of her husband. Failure to do so or running away in such a manner as you two have done brings disgrace upon your family, your husband, and to the community as a whole. To make sure this wanton behavior does not continue or go any further than this, I sentence you both to forty lashes of the whip each." He banged his gavel. "This case is now dismissed. Next case!"

"No! No! No!" I protested. "Please sir, we do not know these people. They are liars and kidnappers. Listen to our own side of the story! Please hear us out!" but we were already being dragged out of the dock by the guards. I was screaming again, struggling with the guards and having hysterics. "Call my real uncle! Call him and you will see. His name is Yousseff Yahya at University of Alexandria! Please call my uncle!" The magistrate was no longer paying us any attention. The next case was already being called. Khalifa and her lieutenants, with very smug looks, surrounded us and dragged us away. Asibi was leaning on me. She was too weak to even stand by herself, not to talk of joining in my protests.

People stopped to look at us making a scene but they did not stare for long. Apparently, it was a fairly common occurrence for people to be screaming and protesting while leaving the *Sharia* Court. The Sharia court? Sadat had been about to make Egypt start operating *Sharia* courts but was it supposed to be for everyone? I had gone to school long enough to know that even during all the patriotism of Nasser's regime the magistrate courts had continued to operate like the secular British system. Perhaps seeing as we were dressed as Moslems they had felt we deserved to be heard in the *Sharia* court. In the *Sharia* Legal System, men tended to have all the powers. There was no need for us to speak since we had a male family representative.

They took us to the inner court of the building complex to receive our prescribed punishments of forty lashes of the whip each. I continued to scream until I became hoarse. I was not screaming because of the beating. It was nothing compared with Ummi's casual punishments, by all counts! I was screaming because I felt so betrayed by my faith in my country, my faith in humanity, yes, and by my faith in God.

By the time our punishments were over, Asibi had collapsed to the ground. She remained there. Rashidat and her mates unceremoniously bundled us into the bed of a small truck waiting nearby. Three of the women got into the back with us. A fourth one got into the front with Khalifa and the driver and we drove off into the dusk. I curled up beside Asibi who was still in a dead faint. Her slim body was really burning up with fever. I pillowed my aching head in the hollow of my elbow and closed my eyes. So this was how our bid to escape had ended. We had been recaptured. I wept myself to sleep because of the hopelessness of it all.

I came awake suddenly when we came to a jarring stop. It was pitch dark. The only light was from the stars and the sliver of a fairly new moon. Asibi and I were roughly dragged down from the truck. We lay huddled where we had been thrown on the ground. I was exhausted, sad, and beyond caring. Asibi was probably too ill to feel anything. The truck drove off a little way but Khalifa and her lieutenants drew near us. She asked them to prop us up into a sitting position. "Okay" she said, "I have been nice to you but you have shown your gratitude by dragging me through these few days of a futile search. Now tell me, where are the rest of the girls and the children?"

We remained mute. She continued in her gentle singsong voice, "Tell me where the others are and I will let you go to your uncle's or anywhere you wish."

I had enough presence of mind not to ask her who she was trying to deceive. For a long time, she talked to us with her syrupy sweet voice. She absolved us of all blame. She made us all manner of improbable promises. At first I was too angry to answer her. And then I became too bored to even process what she was saying. Finally I became too plainly exhausted and I slumped. Asibi made no reply at all. She remained slumped over in an unnatural position from the beginning. She kept slipping down to either side. Khalifa kept asking someone to prop her up again. Eventually she just let her be. Asibi lay there on the cold hard ground while Khalifa concentrated all her enquiries on me.

I must have nodded off because the next thing I knew she slapped my face hard. She began to scream at me in a manner which was totally uncharacteristic of her. Her tone and tactics changed. "Do you think I'm joking here with you? How can you, with just a stroke, undo all the work it has taken us all these years to build? You will tell me where all those girls and children are or I will kill you!"

I sat up, fully alert now. I had never Khalifa seen like this before. She had always been the honey to Ummi's vinegar. Seen in this light however, she was even worse than Ummi had ever been. Even now, she would not soil her hands by doing the whipping herself. "I'm going to keep asking you over and over. Each time you do not give me an answer or you give me an answer that I do not like, I'm going to have Rashidat and Nabeela here beat you or beat your friend over there until you know that I mean business. Do you understand?"

I gazed at her mutely. She asked Nabeela to gag us. By the light of the dawning day, I could see there was no dwelling in sight. There was no other human being or animal nearby. Even the truck which had brought us the previous night was not within sight. I could not even see a highway or a dirt road. And yet Khalifa had us gagged. How were we going to give her any answers if our mouths were tied? I wondered at this but it was just as well. By now, from how her questioning had gone, I had decided that Asibi and I might have been recaptured but that all the other girls and children were hopefully not yet within Khalifa's radar. If this was the case, then the escape had been a success indeed. I was comforted. It was a good thing that she was having us gagged. No one was impervious to torture. If she left us the power of speech, we might inadvertently give her the information she wanted eventually.

True to her word, Khalifa asked us, "Where are the other girls and the children?" Then from the left side someone would whip us, and from the right side, another whip would descend as if to balance the first. Ummi was one person. No matter how much she enjoyed the whipping, her arms soon grew tired. These were four people working in tandem and there were just two of us victims. Ummi tried to whip us on the backs and legs so as not to "mar the goods". Khalifa had us beaten all over the body.

I tried to shield my face with my hands but then she ordered our hands tied to our backs. Inevitably some of the lashes fell on our faces, our heads, our necks... When she felt we were thoroughly whipped on one side, she had us turned over for the other side to be worked on. At a stage she had them whip us on the soles of our feet. She was in a bloodthirsty frenzy. She screeched her orders continuously in a shrill voice like a woman possessed by a legion of demons.

I could imagine how I looked from looking at Asibi. She looked like a bloodied piece of meat covered in parts by a tattered piece of black cloth. Ummi beat to elicit pain but Khalifa beat us to kill us! She had really meant it when she said she was going to kill us. The sun rose, and the day became hot. The motion of the women flogging us seemed to me like a film in slow motion. I had stopped feeling pain a long time before. As for Asibi, right from the first, she had not even groaned, squirmed, coughed, or given any indication whatsoever that she was still alive. They might have been whipping a corpse. I saw Khalifa's mouth opening and closing and realized I could no longer hear what she was saying. People say that at the time of death, hearing is the last sense to go. Unbidden, I remembered Asibi's vision of our escape. Two of us were going to be together. There was going to be "Freedom from pain" as people looked "through" us. It made total sense now! I closed my eyes and floated away. I let darkness enfold me. As if from a distance, I could still see the women holding their whips. Their hands rose and fell rhythmically. Before them lay the pulpy, bloodied forms which did not even resemble human beings. The forms looked just like a picture of the punished, beaten Christ that I had seen somewhere in my dim past. Indeed, we were now free. We were free from our captors. We were free from human injustice. We were free from all pain, free! We had risen above the dust and the ashes. Who said God did not move in mysterious ways in order to answer prayers and to perform His wonders…?

GLOSSARY OF NON-ENGLISH WORDS

Adaadiya Amma	The entrance examination to high school in Egypt
Eid	An Islamic celebration
Hadith	Islamic body of traditions which supplement the Quran
Houris	Beautiful virgins promised to faithful Moslems in paradise
Imam	Moslem Cleric
Inshallah	By the grace of God
Jihad	Religious aggression by Moslems
Kafir	Unbeliever in Islam
Kaffiyeh	Checkered scarf, usually worn over the head by desert communities
Koshari	Staple meal in Egypt made up mostly of sundry ingredients
Nikka	Islamic marriage contract
Sham Ennisim	(Lit) To smell the breeze. An Egyptian holiday to welcome spring
Sharia	The Islamic civil law
Thanaweya Amma	The exit examination from high school in Egypt
Zakat	The act of almsgiving

ACKNOWLEDGEMENTS

Thank you to all those who inspired me, believed in me, and encouraged me not to give up.

Thank you also to those who encouraged me materially, and to those who constructively criticized me. They did more than tearing me apart. They also put me together again. You know why I cannot mention you by name but you know that I am eternally grateful to you and for you nevertheless.

May God's blessings be on you all.

ALSO BY THE SAME AUTHOR

AFGHANISTAN WITH LOVE

A sad accountant, a United States Marine officer, an army chaplain, and a few other people had to go all the way to Afghanistan to find love in the realms of a warrior princess

COCKROACHES FOR SALE

The earth is in search of other planets to expand into and calls down a plague on itself that could wipe out the whole world except for a few people, and a few factors…

BEAUTY FOR ASHES

This continues the story begun in Dust and Ashes and also looks at the intrigues of a society which thinks itself safe and untouchable until intimately confronted with what else is out there.

DISGUISED TREASURES

Somewhat concluding the story begun in *Dust and Ashes* and continued in *Beauty for Ashes*; this story illustrates how even though violence is louder than mercy, mercy still triumphs at the end.

A SNEAK PEEK INTO BEAUTY FOR ASHES

PRISCA, 1985

I was uncomfortable with going to Asyut after our recent adventures there. I also knew that the next time we went there I had to give MD some sort of answers. We settled on going to El Harran for our supplies instead. Other than grains and sugar, there was not really much we could get from El Harran compared to Asyut.

We arrived not long after the vendors set up that morning and we had not really begun to shop. We managed to sell our kids and had bought some corn and sugar. We were still looking around and listening to where the best deals could be got. Suddenly, a truck came to a grinding halt beside the mosque. Maybe it was providence. I had no way of knowing why that particular truck stopped at that particular time, at that particular place. It definitely sounded as if the engine, brake system, or something had some problems. Whatever it was, the men in the truck must have decided they might as well use the opportunity to say their prayers while checking out the problem at El Harran. Who knew for how long they had been travelling or how much further they had to go?

What drew my attention first was the way the truck parked. The driver went to great pains to back into a secluded corner, as if to hide that part from passersby. This worked to my advantage eventually. What really, really drew my attention was that the men who got down from the truck triggered a remote buried memory in me. Perhaps, it was how they looked or moved. Perhaps it was their ugly rifles and how they held them. Whatever it was, they reminded me of the day we had been kidnapped thirteen long years before. They could have left someone on guard, but I did not give this a second thought. As soon as they finished their ablutions and went into the mosque to pray, I signaled Yunana to come closer. I boldly went to the back of the truck and let down the guardrail. The frightened eyes of six girls stared back at me. They were neither tied up nor gagged. The bruises on their heads and faces told me they had been intimidated into silence and submission by some other means.

Putting my forefinger to my lips to signal silence, I motioned for them to follow me. They stumbled out as quickly and as quietly as they could, nevertheless making some noise in the process but nobody challenged us. I motioned for them to get into the carts, three to each cart. While Yunana directed this part of the operation, I closed back the guardrail of the truck. We got out of that market place as fast as possible. We had never done anything like this before but the temptation had just been too strong to resist.

We thanked God in our hearts for whatever intimidation that had kept the girls from protesting or questioning our moves or the cramped space within the cart. We also thanked Him we had not bought much yet before acquiring this new cargo. To lighten the donkey's load, we carried the small sacks of corn and sugar we had already purchased in rough cloth bags slung across our chests and to the back like knapsacks. An astute person would have wondered why we were carrying our load on our backs instead of putting them on the donkeys. The person would then correctly surmise it must be that the donkeys were pulling enough load already in the covered carts. We prayed we would not meet any astute persons on the way. We did not stand about ceremoniously praying. We prayed while on the move, yet reminding ourselves frequently at first to slow down and move as casually as possible when we were still close to the village.

I sweated nervously under my flimsy disguise of a mannish dress and the turban wound around my head to hide my beardless face. I tapped the little donkey on the side occasionally both to direct and to encourage her to take the remaining miles home. She responded by quickening her steps with a renewed burst of energy from time to time. We had never driven ourselves this hard before. This journey usually took us about twelve hours, broken at some rest stops. We had been out since very early the previous day. The donkeys now drew carts which were heavier than when we had set out. This, in itself, was nothing abnormal. We had set out to sell little kids in order to purchase grain and sugar. What was unusual was the grueling pace we had set for ourselves and our animals since leaving the market. We needed to get back to the cave as soon as possible.

When there was no other traffic on the road we went in the middle of the trail. Not that there was much traffic anyway. There were the occasional Bedouins with their animals. Once in a while, we came across a lone camel and its rider. Motorbikes were then making their debut at El Harran but they could not yet manage the sandy trails so we did not have a lot to fear from them. Other more potent fears pursued us but we could not go any quicker. We knew that our cargo was more than just "contraband". We had almost insolently snatched them from right from under the enemy's nose. We expected the bloodhounds to come pounding after us at any minute. We had donkeys to run with but our adversary had trucks to pursue us. Unlike motorbikes, these trucks were fitted for driving on rugged terrain. To them the thick desert sand would be just a mere impediment.

Behind me, Yunana trudged along with the second donkey and cart. Whenever we encountered anyone at all along the trail, we moved well into the sands away from the trail until the other party had passed. This was to avoid eating the inevitable sand and dust they raised in their wake. More importantly, it was also to avoid making eye contact and having to exchange greetings with them. This could "blow my cover". Sometimes, coming back out from the thick sand to the trail was grueling but we had managed well so far. Suleiman had taught us well and had warned us about wandering too far from the track and getting totally lost. Besides, there was also the very real danger of falling into quicksand.

We dared not go to one of our outposts to get rid of our extra load; or to stop, rest, and refresh ourselves and our donkeys. By the oblique way we were taking home we would not come near to any of our outposts anyway. Besides, the food we were bringing was needed almost as a matter of urgency. And yes, we were in a hurry to reach the cave and the relative sanctuary it offered. To better move over the sand, our little carts had been custom-fitted with planks of wood by Suleiman. These made them glide like sleds. If we had to move over packed trails or windswept rock, the going became a torture. Fortunately, we could avoid these hard surfaces by going beside the trail.

I dared to look back again at Yunana. I saw that it was taking him all he had just to keep moving. The poor boy was only about twelve or thirteen years old by our reckoning. Although he was big for his age, he was really more of a scholar. However desperate times called for desperate measures. He did not even look up or make eye contact for me to give him an encouraging smile. We just trudged on.

I tapped the donkey again. When I was just about to drop, we climbed a sand dune, descended, and there was the cave before us! As soon as the people there saw us, and saw how we were stumbling, they ran to our aid. Yunana and I just gave up and collapsed into their welcoming arms. "Six girls... in the carts..." I gasped and allowed myself to practically be carried into the welcoming cool interior of the cave.

In two days, the girls we had rescued were up and about. It took Yunana and I closer to a week to recover and function normally again. Even the donkeys were not ready to travel for some time! The lesson there: there is no getting familiar with the desert. Anyone who will not take life easy in the desert is likely to die sooner rather than later. However it was fear from the consequences of what we had done, which had driven us. It was one thing to go rescuing people who were running away of their own accord and were lost in the desert. It was quite another thing to go kidnapping the victims of kidnappers. Even after we were recovered, Yunana and I were loath to go to that market at El Harran again in case someone had recognized us or noticed our abrupt departure. Our paranoia somehow communicated itself to the rest of the group. From the cave, we hardly ever heard other sounds but we began to imagine that we heard the sound of trucks in the distance. No two people ever heard the same sounds at the same time however, so we knew we were just being skittish.

Suleiman listened very attentively to every passing Bedouin in case there was news abroad of people in pursuit. There was no news. He never dared to bring up the topic himself. Yunana and I stayed holed up for three months while other teams tried to do the procuring of supplies. After three months we decided that the news of our daring escapade must have blown over. For one, reasoned Suleiman, the kidnappers might not have noticed it was at El Harran that their cargo got lost. For another, if one were transporting contraband goods, one could not openly go asking if anyone had seen what was not supposed to have been there initially. Had anyone seen it in the first instance? And so after about three months, we relaxed our vigilance.

When we examined the girls we had rescued, they were really worth rescuing. Six of them were all thirteen years old. They were bright and intelligent girls. They told us they attended the International School at Cairo. They talked of how they had been snatched from beside their school while waiting to go home! As far as they knew, they had been travelling for a day and a night before we rescued them. There were a lot of similarities to what had happened to many of us, and in broad daylight too. The only big difference was that all their parent were very well-to-do and highly placed in society. One of the girls was even American! This time, either the kidnappers had made a real tactical error, were very desperate, or there was some other motive for the kidnapping. The parents of these girls, the Egyptian government, the American government, the intelligence agencies of both governments and probably other individuals, outfits and organizations would be hot on the trail of these girls. If any of them found these girls with us, would they assume we were allied with them or allied with the kidnappers? Who knew? This did not make us more comfortable when we tried to relax our vigilance.

DUST AND ASHES: SUGGESTED QUESTIONS FOR READING CLUBS

What I am advocating is that Christians become more aware, better grounded in their faith, and more tuned to what they believe and what they should be doing about their beliefs so that even in adversity, they would find something to hold on to...
- Introduction to this book

This story is supposed to make Christians more thoughtful about what they claim to believe, and ask themselves if they can really stand under pressure. There is lots of food for thought but the following passages have been suggested by the author as a few things to dwell on. Whether reading individually or as a group, you might want to take the following passages and dissect them by asking yourself these questions:

Do I agree with this statement/sentiment?

Why and why not?

What led up to this statement/sentiment?

What does the Bible have to say about this?

Could the outcome have been different?

If I found myself in this position before reading this book what would I have done?

With forethought, and having read this book, what will I do now?

What would I advise someone else going through a similar situation to do?

What will make this advice difficult in practice?

WHAT WOULD JESUS DO?

1. I am the first to admit that upbringing must account for a lot of my biases. (The Good Old Days)

2. Somehow in our hearts, we had come to think of members of the Coptic Church as not being as serious Christians as we the evangelicals ... (The Upheaval)

3. What I am saying in essence is that it is quite possible that such anti-Islamic messages were being preached from the Christian pulpits but that fortunately for me, I missed them entirely. (The Upheaval)

4. Since my encounter with God, He had been answering all my prayers pronto! It was as if I had made His list of favorite mortals. I had every confidence He was going to answer this one too and we would be rescued by the end of that day. (The Upheaval)

5. What would a child of God do in this kind of situation?... What kind of a Christian was I who would deny my faith at the least sign of torment?...What would it matter to just confess this silly phrase even though I had a totally different belief in my heart? Should I defy Ummi's indoctrination, be

tortured and killed? Had I not been praying for God to be honored in my life? (A New Beginning, Training)

6. We speculated on what must be happening to our Moslem co-captives. "Maybe they will return them to their homes. Do you think they will be kind enough to tell our parents how to find us?"... Opinions were varied... (Training)

7. I tried to tell her stories to while away the time. The stories which came most easily into my head were ... (Training)

8. Sara had become quieter. She was no longer calling for her mother nor did she want to be held by Ester as at the beginning of our ordeal. She must have learned that Ester could not protect her from the harsh realities of the life we found ourselves in. (Married)

9. Where has God been while we have been suffering all these? Did He not see us? Was He not mindful even of Sara and Rawya? No! I don't want anything to do with this God or His Word anymore." ... Truly, at that moment, I felt totally betrayed by God. (Married)

10. One wise man once said that understanding a phenomenon makes it easier to tolerate... (Married)

11. We went to the communal bathroom and had a truly cleansing bath, not with water which had been sanctified by Ummi's incantations, but with the desires of our souls. (Married)

12. "Don't do that" Fawzia shouted. "You are ruining the robe. How are we going to account for it?"... "And how am I going

to explain the fact that I was in charge when this kind of thing happened?" (Stresses)

13. We never saw nor heard about Rawya again …I just chose to believe that God had answered my prayer for her that night. Even if she died, I hoped she was better off (Stresses)

14. I had convinced myself there was no need to ever talk to God again. I had nothing to say. However, looking at the ragged circle of filthy faces turned expectantly towards me, it occurred to me that this was not about me… (On the Move)

15. If only she understood that she was the one who had restored my faith in God and in living! (On the Move)

16. "Out of every evil some good always usually develops."(On the Move)

17. No one wanted to be baptized if it involved any improvisation. "It will be so much like Islam" Khadija said. "You keep improvising things for your own convenience (A Mission Field)

18. …Our captors might think they were killing us but we were finding faith in Jesus Christ as a result of our oppressions. (A Mission Field)

19. This was not simply a case of making the best use of every situation. It was a sense of mission and a purpose for being where I was at this particular time… Someone once said that there was a method to every madness. I saw that there

was a pattern to good for everything that God allowed to happen to a believer. (A Mission Field)

20. …the mysterious ways in which God works is not always pleasant for all the parties involved. (Ramadan)

21. Gone were those fellowship periods. Gone were those periods of quiet camaraderie and spelling one another. We did not so much as have time for ourselves. (Ramadan)

22. Pain and Bitterness! Those were the two main "strong" characteristics of the girls whom we encountered from the other camps. Two of the commoner characteristics though, were despair and resignation. There was a lot of fear but incidentally almost no anger. These girls had been reduced to total hopelessness, and when people are hopeless, every fight and anger tends to die in them. Some of them would not even so much as lift their heads and look other people in the eyes… (Ramadan)

23. Now we went through it again more thoroughly and a bit feverishly, striving to remember as much as possible in case our Bibles ever got totally taken away. We did not know it then but we were doing what persecuted Christians of old did long before us... the more they persecuted us, the stronger we grew… without knowing it, we were holding what big churches would call ordination and leadership training meetings.(Ramadan)

24. Don't ever get discouraged trying to tell others of this hope in Christ. The voices of the ones who want to hear and need to hear are usually drowned out by the few who do not want to hear."(Ramadan)

25. … we noticed that some of the women began to linger at the edges of our circle when we met. I like to think that Bashra's witness got to them and that the Holy Spirit would use it to work in their lives. (Qasim)

26. The bottom line was that God did not mean me to escape at this time. There was still much to be done. (Qasim)

27. But have you considered that you are as much of a captive as I am? Perhaps you are even more so because at least I have a cause. I believe in what I am fighting for but you have no cause that you are really living for. You have nothing that you consider worth dying for… That is the liberating Truth so even though I am in bondage, I am freer than my captors. It is a faith worth living for, Qasim, and also worth dying for (Qasim)

28. Remember, the best way to blindside your enemy is to keep him distracted from what you really intend to do. (Qasim)

29. Most of all I was angry at God! Was He asleep while all this was happening to me? Where was His promise to ALWAYS answer my prayers? Where was the joy in believing in Him? Where were all those miraculous events we read about in the Bible and even in the lives of contemporary Christians of wonderful and miraculous last minute deliverances and rescues? Why were we not seeing our signs? Did we not believe tenaciously enough even in the midst of all the difficulties we had faced so far? Was our faith not of a high enough quality? Had we not been through enough already? Why would God not give us any respite? (P 92)

30. "So when you vow that you would give your all for my service it was only as far as it was at your own convenience, showed you in glowing lights and did not include some specific aspects of your life which you don't want me to touch? Have you considered this could all be part of my plan? When did you stop trusting me? When did you fancy that you could make a better plan than me? Since when did you make yourself my deputy to act when I am unable or indisposed? What sapped my strength? Answer me!!!" (Pregnant)

31. I would realize that sugar-coated evil was still evil nonetheless. (Pregnant)

32. I was assuming that it was my own strength, my convictions, and my charisma that had been keeping them all along. This was pompous and hypocritical of me (Pregnant)

33. It was as if God had turned against me in those days. It seemed He was always harshly rebuking me. (Pregnant)

34. The truth has a way of advertising itself; and the Holy Spirit is the one who gives light to the true seeker, not the clever words of any man."(Pregnant)

35. I could have given any number of answers but again I asked inspiration of the Holy Spirit. (Mothers and Babies)

36. Once, I told this story and someone asked me if I did not feel like gloating. Not at all! I felt so thoroughly humbled by it… I was also very grateful that I had not misled or been an obstacle in any way, maybe by one act of thoughtlessness. (Amira II)

37. It's like a winding road. Until you come to the bend in the road you may not see how it continues. It could also be like a good book, as you used to say. The plot will unfold as you turn the pages, one step at a time. (Hope)

38. "Perhaps if we had hidden in a mosque rather than in a church we would have been less conspicuous and more welcome."(The Cost of Freedom)

39. I was screaming because I felt so betrayed by my faith in my country, my faith in humanity, yes, and my faith in God. (End of the Road)

40. Indeed, we were now free. We were free from our captors. We were free from human injustice. We were free from all pain, free! We had risen above the dust and the ashes. Who said God did not move in mysterious ways in order to answer prayers and to perform His wonders (End of the Road)